One moment of distraction, then a sudden plunge into the unknown. For Alice, it was Wonderland. For Rose, it was the labyrinth of injustice, where every corridor promised a key to justice. Different scenes, same rabbit. Both chasing truth through a world where the rules shift beneath their feet.

So she was considering in her own mind… whether the pleasure of making a daisy-chain would be worth the trouble of getting up and picking the daisies, when suddenly a White Rabbit with pink eyes ran close by her—
Lewis Carroll, Alice's Adventures in Wonderland

POSTMODERNVENUS

A DETECTIVE NOVEL SET IN SAN FRANCISCO

For anyone who's felt broken, betrayed and told to give up: Don't. You are antifragile. *Je pense donc je suis.* I think therefore I am. —W.G. Peterson

DEDICATION — ĪŚVARAPRANIDHĀNA

I wrote this for the hundreds of thousands of survivors across California and beyond who endure, rise, and deserve to be heard. This is my offering—etched in resilience. To my mom—your support has been foundation in this journey. To the survivors and activists who light the path—Virginia Giuffre, Rose McGowan, Chanel Miller, Jade Alectra, and Donna Barrow-Green—your courage fuels mine. To my loved ones—your encouragement means everything. To Dr. Beverley—your belief restored what they tried to erase. Thank you for honoring what others refused to see. With gratitude to the UCSF Trauma Recovery Center, the San Francisco Fire Department EMTs, EVAWI, and the nurses and doctors at Zuckerberg San Francisco General Hospital ER.

POSTMODERNVENUS.COM — 25 APRIL 2025

Barnes & Noble ISBN: 979-8-319-69573-4
KPD / IngramSpark ISBN: 979-8-218-62864-2

Cover design and artwork by W.G. Peterson

First edition: June 2025
Second edition: September 2025

TABLE OF CONTENTS

Postmodernvenus is published by Aura Yoga California, a 501(c)(3) nonprofit committed to advancing justice, human rights law and survivor advocacy. Through storytelling and civic engagement—including *yoga and healing mind retreats and symposiums*—we work to empower voices too often silenced while challenging the structures that perpetuate inequity.

Want to support our mission? *Postmodernvenus* is more than a book—it's a movement for justice, truth, and institutional reform. Your tax-deductible donation helps fund legal education, trauma-informed advocacy, and public resources for survivors. → Visit postmodernvenus.com/donate

INTRODUCTION – THE SCALES OF JUSTICE

Based on a true story.
In San Francisco's cityscape, a heroine emerges—mysterious and divine. Rose Visjonær, with Nordic eyes that burn like bright embers, moves through labyrinthine shadows where crime and deceit entwine. With a fairy-heart face and lips of tender bloom, she sees justice as a chessboard—where souls are pawns in a perilous game.

Amid Banksy's defiant street art and the Barbary Coast's notorious past, she dances through the maze, blindfolded by corruption—where evidence is vandalized and sold, and truth lies aghast.

In this postmodern empire, fallacies masquerade as fact, and the machinery of power manipulates perception, leaving only fractured acts behind. Yet for those brave enough to decode it, fractals of truth begin to unfold. *Fiat iustitia, ruat caelum. Let justice be done, though the heavens fall.* But what happens when the system decides which way the heavens fall—when *fiat justitia* is silenced by *imperium*?

Postmodernvenus is the first novel in a trilogy—an unfolding saga that immerses readers in the labyrinth of the city's broken justice system. To navigate it, Rose turns to government codes, case law, and philosophy—calculating each move like a queen on a chessboard. With unwavering precision, she decodes stratagems veiled as order and outmaneuvers those who mistake her for a pawn.

When the scales of justice tip under the weight of lost and tainted evidence, truth shatters into disillusionment—fractured by the very system sworn to uphold it. This system doesn't seek fairness—it expects obedience. Amid the chaos, Rose rises and plays to win.

"Halls of Justice painted green—money talking."
—Metallica, San Francisco's immortal metal vanguard

In this city, wealth reigns—and truth is buried six feet deep. What begins as a fact finding mission pulls her deeper into the machinery of power—a labyrinthine chess match. For Rose, justice lies not only in victory, but in confronting the system that controls the narrative—its own *fiction d'État.*

By the time she realizes how deep she's in, the doors have already locked behind her. From 2022 to 2024, she advanced her case as a pro se litigant in Superior Court—held to a higher standard than the defendant, forced to navigate a system where the rules shifted beneath her feet.

But Rose didn't break. She became A*ntifragile*, forging something that will outlast those who tried to destroy her.

Government immunity does not apply when the law imposes a non-discretionary duty under Government Code § 815.6—a statute often cited in civil rights and claims against state or municipal agencies.

A story of virtue. Of power.
And ultio tenetur a veritate—justice bound by truth.

WHAT INSPIRED THE TITLE?

Postmodernvenus began within a dream—like a time machine into a cinematic memory, where visionary director Quentin Tarantino sits beside the author in a retro library bar, locks eyes, and says: *Write my next heroine-led film noir, where vengeance is poetic.* The title emerged from a fusion of art history, an art model career, and a moment of subtle irony—incorporating timeless elegance with the edginess of contemporary art and creative storytelling.

Drawing inspiration from the fauvism of Matisse's *Nu Bleu II* and the elegance of Botticelli's *Birth of Venus*, this detective novel explores the intersection of art, identity, and law. Rose becomes unbound—emerging from a sea of chaos into a realm of self-actualization and divinity. Pulled into the system's magnetic force, her pursuit of elusive truths begins.

Through a postmodern lens, Rose confronts implicit bias—disrupting the status quo to do the brave thing. The narrative invites readers to engage with the intricate layers of illusion as Rose navigates a world immersed in uncertainty and equivocal ambiguity.

CHAPTER 1: BLACK RABBIT ROSE

The strongest of all warriors are these two —Time and Patience.
—Leo Tolstoy, War and Peace

"Our previous session left us at the edge of an ominous landscape," he said, his voice calm and deliberate.

"You described *a dark, abstruse forest*—a place where injustice has saturated the police, the prosecutor's office, and the superior court."

He paused, letting the words settle. "Rose, can you help me understand what *forest* represents to you? What emotions arise as you navigate it?"

He sat across from me, comfortably settled in a sleek oversized armchair, his gaze steady and observant—watching not just what I said, but what I felt. The room was designed to soothe and disarm: muted earth tones, soft lighting, and an abundance of green plants arranged with quiet precision. Towering fiddle-leaf figs, delicate ferns, and trailing pothos hung from planters overhead, their vines cascading like silent witnesses.

The faint scent of damp soil lingered in the air, grounding the space in something organic. Something alive.

It was probably meant as horticultural therapy—a gentle reminder that even in sterile, controlled environments, nature still finds a way to reclaim space.

Exhaling slowly, the question rippled through my chest.

"*A dark, abstruse forest* is deceptive… disorienting. Like walking through dense woods where nothing is what it seems."

Silence followed, my voice above a whisper.
"When I went to the police, I thought they'd do the right thing. That he'd go to jail for what he'd done."

The psychologist nodded. "Unfortunately, when people report these crimes, they're often met with retaliation instead of support—discrediting, isolation, trauma. That kind of institutional betrayal can deepen the wounds. In our sessions, we'll unpack the impact of those experiences, including the gaslighting that so often follows."

A pause. Then a quiet reply.

"That book you gave me—it's been really helpful," I said, as a memory surfaced.

"During one of the 2019 Special Victims Unit meetings, Sergeant V. claimed she had *already shown me the case file, the forensic medical kit results, and the photos Henry took of me*. But she hadn't.."

A slow breath filled my chest. "This conversation was recorded—on her police-issued handheld recorder. That audio is proof. Proof she lied to cover up a botched investigation."

A slow breath filled my chest.

"The conversation was recorded—on her police-issued handheld recorder. That audio is proof. Proof she lied to cover up a botched investigation."

My voice trembled—part disbelief, part outrage. "She lied in front of the Managing District Attorney of the Preliminary Hearings Unit and the Victim Advocate. That was December 2019. It was horrible. And it wasn't the only time she's done this."

I shook my head. "That level of dishonesty—it's not just unethical. It's a betrayal of those she was sworn to protect. And she made those misrepresentations casually, like it didn't matter. But it did. That lie rewrote the course of events that followed."

The psychologist leaned forward, voice calm but firm.

"Rose—statements made with the intent to deceive, knowing they're false, or made with reckless disregard for the truth, constitute intentional misrepresentation. Cover-ups exist to conceal both evidence and wrongdoing. In an active cover-up, deception becomes a tool of control. It's not just misconduct—it's an abuse of power."

He paused, watching me. "You've read about the U.S. Olympic athletes who accused the FBI of ignoring years of abuse by Dr. Nassar?"

"Yes. They stood before the Senate and exposed the truth about the FBI and Dr. Nassar. When Maroney spoke, it was powerful—and gutting. What I experienced wasn't just similar; it was the same. They were entrusted with our safety—yet they exploited that power. Those women were silenced. So was I. We lived in it. For so long, I didn't fight— I folded. I retreated into a cocoon of denial. Adapting to his ideology twisted my thoughts. I was disillusioned. Had I been protecting him?"

A pause.

"At times it felt impossible to keep going, but then I'd think of the others—and remember why I had to. There's a painful beauty in uncovering the truth. Beauty that cuts deep."

The psychologist folded his hands, gaze steady. "The hardest truth? The violations don't always lurk in shadows—they sit in power. Behind desks. Wearing badges. Sworn to uphold justice."

"The police. The prosecutor's office. You'd assume they'd do their jobs. But when they don't—who holds them accountable?"

My fingers drifting over the armrest—absent, restless. "I don't know. He took photos of me without my consent, which violates Civil Code § 3344. A friend pointed that out. I'm not sure if the police can use those photos to clear him. I assumed they'd see it for what it was—proof it was planned. Premeditated."

My gaze flickered toward the window, watching a slant of light stretch across the floor. "But they used the photos against me—not him. He took them while I was drugged, not conscious. I didn't consent. And yet they treated them as if I had—as if those images somehow made him innocent."

I thought of *V for Vendetta*—how they turned truth into treason. This system was designed to control. Erase. Rewrite. "I've imagined a few things. Irrational, sure."

"Like taking a full swing at his knees with a wooden baseball bat. Not once—five times. Until he collapses on the Laguna Street sidewalk, kneecaps shattered against the cement. Blood gushing. Then I'd take a blade to his Michelin Pilot Sport tires—slice clean through the rubber of his Porsche 911."
Suddenly aware of how unhinged that sounded, I added, "I've seen too many Tarantino films."

The sun had shifted westward, cascading light across the room. I watched it catch the polished leather of the Psychologist's *Spazzolato* shoes, a perfect shine, like a film noir photograph—surreal.

He studied me, then spoke. "Rose—the visualization of vengeance is always more satisfying than the real thing."

He leaned back, his voice steady, clinical. "Complex-PTSD restructures neurobiology, disrupting emotional regulation and altering behavioral responses. It imprints itself— deeply, somatically. You've experienced it: fear, rage, hyper-vigilance, a nervous system recalibrated for survival. Perception fractures. Temporal processing distorts time," he added, "yet time remains one of our greatest teachers."

The psychologist gazed at me, then over at a stack of books on the end table. With a glint of mischief in his eye, he reached for a well-worn paperback copy of *Pulp Fiction: The Screenplay.*

Flipping to a page he had dog-eared, he cleared his throat and launched into a pitch-perfect Samuel L. Jackson impression:

EZEKIEL 25:17— The path of the righteous man is beset on all sides by the inequities of the selfish and the tyranny of evil men. Blessed is he who, in the name of charity and good will, shepherds the weak through the valley of the darkness, for he is truly his brother's keeper and the finder of lost children. And I will strike down upon thee with great vengeance and furious anger those who attempt to poison and destroy them and you will know my name is the Lord when I lay my vengeance on thee.

Like a tidal wave, the verses he read crashed into me, pulling me back to a reality not long past. I sank into the chair as the flashback hit—Northern Station officers arrived at 11:30 PM, the same day I was at San Francisco General Hospital Emergency Room.

Their tactical boots scuffed softly against the worn wooden floors of my apartment. I was exhausted. One of them began asking questions, and I shivered—terrified to report him. My mind blurred, dissociating, trapped in a loop of unreality. It felt like a rigged game, every move stacked against me, unseen forces warping my sense of control. I couldn't recall everything and panic took hold.

Was this Stockholm Syndrome? Or was I still feeling the lingering effects of whatever Henry gave me with—something like ecstasy or ketamine?

I felt disconnected, as if I were floating outside myself, when the SFPD dispatch officers arrived thirteen hours after the forensic exam at San Francisco General Hospital.

Thirteen hours—a number that felt less like time and more like an omen—as if the velvet curtain at Black Rabbit Rose had been drawn across reality, and I was watching myself from the other side.

Then I caught myself downplaying the incident, as if nothing had happened. I even forgot to mention that Henry took photos of me in his condo.

High anxiety during and after trauma can impair memory consolidation, leaving gaps in recall. Feelings of shame can cause victims to suppress or forget key details. Trauma disrupts the brain's chemical balance—neurotransmitters like serotonin and dopamine— that are essential for memory formation and retrieval.

"Do you want him to go to jail?" one of the officers asked.

I stood there, stunned. The question hit me harder than expected. I felt speechless. Strangely, the only thought running through my head was how grateful I was that my roommates weren't home to witness this.

Nervously I looked around the apartment almost as if the answers might be hiding in plain sight, then turned back to them.

"I don't know, officer. My mind is spinning. I feel confused and hurt."

One officer jotted notes on a hand-sized tablet while the other observed me intently. He made a statement designating me as the victim of a violent crime, then handed me a police slip with the incident case number printed on it.

The words on the police slip seemed to vibrate in my hand—shifting, transfiguring—as if the paper itself couldn't hold the weight of what had happened.

"My vision is off like my mind is playing tricks on me. It got worse when I was driving home from the ER a couple hours ago—I was disoriented, the city's streets were shifting all around me."

Words trailed off as my thoughts wandered, the memory of that drive becoming indistinct.

"Ms. Visjonær, keep this for your records," the officer said, pointing to the police slip. "If you can, call this number tomorrow to speak with the Special Victims Unit. An investigator will be assigned to your case. Thank you for your cooperation tonight. Get some rest." They exited through the exterior gate and walked back to their patrol car, parked along the red curb beside the fire hydrant on Lombard Street. Their headlights flared as they drove away.

"Flashback memories are intense."

"They are. And throughout the investigation, their refusal to acknowledge the felony— *including the police's interpretation of the assailant's non-consensual photos of you as proof of his innocence*—was a calculated evasion of accountability. A tactic that protects the powerful at the expense of the vulnerable."

He paused, thoughtful. "Everything you articulate here is part of the healing process. You're recognizing that acceptance isn't just important—it's immeasurable. Hold onto this and whatever happens don't give up."

Next, he slid a stack of papers across the table. "I've printed out a Master List of Logical Fallacies-thought you'd appreciate it, given your interest and a few new ones that might pique your curiosity: *Ableism*, also known as the *Con-Artist Fallacy*, and the *Alternative Truth Fallacy*, which is essentially a form of *Disinformation Fallacy*."

The psychologist leaned forward, his eyes locking onto mine with an intensity that made me feel like he was searching for something beneath the surface. His voice was low and measured, each word carefully chosen. "The Alternative Truth Fallacy is rooted in postmodernism. Hannah Arendt warned about it in *Origins of Totalitarianism* how authoritarian regimes don't just distort reality, they dismantle it entirely."

He paused, his hands gesturing as he continued. "They don't just suppress the truth; they replace it, fabricating a version so absolute that questioning it becomes dangerous."

His gaze never wavered, his eyes burning with a sense of urgency. "Facts bent into obedience. Sound familiar?"

I held the printed page, my eyes scanning words that seemed to sear themselves into my mind. The narrative was a distorted reflection of reality—authority insisting that events had unfolded in ways they never had.

"The sergeant's claim—that she had already shown me the case file, and Henry's illicit photos—was a lie. A fabrication presented as fact, with no room for doubt or inquiry."

Sartre's concept of *mauvaise foi* or 'bad faith' suggests that individuals—those who make up the system—often seek to escape the moral weight of truth by hiding behind roles or rules. In a related vein, Camus' *absurdism* speaks to the tension between humanity's need for justice and the universe's cold indifference. Together, they illuminate the existential violence of being gaslit not just by a person, but by an institution.

The psychologist replied gently, "Rose, given the weight of these experiences, it's important to find moments—or places—that bring you comfort. Is there a place that helps you feel grounded?"

"Yes. A cold plunge at D.L Bliss State Park, the ocean, or—I keep imagining myself inside Black Rabbit Rose in Hollywood Los Angeles. I've never been but picture it vividly. A magical theatre-lounge with a stage draped in cascading crimson velvet, lit by Victorian chandelier icicles. Inspired by Houdini, master of the death-defying escape, it feels like a sanctuary of illusion and possibility."

"At Black Rabbit Rose, we sip emulsions from long-stemmed glasses or Marie Antoinette coupes—a place where we live while we're alive. The fire-and-brimstone preachers are banished, their righteous venom fading into shadow alongside the false prophets who mistake delusion for destiny." As we sat together, language unfolded between us. The psychologist's gentle nods, the way he leaned forward with a relaxed smile—it all created a sense of ease, a kind of intimate safety.

"The cold water shock likely grounds you in the present," he said, his voice thoughtful, almost enigmatic. "It brings calm and clarity. Whereas Black Rabbit Rose—that's a magical, intentional escape. And it makes sense. You were betrayed of course you'd be wary of anyone who claims authority while wielding fear as a weapon."

"Exactly. The moment you walk in it's like stepping into another dimension free from dogma. I hope they play 'Stardust' or 'Begin the Beguine' while we're deep in conversation, just before the Magic Hour Cabaret begins."

He nodded. "When you're overwhelmed, visualizing a place like Black Rabbit Rose—somewhere safe, enchanting, creatively alive—will help ground you. Let's explore how we can bring that kind of imagery into your daily routine, to help ease intrusive thoughts or memories."

CHAPTER 2:   THE LOSS OF INNOCENCE

A taste for truth at any cost is a passion which spares nothing. — Albert Camus

My Blackberry mobile vibrated loudly against the surface of my drafting table desk. I saw Henry's name flash across the digital screen and picked up.

"Rose— I'm here, come down when you are ready!"

About a week ago he suggested that he would pick me up in front of my apartment building at 8PM to go to dinner. He explained that he lived off of Union Street in Cow Hollow and was only a few blocks away from me so he thought it would be best if he drove us to the restaurant. I agreed. I wore my favorite navy blue cardigan sweater, Citizen of Humanity jeans, wedge heels and a purse.

As I walked towards him parked alongside the curb, the passenger-side window of his silver metallic Porsche 911 Carrera S Convertible was rolled down in anticipation of seeing me. As he looked out through the open window at me.

"Hi, jump-in, great to see you!"

I opened the door, sat into the sleek slate gray leather interior seat and felt the fresh cool breeze of air-conditioning hit my face. The dynamic sounds of classic rock n' roll music saturated the space between us as it played from the elegantly designed Porsche speakers. I put on my seatbelt and shut the door.

Suddenly, the traffic light turned bright green. Henry shifted the seven-speed high-precision transmission into drive and sped through the intersection. At that moment, he glanced over at me and asked:

"Are you sure you're twenty-one?"

I couldn't tell if he was teasing. I was surprised to hear him ask the question again.

"Why—am I too young to ride in a sports car?"

"Can't believe you have one of these," I added, running my hand lightly over the dashboard. "It's been my dream to own one since I was young."

"Perfect. You'll enjoy this," he replied with a confident smile.

Within seconds, he accelerated up the steep incline of Gough Street, then took a swift left onto Broadway, heading toward Chinatown, North Beach, and the Financial District.

"When I first met you," he said, shifting the car into sport mode, "you didn't look old enough to be in college. Maybe you've heard this before, but—you look incredibly young for your age."

The twin-turbo, six-cylinder horizontally opposed engine responded instantly to the lightest touch. I took a deep breath as we flew beneath the golden arch of the westbound Broadway tunnel. Inside the high-capacity conduit, the road was empty—so he pushed it harder. The car's low center of gravity gave it flawless stability, with minimal vibration. The distinct, muscular growl of the engine echoed through the open windows. I noticed he kept them down, even with the A/C running.

We exited into an alleyway in the historic Jackson Square District. He pulled up to a white curb beside a row of urban brick buildings—the kind that seemed to carry stories behind every window.

The drive from my Marina apartment to the hidden restaurant had taken less than ten minutes. I glanced out the window. The night was unusually dark, yet crystal clear. The brightness of the half moon hung above us, casting a cool glow over the still street. The air was calm, with no wind at all.

Henry stepped out of the driver's seat and watched closely as the valet approached, offering his hand to help me out of the Carrera. With practiced ease, Henry tossed the keys over the hood—like he'd done it countless times before.

The valet caught the keys and cheerfully replied, "Nice to see you again, Sir."

The Art Deco **BIX** sign, above the large refurbished wooden doors of the speakeasy supper club, glowed neon blue. It was a peaceful February night; yet the notorious reputation of the lawless and licentious city seemed to hide itself within the brick walls of this district.

The omnipotent history of the Barbary Coast whispered as he pulled the door open. Henry gently placed his hand in the small of my back to guide us through the entrance way. As we walked inside the soaring two-story dining room, a hostess quickly approached and informed us, "Good evening Mr Henry, thank you so much for joining us tonight. We spoke on the phone earlier about two reservations at our bar. Please follow me this way." She escorted us to his preferred location within the repurposed bank building as a live jazz-pianist played.

"Our bartender Mr Taylor will be serving you, enjoy," the hostess said as she slipped away.

Henry warmly smiled at me and said, "I prefer to sit here because of the immediate service and I know the owner. Plus, isn't the set up stunning?"

A timeless Roaring Twenties dance hall mural illuminated the backsplash above the bar. It was an impressive size at about 10 x 30 feet, so it adorned the entire length of the wall. We sat in the cushioned seats towards the end of the bar near the pianist.

"Yes, stunning and imaginative. It feels almost as if I'm looking directly into a surreal vision of the past or a reflection," I replied.

A bartender dressed in a clean-white tuxedo jacket greeted us. He proudly handed out the menus.

"Good evening, Mr Henry. Pleased to see you again. Let me know if you have any questions about the menu. I will be back shortly," he announced.

Delicately Henry scanned the menu in his hand.

"The dried pear Bombay Sapphire cocktail is absolutely delicious. I've had it. Would you care to try it?

I paused, weighing my options. "It sounds lovely but I'll have the margarita," I said, a playful laugh escaping my lips. The visual contrast struck me as amusing—a vibrant margarita with a lime wedge seemed out of place in this refined restaurant.

His eyes carefully examined me.

"Rose, you can have anything you'd like while you're with me."

Little did I know, his words masked the imbalance of power that would soon become chillingly clear. After Henry placed our order, he gazed at me steadily. "Lovely that we were finally able to meet up. I've been hoping to have another conversation with you. The satisfaction of a spontaneous interaction like the one we had a few weeks ago, doesn't happen too often."

As the bartender returned, he methodically placed the fresh napkins along the dark mahogany bar. He positioned the old fashion martini in front of Henry and the margarita next to me. The strong bouquet scent of cherry and whisky from his cocktail wandered in my direction as he gently lifted his glass into the air.

"Cheers, I'm happy you're here with me now! We have the opportunity to talk about life and future work in the city. I understand you are an artist with an interest in advertising and digital marketing as a career and I have so many... a plethora of professional connections I would be more than happy to introduce you to. By the way, the mural behind the bar is by artist Mindy Lehrman Cameron."

"Thank you for inviting me."

Henry continued, "The BIX is iconic; the Deco-inspired style of the supperclub paired with the jazz keeps me coming back, but every time I return it's something new. I never know what to expect. Certainly one of my favorite spots for dinner and drinks. This past Winter I hosted my Christmas Party here for my clients, colleagues and investors."

Henry exuded a comfortable confidence and powerful composure. His body was balanced and strong. He had a tasteful well dressed city style, sharp blue-eyes with a silvery dirty blonde suave haircut. Henry was about 45 yrs old and I was 25.

"Rose, moving to the city from a small town can feel daunting. I would like to show you around and introduce you to some of the things that I like to do. Also I would like to check-in with you to see how you are doing. I admire your ambition and want to be supportive," he explained.

Next, he ordered the appetizers that he liked which were *Steak Tartare* and Dungeness Crab but he never asked me about what I wanted to eat.

Raw minced beef would be the last thing on earth I'd have.

Nervously, I twirled my silver ring around my finger as my hand rested in my lap. He ordered another round of strong cocktails.

"Thanks, I recently moved to the city from Arcata, where I lived with my boyfriend. Now pursuing a Master in Fine Arts degree and looking to break into the industry as a Junior Art Director."

My eyes locked into the evocative image behind Henry.

"Wow that oil painting of the suave gentleman in the black tuxedo and white gloves admiring the lipstick-stained absinthe glass, I can't stop looking at," I confessed. "The sophistication of it and my dad has a poster with the "BIX" logo. Seeing this painting now is surreal—what are the chances?"

As I gazed at *'The Butler in Love—Absinthe,'* an oil painting by Mark Stock mounted above the Grand Piano, Henry turned around to take a look.

The painting seemed to illustrate the man's unrequited love or obsessive desire.

"The olive green color in the painting always seemed kind of eerie to me. Seeing the painting in comparison to the replica reminds me of an artistic philosophy concept: the meaning of a visual message determines the way in which that message will be perceived. Earlier today I was at *City Lights Bookstore* and I bought 'The Work of Art in the Age of Its Technological Reproducibility' by Walter Benjamin," I described.

Henry smiled and replied, "Spectacular, hold that thought." He gestured again for the tuxedoed bartender. As Mr Taylor returned he placed an oversized white dish on the placemat in front of Henry. The tender Steak Tartare appetizer which was mixed with parsley, capers, fresh shallots and olive oil seemed almost alive. Repulsed by the smell and thought of what it was, I flinched and felt like gagging.

"Mr. Taylor, we will have the Courvoisier 'Initiale' Cognac and a glass of Syrah from Rhône Valley." Henry's decadent desire for indulgence influenced every choice that he made.

He paused for a moment and replied, "Rose — sounds like a dynamic book. Your rigorous interest in art is refreshingly sweet; how are you so clever?"

"Everything I've learned is from my travels, education or curiosity."

He smiled at me and professed, "I have a great selection of art history and photography books at my condo with a breathtaking view of the Golden Gate Bridge and the Bay. Now I am curious—Have you done modeling?" Henry's eyes pierced into mine as he intensely waited for my reply.

"Yes—a fine art model for Professor Hollowell's upper-division figure drawing classes at UC Berkeley for a few semesters. I would hold a posture for an hour at a time."

Henry tilted his head, his voice low, curious.

"Impressed. Tell me—how did it feel, to be bare before a room of strangers?"

"Shocking." The word slipped like a confession.

I remembered the silence of the studio—the light on me, the sound of charcoal and pencil etching paper. My body locked into an elegant shape, sweat gathering along my spine and around my neck, time stretching into the abyss. It felt like an exposure, being dissected under their collective gaze. But the longer I held, the more I transformed—stone, statue, specter—into something *more than human.*

Mr. Taylor returned with the fresh cocktail drinks in unique glassware and placed them on fresh napkins in front of Henry. Following that he brought another oversized white dish, this time with a fresh Dungeness Crab appetizer. It was mixed with garlic butter, shallots, chopped thyme and parsley on a bed of lettuce and it looked somewhat appealing but it wasn't something that I liked to eat.

The bartender attentively stood in front of us and said, "Mr. Henry, if there is anything else you would like, do not hesitate to ask," and walked around the bar into the server's doorway.

As I gazed up at the imaginative mural above the altar-like bar, the vibrant colors seemed to pulse to life, swirling with energy. I realized my dizziness was creeping in - it had been hours since I'd eaten, and the drinks were hitting me harder than I'd anticipated. So I asked Henry, "I would like to try the celery root soup, the citrus salad or the entree pasta next. I am hungry and I haven't eaten."

"Fine, sweetheart, when he comes back I will order those for you."

But he never did.

He continued the conversation about modeling. "Holding a posture for an hour would be challenging! And in front of a group of artists and students no less."

"Certainly I could never do it—Why don't you try the Cognac and tell me what you think of it?"

As he handed me the glass, he spoke with casual ease.

"I practice several times a week. My body feels stronger, more aligned—and it's improved my swimming. I even did some laps at the North Beach pool before picking you up."

His blue eyes sparkled as I sipped the cognac, its warmth unfolding across my palate in a velvety burst.

"It has a cinnamon-ginger spice, with a peachy apricot note," he observed.

"I never drink cognac," I admitted. "My aunt lives near the North Beach pool."

He leaned closer, lowering his voice.

"Rose, I've practiced vinyasa at the neighborhood studio for years. Maybe you've been? They host technique workshops on mula bandha and uddiyana bandha—the root lock and the upward lock."

His words became images in my mind: *mula bandha*, the subtle rooting of energy at the spine's base, as if invisible roots drew deep into the earth; *uddiyana bandha*, the hollowing lift of the belly, a quiet fire kindling upward, energy rising like smoke from a hidden flame.

Breath and movement braided together—steady, yet infinite.

He paused, watching me, then slid another glass across the table.

"Try the Syrah. Dark berries, a hint of violet. Captivating—like you."

CHAPTER 3: POETIC ABSTRACTION OF A MUSE

All the world's a stage, and all the men and women merely players. —William Shakespeare

"Excuse me," I said, sliding down from the barstool, creating a measured distance between myself and Henry. My heels seemed to glide across the polished wooden floor, a graceful contrast to the sharp intensity of his gaze. His poised demeanor never wavered, even as a fog began to seep into my consciousness. He seemed to be pacing the drinks deliberately, hoping I'd lose my edge.

It felt like dancing through a dream, an arabesque carrying me deeper into the dining room's vastness—my heels sketching graceful curves across the polished floor as if tracing an invisible ballet. The room itself became a stage and I, an unwilling performer, was drawn toward the wings. Suddenly, my gaze caught on a canvas: dark, mischievous eyes staring out, a clown clutching a ballerina behind the stage, locked in an unsettling embrace. The painting's presence was inescapable, suspended like a spotlighted dancer in midair, fixed on the wall just below the staircase leading to the restrooms.

There was something surreal, even dangerous, about it—as if the scene had been pulled straight from a mystery novel or a noir film. It was unmistakably *The Kiss* by Mark Stock —a haunting piece known to BIX regulars. From its perch beneath the staircase, it seemed to watch the ebb and flow of guests with silent, theatrical disdain.

The clown's expression—gleeful yet grotesque—radiated a twisted delight, while the ballerina seemed caught between escape and surrender. The scene felt lifted from a noir film or a Lynchian fever dream. A shiver ran down my spine as the ballerina subtly turned… and winked at me.

The elusive and surreal image flickered in my mind, as the door to the lady's room swung wide open. I walked towards the illustrious mirror above the white marble sink. I clutched the cool surface for balance and gazed at my reflection.

The light above the mirror bathed my appearance in a glamorous aesthetic. Suddenly the poetic abstraction of a muse looked carefully back at me, ethereal and mesmerizing. My gaze tripped in and out of focus as I observed my eye lashes heavy with Dior mascara, were delicate doll tendrils. Another shiver danced down my spine.

Peut-être que j'étais la muse? Maybe I was the muse?

The thought floated atop a pink cloud, shook my head in disbelief. The golden Restoration Hardware faucet poured cool water, a gentle caress across my skin. As I washed my hands, silky bubbles formed and burst into the air, releasing a subtle rose fragrance that wafted through the haze.

When I returned to my seat beside Henry the dining room faded into fantasy. The world around me seemed to disconnect from reality as he handed me the glass of dark berry Syrah. His proximity felt suffocating.

"Take a generous sip." He encouraged, his voice low, smooth and at ease.

Our conversation meandered through various topics: design, augmented reality, social media platforms and apps, the Silicon Valley scene, fine wine, and the perks of owning a business in the city. Henry's words were laced with charm, making me feel seen and appreciated, but beneath the surface another animal.

Signaling for the bartender again.

"Mr. Taylor, we will have a flight of red from a St. Helena winery of your choosing and one Redbreast whisky."

The atmosphere sparkled with brilliant light, a dazzling array of distractions vying for my attention. The bartender returned, bearing clean wine glasses and an assortment of fancy bottles. Henry nodded, and five ruby-colored wine tastings were poured in sequence. The air was filled with the intoxicating aroma of dark berries - blackberry, plum, and cherry - mingling with hints of cacao spice. Henry's eyes lit up, fully absorbed in the pleasure of the moment.

Mr. Taylor's voice wove in, describing the exclusive offering: "This is Hall St. Helena's most elevated experience, featuring their coveted Platinum Collection wines. You'll taste a barrel sample of their prized Kathryn Hall Cabernet, accompanied by a private seated tasting. The flight includes three Platinum wines, alongside select, highly-rated Cabernets from the Artisan Collection."

Henry continued, "visual design principles and augmented reality will bridge gaps by improving learning and engagement." He wanted to collaborate with modern businesses to stay contemporary and acknowledged the need to integrate new ideas into his model to avoid becoming outdated. As he spoke about work he directed, "The tastings are exquisite — try this one now." He handed me the delicate wine glass as he looked deep into my eyes as he told me that he desired to modernize aspects of his company and align the company vision with the ever-evolving technological advancements. The details that he would include seemed to be preoccupied with success, power and beauty. Enthusiastic about everything that he liked, it was easy to listen to him.

"Rose— This has been fun and I don't want to cut off the evening too soon," he announced. "I would love to relax with you a bit more and share the panoramic view of the Golden Gate Bridge from my condo in Cow Hollow. It is beautiful and I bet you have not seen the cityscape from a sight like that before, have you?"

Deliriously numb I answered, "I haven't."

"Perfect, I will take you, it would be my pleasure," he adamantly announced as he signaled for Mr. Taylor to return his attention towards him. The tuxedoed man walked over to the bar with a gracious expression in his eyes. Henry expressed, "Thank you for the nice evening. I will have the bill."

Mr Taylor walked to the digital cash register system for a moment and came back with a soft leather card holder. Just as he placed it upon the mahogany bar, Henry tossed his credit card on top without any interest in reading the receipt. Next, he signed the bill in grandiose illegible letters and we walked away.

As he pulled open the heavy wooden door of the repurposed building, the history of the Barbary Coast whispered again—this time louder, insistent. I shook my head in disbelief as the sound deepened into a low, thrumming frequency. Henry guided us into the darkness of Gold Street, just as the valet drew the Carrera to the curb.

The young valet sprang from the driver's side, circling the car with brisk precision. He opened the gleaming silver door and addressed me softly: "Miss."

And suddenly, time accelerated.

Henry whipped through the city streets with no discernible interruption in the flow of power. He enjoyed the thrill and optimum connection to the tuning of the chassis, engine and transmission while I was buckled in my seat dazed and confused.

I jolted awake for a moment when he swung sharply off Union onto Laguna. He clicked the garage remote, guiding us into the basement and slipping into a space among the other cars. My eyelids fought to stay open; I moved on a kind of autopilot as he opened the door and offered me his hand.

ART MODEL

We entered the building complex through the secured glass door in the basement and took the elevator to the top floor. Henry carefully unlocked the door, placed his hand in the small of my back to cortège me inside his immaculate penthouse condo.

As we entered the front room, I noticed that every object seemed to be purposefully placed in a well defined location. He had a remarkable attention to detail. I could tell that he loved possessions, not masses of them, but rather a distinct few that he would probably never part with. Henry cherished the quality that they served, maybe because it reminded him that his life was successful.

The glow of fresh white dove paint captured my eye because it highlighted the space as he was directing me towards the wall-to-wall modern windows. Standing close to the interior glass wall, I felt the cool cold temperature on my fingertips and took a deep breath as I was in awe of the city's splendor.

"Beautiful isn't it," Henry said as he turned to walk the other direction.

Perched high above the other buildings I admired the northwestern views of the Marina and the Bay. Lights twinkled across the cityscape as if they were stars falling to earth glittering gold.

It felt like the geometric pattern of the star polygons continued their delicate process of designing adjacent vertices across the surface of the neighborhood's shadowy building shapes. Overall the luminescence of the Golden Gate Bridge took the stage. As she glowed with a historic radiant aura while the dark sapphire waters shimmered under the moonlight in the distance.

Henry walked into the open kitchen, stood at the island and announced, "I am preparing a dessert with organic strawberries that I picked up today at Whole Foods, your favorite, Greek yogurt drizzled with coastal bee honey, and a cocktail."

Artistic ideas raced into my inebriated mind. The view reminded me of the literature I read at City Lights Bookstore earlier that day. I read a poem by the 1890s librarian and prominent San Franciscan, Ina D. Coolbrith:

"Fair on your hills, my City, Fair as the Queen of old, Supreme in her seven-hilled splendor — You, from your Gate of Gold, Facing the orient sunburst, Swathed in the sunset gleams, Throned in an ultimate glory, The City of mists and of the City Of dreams!"

Suddenly I heard him click the remote control. A high definition in-ceiling projection screen dropped behind where I was standing, which woke me up.

"It's breathtaking! The Golden Gate Bridge is magical and I've never seen the city this way before so amazing that you have this place. How long have you lived here?"

"For a few years and I've enjoyed it—Here, pick a movie on Netflix, have a seat on the couch and make yourself at home," he replied.

He handed me the remote control so I sat down on the Briar Sectional Sofa, gazed at the novel projection screen and scanned the wide selection of movies. I chose a comedy and as I was focused on the opening credits Henry placed the dessert and cocktail on the coffee table.

"Try that—I hope it's tasty," he said, unusually thoughtful as he handed me the strawberry dessert alongside a creamy coconut rum cocktail.

I took a bite, then a sip. "Do you like it?"

"Yes, thank you."

"While traveling through Southern Europe, I took so many photographs—they're stunning. Would you like to see them?" Henry shifted the mood quickly.

"Yes."

"Perfect. Sit tight—*sure* you liked it?" he called out, already disappearing into the other room in search of his artwork.

I stared down at the dessert, queasy with hesitation. But hunger won. I took a second bite—ripe red strawberry drenched in honeyed yogurt. I realized I hadn't eaten all evening. Time felt slippery, irrelevant. A third berry followed, devoured without thinking.

I turned my attention to the cocktail—an abstract swirl tropic cream. I sipped. The sharp bite of lime cut through the sweetness of coconut. Stronger than expected. I was already more buzzed than I should be.

"Here are a few of my photos I took in monochromatic color. I played with the variations or shade by altering the saturation and brightness of the base color. The subtleties in the *shades of gray* can be quite remarkable if you look closely..."

Henry handed me the classical European architecture prints. "Look at these," he said.

As I curiously examined each photo, he stood over me, silent. I noticed he didn't fix a cocktail for himself or offer a dessert, but he didn't explain why. He continued, "I traveled to Barcelona, Mallorca, Rome, Venice and Sardinia a few summers ago."

He described his artwork, "It's an extraordinary medium for me to express my interests and talents! I admire your passion for it, too. I remember the day that I first saw you taking photographs on Chestnut Street. You really stood out to me. It's cool that you've read one of McLuhan's books and understand his catchphrase 'The Medium is the Message'. I took an art history class while in college and enjoyed his book. I'm delighted that we share similar interests."

"Gorgeous pictures," I thoughtfully said.

Then he confessed, "I have been thinking about this one idea for a while. I'm impressed you've modeled before. Would you like to model for me?"

"Right now?"

"Yes, if you feel up to it, no pressure," he replied.

My head spun as I was thirsty and needed water so I looked around his living room. Next he directed, "It would be best if you posed in your bra and panties so I can capture the subtle curves of your body. You have a figure sculpted by the Gods of beauty. You embody the nature of a true *Renaissance Masterpiece* at the Getty."

"I will get you a glass of water — hang tight."

Henry placed the water on the table and sat next to me awaiting my reply. As I drank the water, I felt pressured to comply with his request so I said, "I guess so if it's for a few photos."

My powers of reasoning to draw logical conclusions were not there as I undressed to only my white lace Thistle & Spire undergarments. Deliriously I poised my body along the length of the couch as I pretended that I was the *'Sleeping Venus'* painting by Giorgione. While I rested my drowsy head into the palm of my hand, I crossed my legs gracefully at the ankles, relaxed my hand along the curve of my hip and imagined the infinite artistic lines of the female figure.

With his iPhone he captured digital pictures of me and announced, "Rose, you look beautiful but you'd look more refined and evocative if you were natural and in the nude."

Disorientation and cognitive dissonance crashed over me at once as I slipped off my lace bralette and bikini, standing bare beneath his gaze. My heart pounded, a frantic rhythm, my mind scrambling to make sense of what was happening. Then it hit me. I was isolated. The realization struck like a cold blade. Fear. Exposure. Shame. It washed over me in waves, raw and absolute—like Eve after taking a bite of the forbidden fruit.

"That's enough!"

The conflicting perceptions that I felt raced around and cut into my mind. My limited comprehension made it impossible for me to determine who he was or what he was capable of doing. Relentless, he continued to take more photographs.

"Stop!"

I said in anger. I got onto my hands and knees to search the floor for my belongings to put them on. As I struggled to become cognizant of what was really happening, I felt my eyelids rapidly fluttering and my vision did not seem to work.

"Thank you, Rose," he said politely, his eyes fixed on me.

Then his lips brushed the back of my neck. A cold shiver shot down my spine, a somatic jolt that locked me in place.The moment stretched, suffocating. The pungent bite of chlorine from his swim clashed with the crisp, citrusy trace of Fresh Verbena, L'Occitan en Provence soap.

I didn't move. Couldn't. Then he turned me around, his grip tightening on my shoulder. Too tight. His hand pressing, claiming. He leaned in, aiming for my lips—

I snapped my head back.

"No— I don't want this."

My voice came fast, breathless and trembling. "You took those photos because you told me it was forr... I need to go."

Henry barely flinched. "You don't need to feel that way, *sweetheart*." His voice was smooth, practiced.

"Relax. I'll back off—I got a little ahead of myself, that's all. Everything is fine. You're safe here. Why don't you watch the movie you picked?"

COMPOS MENTIS

He exited the room to head to the bathroom so I haphazardly slid some clothes back on. I felt blitzed and did not know what to do so I waited. Next Henry returned to sit next to me on the couch. With rapt attention he stared at me and reached over to grope my bare breast. I pushed his hand off.

The edge of his lips curled into a smirk.

I dismissed him, "Don't."

Without warning he positioned his body over mine and shoved me back as my head knocked back. I punched his shoulder so he forcefully kissed me and rubbed himself on me. Repulsed, I shoved him back again but my body felt weak. He didn't like that so he shoved me back again with more power so my head knocked back on the edge of the couch against the wall. It hurt and this interchange happened a few times.

Henry's voice edged with condescension.

"Are you going to start acting *crazy*?"

Before I could react, he grabbed me, forcing me down beside him. My body went numb. My eyes flickered, rapid and disbelieving, as if the moment itself was glitching.

His voice darkened.

"I can't deal with *crazy*—so stop."

The threat in his tone pressed into me like a blade. My skin prickled with panic, but I fought to steady my voice.

"No— I'm not *crazy*. I don't want this!"

He ignored me. Pulled me in against his bare chest.

"Sure."

A single word, empty, mocking.

A moment passed—then his hand slid under the waistband of my underwear. Fingers pushed inside me.

"Stop it."

I snapped but his grip tightened on my thigh, his fingertips digging into my flesh. He snickered. I wasn't a person to him—I was a thing. A subordinate subject. A body to own.

No empathy. No remorse. No hesitation.

He shifted down, his breath hot against my skin. His tongue, unwanted, moving over me as he shoved his fingers deeper—violating, invading. Then lower. His fingers forced their way inside me from behind.

Something inside me broke. I lashed out, kicking hard against his chest, aiming near his throat. He dodged, laughing. Then his pants were gone.

He climbed over me, pinning me beneath his weight. His body is a cage.

I thrashed, heart pounding so hard it felt like it would burst through my ribs.

"Stop it! Stop it! Get off me! That's enough!"

My words were useless.

The psycho wasn't listening.

He did not listen or care as he jolted his seemingly psychopathic face less than an inch from mine and breathed on me. He mocked me in contempt. His crystal clear eyes mutated into a vacuous animalistic stare as he inspected his new prey. His nonverbal communication was intimidating. I managed to position my knee into his sternum in the vain attempt to leverage him off. He reached down to open the fly of his boxer-briefs to expose himself.

He violently penetrated me as I was absolutely nauseous and cried, "Get off me get off me. You don't have my permission to do this."

He glared at me, his voice low and menacing, "Next time, I'll ask your permission."

His tone was ominous, a threat rather than a promise. The heat rose from his body like a wildfire. My body uncontrollably quivered. My eyelids fluttered rapidly and it felt like I was having a seizure. He looked down at me again.

"I've told you before — I don't have time for you to act out."

He stuck his fingers up my butt and wrapped his other arm underneath and around my ribcage. He intimately cradled the back of my head in his right hand.

"Stop please stop," I begged as I detached from my body. I surrendered as he came inside me and on my abdomen after a few minutes.

His semen was all over me. I was hysterical yet paralyzed. My vision blurred, my breathing became erratic and my body was subtly convulsing. So he immediately wrapped himself around me to spoon my body and control my reactions.

I quivered as he breathed deeply in my ear. As I listened to the rhythm of his breath slow in pace, he relaxed into a satisfied state of being.

My eyes darted around the room, scanning for an exit. The front door felt miles away, unreachable. My body refused to obey, as if severed from my mind. I wanted to move, but nothing happened.

For what felt like thirty minutes, he lay there, snoring—his heavy arms locked around me like dead weight. I was trapped, immobilized in a waking nightmare.

Then he stirred. And it started again.

Cold sweat broke over my skin as he forced himself inside me a second time. My body quivered, hollow and defeated. Escape wasn't an option. If I tried to run, he'd do it again. If I made it outside, what then? Would I even be safe? Would someone else on the street see my fear and take their turn?

Henry drifted back into sleep, his arms tightening around me, pressing me against his chest. I was trapped inside his body, inside my mind. My sensory perception was high and—irrational.

And then, something shifted.

The doors of perception swung open.

Everything became vivid, yet impossibly surreal. My mind fractured into something else, something deeper. I saw myself—an avatar walking through a labyrinth of tangled gardens and towering hedges.

Along the dusted pathway, a group of circus clowns appeared. Their faces were painted in elaborate, vibrant hues—yet their eyes remained cold, hollow. They whispered among themselves. Low, conspiratorial. Everything was a secret.

The elephants moved inside the maze before me, their hides were a weathered charcoal, with subtle wrinkles etched into their skin like a treasure map. Despite their enormity, they exuded an aura of innocence, as if they'd stumbled into this labyrinthine world by mistake.

Their eyes seemed to hold a deep sadness, a longing for escape from this bewildering place. As they moved, their massive footsteps echoed through the maze, harmonizing with the strange hum that still vibrated through my mind.

I squeezed my eyes shut. *This isn't real.*

Trapeze dancers in red tutus shimmered like fiery jewels against the dimmer backdrop, their layered netting fluttering like delicate wings.

The same costumes I designed for *Queen of Hearts*—the contemporary *Pas de trois* I choreographed only 3 years ago.

As they hung upside down, their laughter echoed through the space, euphoric and weightless. It was infectious, making me feel carefree and buoyant. One of the dancers turned toward me, her smile luminous. Her teeth were brilliant white, and her vibrant crimson lips curved upward, radiating joy. For an instant, our gazes met, her eyes sparkling with mirth.

"Take me away to *St. Barthélemy*—I wear my heart on my sleeve!"

An echo of something I'd once known.

Had I been there before? Or was my mind grasping at pieces of a world that didn't exist? I blinked but the vision remained.

I was derealized, adrift in the liminal space where past and present collapsed, where reality dissolved into abstraction. Falling into a realm where *le rêve est réalité, et la réalité est illusion*—where dreams were reality, and reality was illusion.

CHAPTER 4: S.A.R.T. FORENSIC EXAM

There is no honest way to explain it because the only people who really know where it is are the ones who have gone over. — Hunter S. Thompson

The early morning of February 23rd, I felt lifeless as I sat at my drafting table, trembling, staring blankly through the dusty bay windows of my second-floor bedroom. The city was already awake, the wind rattling the glass like a ghost.

A medium-ripe banana sat in front of me—the one he had given me. For a second, it multiplied, replicated itself—Warhol style. Maybe Warhol had it right, his fascination with consumer culture, and mundane objects like bananas need more consideration than what they are given.

The *Peel and See* Velvet Underground banana *is* this banana I thought, carefully.

My calendar notebook was open on the desk. Just as I blinked my eyes, the black Times New Roman letters from my calendar seemed to enlarge and float into the air. It was metamorphosing into psychedelic colors and forms. Chills went down my spine as I breathed slowly to concentrate.

Outside, the morning fog had already swept through the Marina–Cow Hollow neighborhood, blanketing Lombard Street and muffling the hum of U.S. Route 101. The traffic below moved with indifferent urgency, distant and almost unreal. I watched the cars glide past, their motion a sharp contrast to the stillness hollowing me out from within.

My grad school assignments sat in front of me like hallucinations—distorted projections, meaningless in that moment. The world outside felt more vivid, more pressing, than the quiet gnaw of my own unrest. Reality blurred with something more surreal, echoing *Fear and Loathing in Las Vegas*—where perception fractures and meaning slips sideways. The emptiness I felt was existential, where everything around me seemed to move with purpose, while I remained stuck in the void of my own disconnection.

The kelly-green glow of my digital clock shifted to 6:30 AM.

I reached for my phone and called Kristie. She picked up on the second ring.

"Hi. I'm thankful you answered. I know it's early."

"Good morning, Rose—how are you?" Kristie said, her voice light, cheerful.

"I am having body chills. My vision is weird and I am delirious."

My grasp tightened around the phone.

"Do you remember that guy from the Marina a few weeks ago?"

"You mean the one running his mouth while you were trying to take photos for class? And the same guy drinking wine in the middle of a workday?"

"Yes, that guy. I was with him last night—he took me to Bix in FiDi. Said it was dinner, but all he ordered were beef tartare and Dungeness crab, knowing I'm vegetarian. We talked about work, marketing, art… and then things got strange. I think he drugged me. I am shaking—can't control it. I feel humiliated and scared. He took photos of me in his condo. He got violent. Forced himself on me. I watched his eyes change color—from light icy blue to black eyes. How does that even happen?"

A predator's gaze can change, go vacant, turn black. It's not the iris that shifts, but the pupils—blown wide, absorbing all light, erasing color. Some say it's the body preparing for attack, hunting, killing. Others say it's something worse—a complete detachment from morality, from reality.

Kristie's voice cut through the silence.

"He seemed like a creep."

"Remember at lunch after you met him? I told you I had a bad feeling! And you didn't listen to me."

She exhaled sharply, frustration laced with concern. "I'm not an expert, but it sounds like you were raped. You need to call the RAINN National Sexual Assault Hotline and talk to someone—someone who knows how to help. You can't do this alone."

Her words landed, a truth that left no room for argument.

"Okay."

I replied blankly, staring out the dusty window.

"Like, now," Kristie pressed.

"I don't know the number. Hold on, let me check."

A pause.

"I found it—1-800-656-4673."

We hung up, and I called RAINN. A Crisis Counselor answered. For thirty minutes, I described what Henry had done to me.

"Get to San Francisco General Hospital ER as soon as you can," she advised. "A SART nurse will be there to assist with the forensic exam."

"Ok."

The call ended.

The thought of navigating across the city to the Zuckerberg San Francisco General Hospital Emergency Room—a place I'd never been before—felt impossible.

But I did it anyway.

When Location Services are enabled, a Location icon will display in the status bar. My BlackBerry's GPS voice-guided turn-by-turn directions guided me through the labyrinth of the city's busiest streets. The familiar robotic voice cutting through the haze in my mind.

I was surely running on autopilot.

Forty-five minutes later, I pulled up to the patient entrance.

The white curb marked the drop-off point—San Francisco's busiest emergency room, its only Level 1 Trauma Center. The two reddish-brick buildings, relics of 1974, worn by time. In a daze, I parked. Locked my car.

T.S. Eliot's *objective correlative* surfaced in my mind—the idea that emotion isn't spoken but reflected in the world around it. A landscape that holds the unspeakable. The *dissociation of sensibility*. Metaphysical poets weaving the most disparate ideas together, bound by oppressive violence. Wasn't that what had happened to me?

Henry's transgressions had happened only hours ago. Now I stood at the threshold of the hospital—stern, unyielding, but not indifferent. It wasn't warmth, but it was structure. It wasn't comfortable, but it was better than being with Henry.

An administrative voice broke my thoughts.

"Hi, Miss. How can we help you?"

"I was raped this morning, and need do the exam. I was told this was the only hospital that does them."

"Yes. What is your name?"

"Rose Visjonær."

"And your birthday?"

As I stood at the Registration Desk, a faint haze crept over my vision. The question felt like a distant echo, and my legs wobbled beneath me.

"April 20th."

I grasped the corner of the desk, desperate for support. A nurse rushed to my side, guiding me to a private room with a gray door. She led me to a seat on the edge of the examination bench, and I sank onto it, my body weakened.

"Rose, go ahead and have a seat on the exam table. We're going to start your forensic medical exam and run a toxicology screen. The doctor's been notified and will be in shortly. You're in good hands. Let me grab you a bottle of water—just sit tight, okay?"

She offered a small nod, then closed the door behind her.

I glanced around the sterile white room, the walls too bright, too clean. The hospital gown felt stiff against my skin as I pulled it on, then eased myself onto the exam table, eyes drifting closed.

I must have dozed off—ten minutes, maybe less.

A knock at the door startled me.

"Miss Visjonær, are you dressed?"

I pushed myself upright, fingers patting my hair down instinctively, as if tidying up could make me feel more in control.

"Yes, I am."

Panic settled in—not about the exam, not even about what had happened. My mind fixated on missing class. My copywriting class. Guilt sank in like a stone.

I shifted in the itchy hospital gown, trying to ground myself in something tangible.

"Can I call my professor?"

I asked, glancing at the SART nurse. "Don't want to miss my class without letting them know."

She gave a nod. "Yes, that's perfectly fine."

I dialed the School of Advertising at the Academy of Art University, my fingers instinctively finding the familiar buttons on my BlackBerry.

The Admin Assistant answered on the first ring.

"Goodmorning, the School of Advertising, this is Laura. How may I direct your call?" she said cheerfully.

"Good morning it's Rose, may I speak to Dr Shakespeare?"

"Hi Rose, why do you need to speak with Dr. Shakespeare? Your class starts in less than fifteen minutes. Why not talk with her in person?"

I gulped back tears.

"I can't. I'm in the ER."

A pause.

"I need to talk to her now. Is that okay?"

"Yes, that's fine I will transfer you to Dr. Shakespeare's direct line," Laura quickly replied.

I waited as the call transferred, hyper-alert as the phone was pressed against my ear.

Next a heavy wave of shock washed over me, my eyes overwhelmingly swelled with tears.

Click, the attended transfer complete.

"Good morning, Rose—how are you doing today?"

Dr. Shakespeare's voice was smooth, professional. The sound of her voice comforted me.

"Hi, good morning, Dr. Shakespeare—I won't be in class today. I'm in the ER. I was raped."

The words rushed out unfiltered, and raw. An unrestrained truth hurtling into the void like a speeding motorcycle.

A pause.

"I'm concerned to hear this," she said carefully.

"It's absolutely fine you miss class today. I am proud of you for taking action—seeking emergency medical care and reporting the incident. This is important and your safety is priority"

Her words impacted me, the silent tears began to fall down my feverish cheeks onto my blue hospital gown. I wasn't expecting validation.

"Thank you. I'll be back next week to class."

My voice wavered, I felt shaken out of ordinary perception, like reality had fractured slightly.

"Take care, Rose. I'll be thinking of you."

She hung up.

I inhaled and exhaled sharply.

The ER lights softly buzzed overhead, sterile and cold.

"How did you sleep last night?" the nurse asked.

"I didn't really sleep."

Every time I closed my eyes, I was transported back to Henry's condo—floor-to-ceiling windows framing the twinkling lights of the Marina. Flashbacks and nightmares bled into my waking life, hallucinations flickering beneath the hospital's harsh fluorescent lights.

While I was with him, sleep came only in fragments—thirty minutes, maybe an hour at a time. And each time I resurfaced, his face was there, staring at me. His eyes would shift —ice-blue one moment, pure black the next.

I blinked, trying to focus on the nurse, but everything felt distant—like I was swimming in deep water, suspended between worlds.

I wasn't in the ER. I was in his condo.

The air carried the sharp bite of chlorine and fresh verbena soap—chemical, clean, suffocating. That scent clung to my skin, burrowed into my strawberry blonde hair, my consciousness—it refused to let go.

The vision of Henry haunted me. Chlorine clung to him like a shadow, a pungent trace of his late-afternoon swim at the North Beach Swimming Pool. When he picked me up outside my apartment and I slid into the passenger seat of his Carrera, it followed— inescapable.

Now it was everywhere—saturating the stark white ER walls. Embracing me. Surrounding me. As the rush came.

"Rose?"

The nurse's voice cut through. I forced myself to nod.

"I wanted to leave," I replied as the tears fell.

"But my body wouldn't move. Fear settled deep in my bones. If I tried to leave he would do it again! Well he did. He raped me twice."

"Rose, I can only imagine how overwhelming it must feel. I am sorry but I want to make sure you're comfortable with what's going to happen next."

"Can you take a deep breath and review the sexual assault forensic medical form with me? It explains the procedures we'll be doing today. I need you to sign off on it if you're okay with moving forward. We'll get through this together, okay?"

The nurse handed me the CALEMA-923 form, along with a pen. I scanned the pages, signed my name in each designated box and line.

The examination lasted six hours.

Every interaction with the SART team and nurses mattered—they provided medical care, emotional support and safety. They drew my blood through venipuncture for serologic testing, screening for infections that could compromise my immune system. Microbiology swabs were taken for DNA collection. I consented to both the forensic medical exam and the toxicology screen, allowing them to record everything through California's standardized forensic forms.

I was given a regimen of SAEK prophylactic medications administered as part of post-assault medical care, and I was prescribed Oxycodone for pain.

"I've also contacted the on-call therapist from the University of San Francisco Trauma Recovery Center," the nurse said, her voice calm but professional.

"It's standard protocol for victims of violent crime, including sexual assault. There's no pressure, but if you'd like, you can speak with them. It's entirely up to you—whatever you feel most comfortable with."

Anna Ovchinikov Brown, the on-call therapist from UCSF's Trauma Recovery Center, arrived while I was still undergoing the SART examination. Her presence is steady and compassionate. She spoke about the importance of self-care and healthy coping mechanisms, explaining that I was eligible for Trauma Recovery Counseling since I would be registered with CalVCB.

"Rose, you can begin counseling with me at the center," she said as she handed me the save-the-date card.

"Please keep this with you. I am grateful to have met you today. I see so much strength in you, and I look forward to working together. Take care."

The SART Nurse collected evidence—blood, urine, and swabs for biological samples. I was given a full course of anti-STD medications, and took the emergency contraceptive pill Plan B.

I could already feel the nausea. Next, I was given the ER's medical discharge paperwork and instructions to follow.

The city's rush hour traffic swallowed me whole. I had no clue how everything would come crashing down all at once when I left the safety of the nurse's care inside the ER.

My GPS recited proper directions—turn left, merge right, continue for a half mile—but the words seemed to be in another language. A disconnection between the auditory input and the brain's processing of that input. Maybe this is auditory disassociation?

I failed to follow the directions. My mind zigzagged, unable to process the streets unraveling into an endless maze. My BlackBerry's GPS droned on—turn left, merge right —but the directions barely registered. I got very lost.

I ended up somewhere in the Mission District, east-central San Francisco, where the streets pulsed with Spanish-Mexican history. Bold murals of revolutionaries and saints painted across alley walls, their watchful eyes.

Feverish, I called Miles, the one friend I knew who knew this city inside and out. My voice shook as I told him what happened. He was quiet for a second—then steady. He guided me home. Without him, I might've circled the streets for four hours, trapped in the disorienting fog.

It took nearly <u>two hours to drive three miles.</u>

By the time I reached my Cow Hollow apartment, my legs felt detached as if I were walking on borrowed bones. The black iron gate loomed ahead—I slid the key in, pushed it open, and stepped through. My gaze traced the steep marble staircase leading to my front door. Each step felt like a battle.

Unlocked the second door, stepped inside and walked straight into my room.

I undressed and stumbled into the shower. Turning the knob to high, the scalding water hit my skin—but it did nothing to erase the pain or the memory that haunted me.

In trauma, the amygdala floods the brain, overriding the hippocampus and shattering memory into fragments. Still, I followed the counselor's advice: call the police. Dial 911.

At 11:30 p.m., the buzzer sounded. I let in two San Francisco officers. They stood in my entryway, dark navy uniforms pressed, silver badges catching the light. One wore a precisely groomed mustache. Their posture was stiff, their presence all formality and protocol.

I felt intimidated, so I simplified the story—leaving out details, like how Henry had taken photos of me in his condo. At first, I was too scared to give his full name or phone number. Suddenly, I imagined—with eerie clarity—how his influence and connections would protect him from facing any real consequences.

When consciousness is altered—by drugs or trauma—memories return slowly, like puzzle pieces falling into place. Speaking to the officers triggered a stress response. I felt like *I* had done something wrong.

They handed me an SFPD incident report number and the phone number for the Special Victims Unit.

"Call this number this week. A detective will be assigned to your case. Thank you, Miss Rose." Then, they left.

CHAPTER 5: SECOND ER VISIT – DR BARTON'S ASSESSMENT

She once believed that the damage to her mind and heart was permanent, until she met wisdom, who taught her that no pain or wound is eternal, that all can be healed and that love can grow even the toughest parts of her being. — Yung Pueblo

Woke up to a sharp pain twisted through my abdomen, running along my side. An unbearable itch followed, spreading beneath my skin. I had never felt anything like it before. Was it from the assault? An allergic reaction to the seven or more SAEK medications?

I couldn't move well so I dressed carefully, took a prescribed Oxycodone by the nurse and made my way down the steep marble staircase as quickly as I could. I swung open the black exterior gate and stepped onto the cement sidewalk on Lombard Street. The morning traffic rushed by, cars speeding to their destinations. Disoriented, I walked endless streets, searching for my car. Where had I parked it?

The advection fog rolled into the Marina's Cow Hollow neighborhood, casting a gray veil over the city. The salty scent of the Pacific Ocean filled the air as I walked down Lombard Street, a six-way thoroughfare that was part of U.S. Route 101. The city's vibrant colors seemed muted, blending together in a monotone haze. My gaze scanned for where it might be parked. After twenty minutes of searching and walking in zig-zags I realized that it was not there. The Municipal Transportation Agency or SFMTA must have towed it.

I fell hard onto my knees, cradling my head into my hands as my tears melted into the dirty Lombard Street sidewalk. As I hyperventilated, my heart pounded, and bright flashes of light flooded my ability to see. Did they tow my car because it was street cleaning day?

I dial 911. The early morning street lights spun, into a tornado of colors, as an operator answered the call.

"Nine-one-one operator – what is your emergency?" a female dispatcher asked.

Gasping for air I could not articulate a sentence; so I stuttered involuntarily, ""Ie-ie-ie-ie am having a panic attack. I don't know where my car is. Please help."

"What is your name?" the dispatcher exhorted.

I gasped again as I pressed all of my body weight into a cement wall so I could stand upright. The cars driving down Lombard Street sped vapidly as I was struggling to speak.

"Miss what is your name?" she reiterated.

"I cannot breathe," I replied.

"What is your address?" she inquired.

"Lombard Street my-my car was towed this morning and N N I need to go to the hospital," I said. "I understand and I am trying to help. What is your name, miss?"

"Rose."

"Thank you, Rose. You need to call Yellow Cab. Tell them to take you to AutoReturn, it's located on 7th Street. You will need to pay the fine. I know this is hard; but if you wait another day to retrieve the vehicle it will accrue more fines. Next you need to drive to the San Francisco General Hospital Emergency Room. Do you understand?" the dispatcher asked.

"Yes, go to AutoReturn first?"

"It is your choice, ultimately. It sounds like you do not need police assistance. So I will be erasing this call from the record."

"What? Why?"

"*Good luck*," she said and hung up.

I followed the 911 operator's instructions and called Yellow Cab. As I waited for the cab to arrive, I took another Oxycodone. It took five minutes for the cab to arrive. As I grasped the metal handle to the idiosyncratic yellow door, I fell into the plastic seats and held my bag close to my chest for comfort.

"Good Morning Miss, where are you headed?"

"AutoReturn on 7th Street."

"Sure thing. 450 7th Street," he replied.

He abruptly accelerated the Ford Crown Victoria Yellow Cab up Gough Street.

Once we arrived, I paid the driver in cash and exited the cab.

My stomach twisted as I opened the heavy glass door to the infamous Impound AutoReturn. The fluorescent lights buzzed overhead, casting a sterile glow across the linoleum floor. I felt like I'd stepped into a nightmare video game—one designed to break me.

A winding maze of black stanchion tape led to the AutoReturn Cashiers, like some dystopian side quest designed by Kafka. I moved through it like an avatar, each step surreal, the walls too close, the silence too loud. I glanced at my phone: 8:00 a.m. sharp. The digital numbers glared back like a checkpoint timer, counting down in a game where the prize was my own impounded car—and a sliver of my autonomy.

"Hello. I believe my car was towed this morning."

"What is your license plate number? And the car model?"

"22CGCW8 and it's a dark blue Honda Civic."

"Yes, we have it here," she replied as she rapidly typed on her keyboard attached to a DOS desktop.

"That will be $541. How would you like to pay cash or credit?"

She asked as she peered through the bulletproof plexiglass at me.

"Credit."

I opened my wallet and slid the card into the small metal cup beneath the plexiglass.

"Thank you."

"Do you know what time it was towed?"

"Looks like it was just before 6am. Please sign this copy and here is the one for your records. You will need to exit out that door and take a left into the impound yard."

I exited through the side door and waited beside a towering silver fence laced with barbed wire and studded with security cameras.

Soon after, my car was released. I walked into the tow yard where a security guard pointed toward it—parked in a massive lot among rows of other impounded vehicles. I slid into the driver's seat, started the engine, and headed straight to San Francisco General Hospital. When I arrived, I parked in the garage near the entrance.

As I stepped out, the world around me began to distort, like a kaleidoscope turning. In a dissociative daze, I drifted toward the San Francisco General Hospital ER registration desk. The world began to spin again, and I felt myself slipping out of my body—watching from above, as if I were merely a spectator to my own unraveling.

"Hello, how can we help you?"
One of the women at the registration desk spoke, her voice drifting through the air like a distant melody. Overhead, the lights pulsed and flickered, casting an otherworldly shimmer across the ceiling. My mind spiraled—thoughts unraveling like a runaway train through a fractured dream, images flashing in and out of coherence.

"I don't want to live anymore," I whispered. "There's an intense, insufferable burning."

I gasped. Suddenly awake. A white hospital bed beneath me. The stillness was eerie, as if time had stopped. I looked around, disoriented—my heart rapidly pounding. Did I black out?

A line drifted through my mind, soft as a whisper: *"With your feet in the air and your head on the ground, try this trick and spin yah your head will collapse, but there's nothing in it, and you'll ask yourself, where is my mind?"*

An angel approached, her presence illuminating the space with a soft, otherworldly shimmer. She moved with grace, a hush in her footsteps, as if her arrival had parted the air itself. Light seemed to follow her, pooling around her like a halo.

She looked at me gently as I cried. I wasn't sure if this moment was transcending reality or if I had slipped into some divine hallucination.

"Is this an illusion?"

"Rose—I'm Dr. Barton. I work here at San Francisco General Hospital. I'm glad you're here and safe. How are you feeling?"

I shook my head, unable to speak.

Dr. Barton flipped through the pages on her clipboard, scanning my triage notes, patient history, and vitals. Her questions were careful, almost reverent—tending not just to my injuries, but to something deeper. She moved like someone who had seen darkness and chosen to bring light.

She paused, eyes steady with concern. "I see you were here just two days ago. That makes this your second visit in a week."

Her tone softened. "I want to reassure you—I'm here to help. For now, just rest. I'll check on you in a few minutes."

I felt submerged, as if I'd slipped beneath deep water. The world above was distorted—sounds warped, muffled, distant. Fluorescent lights flickered overhead, their glow filtering down like sunlight through waves. My body felt weightless yet immobile, tangled in thin, scratchy sheets like seaweed clinging to my limbs. Breathing was a struggle—the air thick, heavy, pressing hard against my chest.

Thoughts drifted in slow motion, like silt rising from the ocean floor. My heartbeat echoed in my ears like sonar—steady, distant, unreal. Time no longer passed—it floated. I wasn't sure if I was dreaming or drowning.

A soft beeping from the monitor pulsed like a sonar ping, somewhere far above me. I was suspended below language, below thought, in a quiet current of forgetting. My body remained on the surface, but my mind had sunk deeper—adrift in a tide that didn't want me to rise.

She returned not long after, her presence once again casting calm across the chaos.

"Rose," she said softly, a whisper through the storm.

"I need you to promise me something— a vow to keep you warm."

Her gaze met mine, steady and bright, a lighthouse cutting through the night.

"Be gentle now, when you go home, move slowly, let yourself roam. Give to yourself what you'd give to a friend, Patience, kindness—let the healing begin."

I nodded slowly, the heaviness pulling me down, as if my body were sinking beneath invisible currents. The sheets felt heavy, the room quiet. The IV beside me, steady and low. And then—the world faded.

Like light dissolving into the vast Pacific Ocean.

CHAPTER 6: THE SFPD CRIME LAB

Forensic confirmation bias describes how an individual's beliefs, motives, and situational context can affect the way in which criminal evidence is collected and evaluated.—News-Medical.net, Forensic Confirmation Bias

Injustice doesn't always need a shredder. Sometimes all it takes is a blank form left unsigned—leaving the truth trapped in blood the crime lab was never told to test.

Early Monday afternoon, after my first class of the day, I followed my usual route toward the AAU Library and Computer Lab on New Montgomery Street in the Financial District. As I turned onto 2nd Street from Mission, my BlackBerry Curve 3G began to ring. I answered.

The voice on the other end was calm and professional. "Hi, Miss Rose, this is Detective Viscari from the SFPD. I've been assigned to your case. Is this a good time to talk?"

I adjusted my heavy shoulder bag as I continued down 2nd Street toward New Montgomery, still stunned to hear from him.

"Hi, Detective. Thank you for giving me a call, and yes, it's fine."

"The commanding officer of my unit asked me to check in with you. How are you?" Detective Viscari's voice sounded reassuring, but with a note of formality.

"I'm okay. Just finished class and was heading into the library to study." I scanned my student ID at the secure entrance of the AAU building and walked past the Campus Safety Team into the lobby.

"Nice. I won't take up much of your time. Are you available this Friday, March 5th, to come to the Investigations Division and Crime Lab?"

"Friday? Yes, in the afternoon I am," I replied, mentally checking my schedule.

Fast forward to Friday—Detective Viscari arrived outside my Cow Hollow apartment building on Lombard at 1 o'clock, right on schedule. As he stepped out of the undercover cop car, he gave a nod and announced,
"Great to meet you, Ms. Rose. Thank you for your cooperation. How are you feeling this afternoon?"

We shook hands.

"Hi, Detective Viscari," I replied, my voice tinged with both relief and uncertainty. "I appreciate you being here. What I went through was terrifying, and I just want to feel safe again."

My words trailed off as the weight of it all pressed down on me. "He lives in my neighborhood... only a few blocks from here."

The detective nodded, offering a warm, reassuring smile. "You're safe now. I'm here to get to the bottom of this ordeal." His voice was steady, grounding, like a promise that things would get better.

Behind him, his undercover and retrogressive '90s cop car sat idling at the curb—a gold Ford Crown Victoria, the unmarked staple of SFPD in that era. It had that well-worn, city-issued look—faded paint, steel wheels with scuffed hubcaps, and a short police antenna poking up from the trunk, just enough to give it away. The police radio crackled faintly behind its tinted windows.

He opened the car door so I sat down in the worn cloth seat and intensely looked-out the windshield of the cop car.

As he drove us through the city he said, "You're doing the right thing and I will ensure your privacy throughout the investigative process. In the folder here in the middle seat I brought a pamphlet for you that includes resources available to you for help or information. We have the Prosecutor's Office, Victim Services and Advocacy, SFWAR, the UCSF Trauma Recovery Center, a few local support groups and 24-hour National Hotline Numbers. You are taken care of."

"When I was at the ER doing the forensic kit, the nurse said I could speak with a psychologist from UCSF Trauma Recovery Center. I agreed. We spoke for a while and I like her. She scheduled a time to see her at the Center so that will be on Monday next week."

"That's great news and we're here," exclaimed the Detective as he parked the undercover cop car at the white no-parking zone in front the Hall of Justice building at 850 Bryant Street. He swiftly exited the car and opened the passenger side door. I snatched my shoulder bag off the cloth seat and exited the car. As I stood on the sidewalk, I bewilderedly gazed up at the multi-story gray Hall of Justice building and then looked at the Detective.

"I know you're new to the city, have you seen this building before?"

"No, not at all."

While examining the exterior of the enigmatic building I noticed a carved transcription in the graystone; so I asked, "Detective what is that emblem?"

"It's the Seal of San Francisco which was adopted in the 1850s I believe. It features a sailor and a minor flanking a shield that bears a steamer ship entering the great Golden Gate. Above the shield a Phoenix foretells of the great fire to come in 1906 and below the shield is the city's motto – Gold in Peace, Iron in War. The seal is made out of a 42 ton block of white sierra granite if I remember correctly," answered the Detective.

"Here let's get inside. How are you doing, kid?"

"Yah I'm fine, maybe a little overwhelmed."

"That's understandable, it will be alright," he replied as we walked up the large graystone staircase.

"This is the police headquarters, and historically speaking, it's the 3rd building to serve as headquarters for the San Francisco Police Department."

He opened the glass door to enter the building. As I walked into the lobby I saw a security line, several guards and the concealed weapons detection machine. The Detective pointed towards the security line and said, "Looks as though there isn't too much of a line right now, just place your bag in one of the bins, so it can be scanned and I will meet you on the other side."

"Okay," I said as he smiled.

Quickly I walked into their black tape labyrinth of a security line, stood behind someone as I picked up a grimy bin to empty my pockets and have my bag scanned. I walked awkwardly through the weapons detection machine and looked at the security guard.

He nodded his head, "You're good to go."

I picked up my bag from the bin and saw the Detective confidently standing nearby the lobby's set of elevators speaking to a uniformed police officer. He gestured for me to walk up to them and said, "This is Officer Tim Pelosi and he is one of my long time friends."

"Hi Miss Rose, lovely to meet you. I will let you guys get to it, but it was good catching up," Officer Pelosi said as he waved and walked down the hallway.

"Yes. So our Crime Lab is located in the basement of this building. We'll use the police and technicians elevator which is separate from the general passenger elevators."

He adjusted his leather shoulder strap bag as he led us towards the silver metallic elevator. He pressed the push button and the doors opened with a distinctive ding.

"Right this way," he directed.

An oversight panel, consisting of 19 volunteer jurors, found the Police Department's management of the lab resulted in bungled forensic science, theft in the drug-analysis lab and the embarrassment of two criminalists failing a national proficiency test.—'SF's Crime Lab Shouldn't Be Run By Police', Journalist Evan Sernoffsky at the SFGATE

The doors closed as we walked into the strange liminal space of an elevator cab. The ride was less than a minute. The silver metallic doors reopened; so I exited the elevator into a vastly dim and vacant basement hallway within the Hall of Justice. I sighed in disbelief. It felt like I was inside a movie or a dream and this was not my life.

Gradually we walked towards a large rectangular window. Bright halogen light poured through the double-pane glass as the white-coat forensic science technicians seemed busy doing tests on the laboratory equipment.

The Detective described, "These are our forensic technicians. They analyze evidence with various testing methods and laboratory findings, to procure and document evidence for the police department. It helps us identify the most relevant clues to a case. The evidence varies and may include blood, saliva, fibers, drugs, alcohol, or firearm residue. Our Crime Lab detects, collects and processes these samples for further evaluation."

"Your rape kit is being processed here at the crime lab," Detective Viscari said, his tone measured, routine.

"Good, you got to the ER that morning—evidence collected in less than 48 hours can be a powerful tool in bringing a perpetrator to justice."

"I hope so," I swallowed hard. "We were at the BIX for two hours, he kept ordering drinks—he said he knew the bar manager. It was excessive. Next he drove us to his condo in Cow Hollow. I might have been drugged. I was disoriented and hallucinating. Then we got to his place."

I hesitated, my pulse quickening.

"I yelled no but he ignored it. He mocked me. His eyes seemed to morph from blue to black."

I forced myself to repeat Henry's words to Detective Viscari, *"Are you going to start acting crazy? Because I cannot deal with crazy."*

The memory sent a chill through me as I stood in the hallway of the basement Crime Lab and continued, "He grabbed me hard, but his breathing never changed. Steady and calm while my whole body went numb. I think he drugged me."

"'Since you underwent the rape kit and medical forensic exam at San Francisco General Hospital ER, the Crime Lab will be able to develop a DNA profile of the perpetrator," Detective Viscari said, his expression reassuring.

I gazed through the glass at the forensic technicians, feeling a sense of relief. "A toxicology report will also be processed," he continued. "You did the right thing, coming in right away - that's critical for evidence collection."

His words comforted me, and I trusted that everything was being handled properly by the SFPD and the Detective.

"Thank you."

A pause.

"I felt frozen, numb. Whereas, he seemed to experience a sense of catathymic relief... and he did it again, violently. Afterward, I had overpowering visual hallucinations."

Viscari exhaled, his tone steady but firm.

"Sounds terrible, but you're doing everything right. You got medical attention, and now you're working with us." He motioned for me to follow him down the dimly lit hallway.

"I want him to go to jail."

"I don't remember if I told that to the Northern Station dispatch officers when they came to my apartment at 11:30 p.m., after I got back from the ER. I was so exhausted. I actually had to go back a second time because I was in pain."

Viscari gave me a nod. A hint of disinfectant drifted in the air, a reminder of the sterile environment.

"I'm proud of you for reaching out for help. You're safe now."

His expression seemed sincere, but I sensed a hint of withholding, a truth hidden beneath the surface - one he wouldn't share with Rose. Then, after a pause, he asked, "From what I understand, you're in graduate school? What are you studying?"

"Yes, working on a Master of Fine Arts," I replied. "My goal is to be an art director at an advertising or design firm. That's why I moved to the city."

"That's impressive. You must be sharp," Viscari said, his eyes crinkling at the corners as he smiled.

He gestured for me to walk with him, and we headed down the long, sterile empty hallway and flickering fluorescent lights.

The hum of machinery thrummed through the corridors, a steady heartbeat that seemed to pulse with an otherworldly energy. We traveled past another window, its glass pane reflecting our images like specters. An empty room with microscopes, gas chromatographs, mass spectrometers, spectrophotometers, thermal cyclers, DNA sequencers, real-time PCR machines, DNA extraction instruments, fingerprint comparators, evidence dryers, fume hoods, autoclaves, photomicrography equipment, and crime scene reconstruction software.

Overthinking, overanalyzing separates the body from the mind, lyrics echoed in my thoughts as I gazed at the elaborate tools. The metallic elevators loomed ahead, their doors sliding open with a whoosh, an empty invitation.

Viscari's eyes locked onto mine as we stepped inside, he stood over a foot taller than me, the doors closing behind us like a seal, enveloping us in an eerie silence.

"I need you to write a detailed narrative statement about what happened. Type it up, be as specific as possible, and I'll include it in the case file. Will you do that for me?"

"Yes, I will."

"My job is to keep you safe—to prevent and investigate crimes that threaten public safety and social order. I've been doing this a long time. Your cooperation makes the process smoother." Detective Viscari's voice was steady, practiced.

"I imagine it's been a long day for you. How about I drive you home?"

"Okay"

As we moved through the Hall of Justice's hallways and into the 1960s-era lobby, Viscari greeted nearly everyone we passed—officers, prosecutors, defense attorneys. He shook hands, exchanged quick words, and made introductions. I watched as they nodded at him in passing—some out of respect, others with something harder to read.

I walked beside him, the fluorescent lights buzzing overhead, and a chill worked its way down my spine. The scene played out like a ritual: a man at ease in his domain, every gesture designed to inspire confidence.

But beneath the civility was something hollow. Little did I know, the same man assuring me of my safety, would never submit the one-page request form that could have sent my kit to the SFPD Crime Lab.

During an active criminal investigation, the forensic evidence collected from my body at San Francisco General Hospital Emergency Department—critical to pursuing charges against Henry—was never submitted for analysis, rendering prosecution impossible.

As we left 850 Bryant—the Hall of Justice looming like a relic—Viscari opened the door of a gold Crown Victoria, its presence heavy with law and intimidation. I slid onto the cool leather seat as the engine rumbled to life. We pulled away from the courthouse, threading through SoMa's late-afternoon shadows toward Cow Hollow. His words slipped into background noise, the city's twists and turns numbing me into a world of dissociation.

Back home, I looked around my neatly organized room.

Everything was in its place, but nothing felt right.

It was as if reality had shifted just slightly—subtle enough that no one else would notice, but I did. So I reached for my vintage-red 1986 *Nishiki* 10-Speed, carried it down the hallway stairs, locked the gate, and jumped onto the bike.

As I shifted gears on the cassette, the motion sent a charge through me—a brief, electric sense of control.

Flying down Chestnut Street I cut right on Divisadero heading toward Crissy Field.

The wind pressed against my skin, and I let it push me forward. I rode past Fort Point, past Battery Vista, my breath deepening, steadying. Then I reached the Golden Gate Bridge's bike-access path. I pushed harder. The city fell away behind me as I crossed over the steel expanse, the water below dark and endless. I kept going.

Up into the Marin Headlands, climbing toward Hawk Hill. My legs burned, but I didn't stop. Not until I reached the peak—923 feet above it all.

From up here, the city was nothing but a distant skyline. The chaos, the corruption, the walls that closed in on me—all of it small, almost insignificant.

For the first time in days, I could breathe.

CHAPTER 7: UNIVERSITY OF CALIFORNIA, SAN FRANCISCO (TRC)

She expected the world but it flew away from her reach. So she ran away in her sleep and dreamed of paradise. —Paradise by Coldplay

Now, it had been a week since the Detective drove us to the SFPD Crime Lab in the basement of the Hall of Justice. Beneath those thick concrete walls, unfathomed secrets hid from the surface—concealed unless you knew exactly what to ask. I didn't. I'd never even been to Bryant Street before.

Actually—that's not true. I had been to Bryant once, to retrieve my towed car from the notorious AutoReturn impound. The memory made me shudder.

I dug through my tote and pulled out the glossy bifold pamphlet the UCSF TRC psychologist gave me at the ER. It read:

The UCSF Trauma Recovery Center envisions a world where every survivor of violence gets the help they need to heal. We eliminate barriers to healing and inspire survivors to embrace hope. Our mission is to serve adult survivors of violence and traumatic loss. We provide respectful, compassionate, and effective mental health and support services.

That Monday morning, I began counseling with Anna Ovchinikov Brown at the UCSF TRC in the Potrero District. I was relieved to see it was the same psychologist who had sat with me for nearly an hour during the ER exam. We met in a tiny therapy room where she quietly took my intake.

Underneath it all, I was searching—for tools, for meaning, for a spiritual and philosophical path of insurmountable value. Something to help me explore the deeper secrets of existence.

She looked at me gently.

"How have you been since I last saw you—Rose?"

"I want him to go to jail."

"I told my boyfriend not to share what happened—but he did. I found out the hard way. After a family wedding in Half Moon Bay, his mother told me I was an embarrassment, that I didn't deserve her son, and I was no longer welcome in their home. Since then, nightmares, insomnia, and intrusive thoughts. The emotional toll is taking a physical one."

In Brown's psychological notes, she wrote: Patient is experiencing trauma-related symptoms. Feels unprotected and out of control after the assault and the blaming reaction from someone she trusted. Displays dissociative symptoms. Shock index (SI) should be monitored.

Note: Derealization and depersonalization present.

"I'm sad but hyper. I can't focus or finish assignments. I hear her voice—his mother's insults—echoing in my mind constantly. I don't have friends I can confide in, except for the TRC counselors. No one seems to understand what it's like... or maybe I'm just imagining that.

He raped me to validate a false sense of masculinity and entitlement. He's a con man. And sometimes, if it weren't for this center, I don't know if I'd want to keep going. This feels unbearably isolating."

"What do you do for self-care?" she asked gently.

"I ride my 10-speed Nishiki road bike up to Hawk Hill in the Marin Headlands—to watch the city from a distance. Then I drop into the one-way, five-mile Bunker Road Tunnel. It connects two old military bases and feels mysterious once you're inside. After that, I fly downhill into Sausalito, then climb back up to the Golden Gate Bridge. I ride to escape the thoughts—but they always return.

I've also been practicing Bikram Yoga in the Marina. I might sign up for their hot yoga challenge this month, not sure yet."

The Marin Headlands is known for its dramatic coastline and fog-swept hills. Jagged cliffs rise from the ocean, and foghorns echo through the mist like distant memories. I remember the rolling hills of coyote brush and sage—how the wind carries silence between waves.

My first visit to the Marin Headlands came in sixth grade, a four-day school trip that felt like stepping into another world. I wandered its wind-swept cliffs and rugged coastline without knowing the deeper truth—that these hills had long held the footsteps and stories of the Coast Miwok people, who lived here for thousands of years.

The Headlands carry layers of memory: the quiet persistence of indigenous life, the restless arrival of European explorers, the echo of artillery silos hidden in the hills during the Cold War. Each era leaves its mark, yet the land remains steady, whispering resilience. It invites you to pause, to lean into its silence, to let curiosity shape the way you see.

'What did you love about your Nishiki?'

'I'm not familiar with that bike—it sounds like it gave you a sense of freedom,' Anna said.

'It did,' I replied. 'The 1973 Nishiki originally belonged to my mom. She passed it to me in college, and when I moved to the city for graduate school, it came with me. It's a classic, built by a renowned Japanese cycling company that rose during the bike boom of the '70s and '80s, competing with Schwinn itself. When I ride it, it feels like more than motion. It feels like freedom.'

<u>MAY</u>

If you were to ask me, after all we've been through—do you still believe in magic? Yes, I do. Of course I do. — Coldplay, Magic

By May, I was seeing Dr. Erika Smart twice a week, with psychiatry sessions to boot. I had a history of trying to end it all, a dark thought that came creeping back. My life felt like a ghost story, something I couldn't shake.

The doctor's eyes, steady and sharp, locked on mine as she asked, "Rose, how are you feeling today?"

I sighed, my chest tight. "After his mother told me I didn't belong—said I wasn't good enough for her son—it just felt like all the air had been sucked out of the room. Like my life was meaningless, like nothing I did mattered. And then... then the Detective handed me a folder. Photos. Photos of women beaten and left for dead. He told me I wasn't a 'real victim.' It was too much. At midnight, I found myself at the Golden Gate Bridge." My voice cracked, but I forced it out.

"The fog, thick and cold, wrapped around the first tower's railing. I swear, I saw two Arctic Wolves. Their fur gleamed like silver under the streetlights, their eyes, blue like a storm, cut right through me. They were coming for me. I didn't know if it was real, but I ran. I ran like my life depended on it. By morning, I was in the SoMa hospital. You probably spoke to them." I paused, trying to steady myself. "I can't get away from him. He lives just around the corner. Every time I turn, I see him, smiling, like nothing ever happened. How am I supposed to heal when I can't escape?"

Dr. Smart's expression softened, but her eyes stayed focused. She jotted something in her notes before meeting my gaze again. Her voice was warm, but firm. "Rose, your descriptions— they're vivid. You have a creative mind. And it's clear that it's still with you. But please know, you're not alone in this. You have people to reach out to."

She paused, letting the silence hang. "What have you been working on lately?"

I shifted, uncomfortable.

"I've been trying to keep busy. Obsessing over projects. Diving into philosophy, looking for something that makes sense. But everything else? It's like it doesn't exist anymore. I was always the straight-A student. UC Berkeley alum. Perfect. But now? Now, I'm lost. Nothing feels real."

"Sleep is a joke. I drown the restlessness with alcohol or I push myself at the gym, trying to outrun this feeling. I'm desperate for a way out, but I'm scared. I'm scared because I can't escape what's happened. I don't know how to find the me I used to be. I feel trapped in a loop of my own making."

I took a deep breath, forcing the words out, my voice shaking. "I saw him yesterday. He was driving his Porsche down Chestnut Street while I was getting coffee. I froze, and couldn't breathe. Another time, I had to duck into the nearest restroom, just to catch my breath. It's like I'm paralyzed, knowing he's still out there, doing the same thing to other women. He hasn't faced any punishment for what he did to me. And every time I see him, or think about him, it's like I'm right back there. It's real. It's not just a nightmare."

The doctor nodded, her gaze never wavering from mine.

Dr. Erika Smart PSYD Intake: Patient presents with clear, articulate speech; mood fluctuates between tearful, detached, and euthymic. Reports recent suicidal ideation (SI) and impulsive, inappropriate combination of codeine and alcohol, likely an attempt at a suicidal gesture. Exhibits passive homicidal ideation (HI), with fair insight and limited judgment. Cognition intact.

The patient meets diagnostic criteria for PTSD and depressive episodes with fluctuating hypomanic features, suggesting Bipolar II Disorder. Reports increased alcohol consumption as maladaptive coping for anxiety and distress. Concerns about impaired impulse control, risk of self-harm, and mood destabilization. Recommend pharmacological intervention, including mood stabilizer (e.g., Lamotrigine) and SSRI/SNRI. Strongly advise against benzodiazepine use. Referral for trauma-focused therapy, DBT skills training, and structured psychiatric follow-up. Close monitoring for SI/HI escalation.

SONY ICD-PX312

The Detective pulled up to my apartment in the unmarked gold Crown Victoria as a haunting sense of déjà vu swept over me. He opened the passenger door and gestured me inside. As I slid into the passenger seat, the cool leather interior enveloped me, its familiarity momentarily calming, a sense of reassurance that would soon prove misplaced.

He turned on the engine, the radio was already on Billie Holiday's voice echoed through the speakers. He navigated the streets to North Beach, expertly maneuvering into a spot reserved for firetrucks, marked by a bold red curb. With a courteous gesture, he stepped out and opened the door for me.

'Ready for a coffee break?'

He asked, his tone disarmingly friendly. I nodded, we walked toward the wooden framed glass door, the sounds of the vibrant neighborhood filling the air.

Caffe Trieste, a spot that had always felt like a quiet haven in the city, was lined with black and white photographs of vintage San Francisco and artistic portraits, giving it a timeless feel. The rich scent of espresso beans mingled with the soft buzz of conversation as we entered, the walls echoing the history of the place. We walked up to the counter, where the barista greeted us with a smile.

"Good morning, what can I get started for you two?"

The detective ordered his usual—a cappuccino. I ordered an iced coffee. He paid, and we made our way to the seating area.

Along the wall under the large window was a long, wooden bench, its smooth surface worn by years of use. The café's round tables, adorned with classic solid beechwood bentwood chairs, added warmth and character to the space. I settled onto the worn wooden bench, feeling the gentle curve of the wood beneath me, while Detective took a seat in one of the chairs across from me, his eyes fixed intently on mine.

The barista returned and carefully placed our coffee drinks on the table between us.

"Goditi il tuo caffè!"

Viscari leaned back slightly, stirring his cappuccino.

"How's grad school at the Academy of Art?" he asked, his voice casual but laced with genuine interest.

I shrugged, taking a sip of my iced coffee.

"I've been plodding along, spending endless hours at the school's library…it's in the New Montgomery Building. I've been working on an Adobe Photoshop and InDesign assignment but sometimes get lost day dreaming."

Viscari's expression turned thoughtful, his hazelgreen eyes studying me.

"Daydreaming, like drinking espresso, is a catalyst for creativity," his expression softened, and he offered a warm smile.

"You're doing great, kid," he said, his voice low and encouraging. "I grew up in North Beach. I was never an artist myself, but my sister loved painting. She'd spend hours capturing the vibrant colors and history of the neighborhood, the sounds, the smells... it was her way of seeing the world."

I could tell he was trying to lighten the mood, but there was a seriousness in his eyes that hinted at something else. He set his cappuccino down, his fingers resting on the edge of his cup. His gaze drifted out of the window, where the sounds of the city filtered through the glass, then back at me.

"There's something I need to ask you to do," he said, shifting to a serious tone.

"I'd like you to do a pre-text phone call with Mr. Henry."

I froze for a moment, the words hanging in the air as dread poured over me. My fingers tightened around the cool iced coffee glass, the ice clinking softly.

"A pre-text phone call?"

Detective Viscari's eyes never wavered, his tone steady, though I could sense the weight of what he was asking.

"Yes. It's a tactic we use. You'll call him, pretending like everything's fine. Just casually check in, like you're talking to an old friend, make him think there's no tension, no pressure."

I swallowed, my throat dry.

"And… what am I supposed to say?"

"Keep it simple. Ask about his day, make small talk. But while you're doing that, I want you to lead him in a direction. Get him to talk, to say things he wouldn't otherwise. We'll be listening in. It's your chance to get him on the record."

The gravity hit me like a tidal wave.

My thoughts juxtaposed themselves in my mind.

I couldn't believe what he was asking me to do.

The thought of talking to *him* again—the thought of hearing his revolting voice over the phone made me almost gag. A cold shiver crawled up my spine. The idea of Henry admitting it, or worse, his denial drenched in lies and manipulation, made everything inside feel suffocating.

Gripping my glass, suddenly unsteady, as if the very act of holding it was the only thing keeping me anchored to this reality. My thoughts sped through my mind like shooting stars at the speed of light, each one flashing faster than the next.

Viscari leaned forward slightly, his expression softening just a touch.

"He'll talk. They usually do. They're always sure of themselves. Just stay calm, keep cool, Rose. We need him to admit what he did—that he raped you. It's the best shot we have to build the case. We need to hear it from him, on record."

The weight of his words hung in the air, the gravity of what I was being asked to do frightened me.

"You *really* think he'll admit it?" I asked and paused for a moment, "I doubt that."

The detective reached into the left inside pocket to his lapel corduroy blazer pocket, pulled out a Sony ICD-PX312 digital voice recorder, and placed it gently on the table between us.

"They think they're smarter than us, but sometimes will slip up." His voice was firm now, a quiet confidence threading through his words.

"You'll do fine, kid. Trust me."

CHAPTER 8: MR. HENRY METS THE POLICE DETECTIVE

Victor Lustig proved the power of mystery. People are attracted to those who seem mysterious, so cultivate an air of mystery yourself. Be vague about what you're doing or plan to do. Don't show all your cards and you'll create an atmosphere of anticipation — people will pay attention to see what you do next. Use mystery to deceive, enthrall, and intimidate. – 48 Laws of Power, Robert Greene

The day was off to a strong start, a rhythm of success building under Henry's feet.

Momentum was his fuel, and today, it surged through him like never before. After months of relentless effort, key accounts were finally locked in, pushing the firm into the black. The pipeline was brimming, opportunities lined up like prized chess pieces. They weren't just succeeding—they were dominating the field.

And now, the afternoon's meetings would seal their place in venture capital heaven, a realm of high stakes and greater rewards.

Midway through a presentation, as his sales team laid out their latest triumphs, Henry's phone buzzed, breaking his focused concentration. A quick glance at the screen—an *unknown number.*

Could be a client. Could be an investor. Could be a chance to push even further. Henry's thoughts raced as he turned away from the table, excusing himself, and answered.

"Hello?"

The voice on the other end was calm, measured, and unmistakably authoritative.

"This is Detective Viscari with the San Francisco Police Department. I'm investigating a case. Do you have a minute to talk?"

Henry's posture didn't change, but his mind flicked to damage control.

"Sure thing, Detective. Just give me a moment."

Keeping his tone even, he hit mute, glanced at his team, and flashed a quick gotta-take-this look. A couple of nods, no questions. He slipped out of the glass-walled conference room, the hum of the meeting fading behind him.

Once in the hallway, he kept moving until he found an empty stairwell. He exhaled, checked his watch, and unmuted the call.

"Sorry about that, I can talk now."

Viscari's voice remained level, stripped of any small talk.

"No problem, this will only take a minute. I'm the lead detective on this case, and I need to ask you a few questions in person at my office at the Hall of Justice."

Henry's grip on the phone tightened instinctively, his knuckles going white. Stay steady, he told himself. This was just a routine call—nothing more.

"What's this in regard to, Detective?" Henry's voice stayed controlled, though the weight of the unknown crept into his words.

"This is in regard to a report that named you," Viscari replied, his voice calm but measured. Then, a pause—a beat just long enough to let the weight of his words settle.

"Where were you on the night of February 23rd?"

February 23rd. Tuesday night.

Henry's mind ran the numbers, flipping through his recent memories like a Rolodex. The hours of that evening—empty. A fog of forgetfulness. Nothing stood out. He stalled, unwilling to reveal uncertainty.

"I'd have to check my calendar. Was that a Thursday?"

"No, a Tuesday," Viscari corrected, the finality in his voice unmistakable.

"Do you recall going out with a young woman by the name of Rose?"

And there it was.

Henry's expression didn't shift, but something coiled in his chest.

"Yes. What seems to be the problem, Detective?"

Just enough concern. Just enough curiosity. Innocent, but not overeager.

"Well, that's what we're trying to figure out. Can you come down to the station? I'd prefer to ask you these questions in person. What day works for you?"

Henry glanced at his watch again. Keep control of the timeline. Set the pace.

"Thursday, May 27th works for me."

"How does 2 o'clock sound, Mr. Henry?"

"That works. I'll have my assistant rearrange my schedule."

"Thank you," Viscari replied.

The line went dead.

Henry stood still, phone still in hand, staring at the blank screen. What the hell had Rose told them? His mind raced, combing through every detail.

He bolted down two flights of stairs, pushing through the heavy exit door onto the street for fresh air; his body began to betray him, a light sheen of sweat spreading across his back, darkening his carbon-brushed cotton t-shirt as it clung to his skin.

Detach. Assess. Execute. A principle Henry lived by long before he ever heard it on a Navy SEAL's podcast. The Detective's disruptive call was already being filed away—categorized, neutralized. Tools to wield, refined for his corporate and personal agenda. Like everything else he touched, he repurposed them, bent them to his will. He exploited discipline the way he exploited people—Black Rabbit Rose was no exception.

A leadership mindset, twisted to serve his ambitions. The next meeting—2 o'clock. New investors. Real money. A one-night stand from months ago would not unravel the empire he was building.

His mind was already mapping the week ahead. A cocktail hour at the Battery. And, of course, the grand crescendo—next Saturday's gala at the San Francisco Opera House. *Belle Nuit: A Night of Merola.* A stage draped in refinement, where power moved in whispers beneath the shimmer of crystal chandeliers. He made a mental note to confirm the wine selection for his table. A small but important detail.

Optics were everything. By next weekend, he'd be in a tuxedo, sipping champagne, exchanging handshakes with city elites, nodding along to Puccini arias. His name printed in the program under *Patron Sponsor.*

By next weekend, this would be nothing—just another moment, neatly compartmentalized. Boxed away.

Henry rolled his shoulders back, ran a hand through his dark-blonde hair, and exhaled slowly. Then, with the same calculated ease as always, he stepped back inside his office. The day wasn't over yet.

HENRY'S ILLICIT PHOTOS

Mr. Henry drove his flawless metallic gray Porsche 911 Carrera into the parking garage just around the corner from the Hall of Justice at 850 Bryant Street. He never leaves his prized car on the open city streets unless he's in the Marina or absolutely pressed for time. Typically, he parks in a valet or a covered space—his Porsche is his prized possession, and it deserves all the care he can manage.

As he walked the short distance from the garage to the Hall of Justice, Henry reminded himself why he limited his visits to the SOMA district. In less than a mile, he encountered dozens of homeless panhandling along the sidewalks, garbage scattered in all directions, and—worst of all—unsightly smears of feces. If the maze of obstacles and their accompanying stench weren't enough, the streets themselves were cracked and pitted, navigated at high speed by traffic weaving through it all.

Approaching the building's entrance, he passed through the security checkpoint. Placing his European leather bag on the X-ray scanner, he stepped through the metal detector and received his bag back from the officer.

After a moment of composure, Henry made his way toward the elevators. He pressed the UP button, the harsh *ding* of the call echoing in the still air. He scanned the area for any movement, feeling the weight of the space around him. The elevator doors—heavy from decades of use—finally groaned open with a reluctant sigh.

A handful of clerks, lawyers, and other court attendees shuffled out, their expressions indifferent. As the it emptied, Henry stepped forward, the faint metallic of the elevator mingling with the stale air, and waited for his turn.

A woman ahead of him pressed her floor's button, smiling as she entered.

"What floor?" she asked politely.

"5th floor, please," Henry replied, offering a smile in return.

At the 5th floor, the elevator doors slid open, now empty except for Henry. Stepping out, he made his way toward the Special Victims Unit (SVU). With each step, the tension of the upcoming appointment settled in. His heart began to race, though whether it was guilt or nervousness, he couldn't tell. He pushed the feeling aside, focusing on the task ahead.

He arrived at the office and grasped the silver doorknob. Stepping inside, he surveyed the room—an assortment of posters with Public Service Announcements and other proclamations lined the walls. A receptionist glanced up casually as he entered, giving him space to speak first.

"I'm here to see Detective Viscari for a 2 o'clock appointment," Henry said to the receptionist.

"I'll let him know you're here. Please take a seat in the waiting area—he'll be right with you," they replied.

Henry settled into one of the stiff green lobby chairs beside an end table stacked with old magazines. He picked up a National Geographic, flipping through the pages without absorbing a word.

Instead his gaze drifted, scanning the room. The atmosphere was stark, outdated—the kind of place where time hung heavy, thick with unsolved cases and lives ruined. Maybe it was the nature of the business of the Special Victims Unit, or the prospect of a drunken night coming back to haunt him, but the bleakness permeated his body as he anxiously waited.

A few minutes later, Detective Viscari appeared in a charcoal-gray suit—worn casually, the top button of his shirt undone, no tie. His face was unreadable, his movements deliberate as he extended a hand.

"Mr. Henry. Thanks for coming in."

"Pleasure to meet you, Detective Viscari."

Henry stood, shaking his hand firmly.

"Follow me," Viscari said, leading him past rows of cubicles where administrators typed away, their faces impassive. The rhythmic clatter of keyboards filled the space, a low hum of routine indifference.

The detective opened the door to his office and stepped aside.

"Have a seat."

Henry surveyed the room—beige walls, nearly bare. A metal desk with a desktop computer stood against one side, while a second table sat in the center, an emerald-green Georgetown Swivel-Tilt chair neatly tucked between them. No clutter, no personal touches—just a space meticulously designed for business.

He stepped inside, the door clicking shut behind him.

"Please, have a seat."

Viscari lowered himself into his chair. Henry released the strap of his European leather bag and set it atop the desk before sitting down. His hands rested in his lap, eyes scanning the room. Framed certificates from the Police Academy lined the walls, along with a few photographs—Viccari alongside other officers, frozen in time, their expressions unreadable.

After a few minutes of small talk to ease the tension, Detective Viscari reached into a drawer and placed a Sony M-450 Microcassette Handheld Voice Recorder on the table between them.

"I'll be recording this conversation for evidentiary purposes," he said, his voice firm. "Will that be alright with you?"

"Yes. That is fine," feeling anxiety wash over him. He breathes deeply to steady his rattled nerves.

"For the record, Mr. Henry has given consent for this conversation to be recorded. Is that correct, Mr. Henry?"

"That is correct," he replied, doing his best to sound composed. He could feel sweat forming at his brow.

With that confirmation, Detective Viscari clicked the recorder on and picked up his pen, eyes scanning Henry as he readied his notepad.

"On the night of February 23rd, you went to the BIX with a young woman by the name of Rose. Is that correct?"

"Yes, that is correct."

First mental checkmark. By confirming the meeting, Henry had already placed himself in a particular category in Viscari's mind.

"How did you meet?"

"Several weeks before that night. I was out with colleagues at the California Wine Merchant on Chestnut. Rose was walking by with her camera, and I struck up a conversation."

"What did you talk about?"

"I asked Rose what she was photographing. She said she was a grad student working on a class assignment. I'm a hobbyist photographer, so I was intrigued. I asked if I could see her photos, and she handed me the camera. We talked about photography, and I offered to buy her a glass of wine."

"What time was this?"

"Around three o'clock. My team and I were celebrating a win."

"What do you mean by 'win'?"

"We secured another round of funding. A major milestone for the company. I personally invented the patented IT service we provide, and we just got an infusion of capital to scale it worldwide."

Detective Viscari leaned back slightly, pen tapping idly against his notepad. "Impressive. I might know some professionals in your field, but that's neither here nor there."

His tone shifted. "Are you aware of the allegations against you?"

Henry exhaled smoothly. "I might have an idea, but please, enlighten me."

"I need to collect facts about that evening at the Bix and what happened afterward. How did you both arrive at the restaurant?"

"I drove. Rose lives in my neighborhood, so she agreed to be picked up outside her apartment complex on Gough."

"What time was that?"

"Around half past seven."

"And how did the night go?"

Henry gave a light chuckle. "Bix never disappoints. I've had many wonderful evenings there."

"What appetizers did you order?"

"Beef tartare and crab cakes, which are my favorites."

"And the drinks?"

"Several rounds of cocktails. Mr. Taylor was our mixologist. We had a flight that included a Saint Helena Syrah and a Cabernet Sauvignon. Fantastic wines." He offered a practiced smile. "Forgive me, we may have had a little too much to drink."

"Approximately how long were you at the bar?"

"We were there for quite a while. It seemed like we had a lot in common. We talked about everything and nothing. I told her about the view of the Golden Gate Bridge from my condo because she kept professing her love for it. I think I drove us back to my place around midnight."

"And what happened then?"

"I parked in the basement garage of my complex and we went up to my condo. I offered to make her a nightcap and I showed her the view from my balcony. It was a gorgeous night."

"How did Rose's level of intoxication seem to you?"

"She seemed buzzed but not out of control. Certainly not as bad as you can see on your average Thursday night in the Marina," Mr Henry smirks as they softly chuckle in unison.

The Detective replies, "Seems like a nice evening."

"I thought it went well."

"What happened next?"

"During dinner at the BIX she told me she had done art modeling. I took the opportunity to show her a few of my Art History coffee-table-books that I've collected over the years. And, I showed her printed photos I took on a recent trip to Barcelona and Madrid. She seemed to enjoy it."

The detective nodded, expression unreadable. Henry took it as his cue to continue.

"I asked if she'd like me to take photos of her."

A pause. He tilted his head slightly, a slow, deliberate movement.

"And she said yes?"

Viscari's voice was even, but there was weight behind it.

Henry exhaled through his nose, almost amused.

"She told me she did art modeling. She didn't hesitate. Just took off her clothes, stretched out across my couch—completely nude—and posed."

He let the words settle, watching the detective's reaction.

"Took a few photos of *Rose on my iPhone* and had a feeling I'd need them printed for our meeting today."

A smirk ghosted the corner of his mouth.

"Would you like to see them?"

Viscari didn't blink.

"Yes."

Henry reached for his Tuscany leather bag, unbuckled the clasp, and pulled out a business envelope. He placed it on the table and slid it forward. "Have a look."

The detective took the envelope, unfastened the reinforced metal closure, and methodically arranged the prints across the table. His fingers dragged briefly over his scalp before he adjusted his glasses, leaning in to examine them under the sterile fluorescent light.

Henry watched, his expression unreadable.

"I'm sorry for the misunderstanding," he continued, voice laced with faux regret. "But I have proof it was consensual. These were taken straight from my iPhone."

Viscari picked up a photo. Across the desk, Henry watched intently—first the detective's reaction, then the photos themselves. Rose, sprawled out, her body languid, her expression glazed. Her youth, her sensuality—captured in black and white—fed into his self-indulgent narrative. She was the submissive subject, her intoxicated gaze locked in a daze, reinforcing his own sense of dominance.

Henry broke the silence.

"She told me she did professional art modeling while in school. Nude modeling."

Detective Viscari shot him a sharp, measuring glance.

The overhead fluorescent light hummed faintly, casting a sterile, almost clinical glow over the room.

Viscari barely looked up. "What time did you take these?"

"Around 1 a.m.," Henry replied, glancing down at the timestamp on his phone.

The silence stretched.

Detective Viscari's fingers tightened slightly around the edges of the photo, the paper crinkling ever so slightly under his grip.

Viscari exhaled slowly through his nose, his expression unreadable as his pen tapped rhythmically against his notepad. He had seen this before—the rehearsed justifications, the clinical detachment, the entitlement cloaked as admiration.

"And she didn't object?"

The Detective's voice was flat, yet there was a subtle edge to it, something beneath the surface.

Henry's lips curled at the edges, just enough to hint at a smile.

"Of course not, Detective."

He gestured toward the photos spread across the table.

"I'm sorry for the misunderstanding, but this—" he tapped a single image, "this proves it was consensual."

RENAISSANCE NUDE

In Henry's photos, Rose lay exposed, stripped of agency, sprawled naked on his sofa. Her body was relaxed, but her eyes—distant, unfocused—told a different story, one of detachment and disconnection.

Henry's tone was almost amused, as if he were relishing the moment.

"She was overtly seductive, wouldn't you say, Detective?"

The subtext was clear—he wanted Detective Viscari to see her as he did: not as a victim, but as an object. A conquest. Something taken, not harmed, he thought.

His words were deliberate, a calculated effort to control the narrative before it could turn against him. But the photos told another story.

A Renaissance nude—aa *Postmodernvenus*—yes. As Rose lay there motionless, her ocean eyes vacant and unfocused, her expression dazed and unnatural. A stillness that wasn't quite right. She was intoxicated, unmistakably so.

Henry, of course, saw something else entirely.

To him, Rose's human form wasn't a being with autonomy, but a noir composition—something to be arranged, captured, owned. He wasn't a man who had taken what wasn't his. He was a masterful artist, rendering his subject eternal.

The male gaze at its most insidious: not just power in perception, but power in control. The ability to dictate reality itself.

The fluorescent light buzzed softly overhead. A faint hum, like the sound of a machine left running too long. Henry smoothed his tie, tilting his head as if admiring his own work. His voice came light, almost bemused.

"Sorry she feels that way."

A pause.

"Maybe I should buy her some *roses*, Detective?"

CHAPTER 9: THE DA CLOSED YOUR CASE – INSUFFICIENT EVIDENCE

In a world where the powerful play their games of corruption and greed, the music will still be beautiful, as it always has been—silent in its resistance, constant in its clarity.
—Kurt Vonnegut

The Detective calls to meet about the investigation. After a back-and-forth over text, we settled on 3 PM. Right on time, he pulled up in an unmarked gold 1990s Ford—clean, low-profile, effortless. The light gold paint shimmered under the afternoon sun.

The tinted windows kept their secrets, hinting at an unsolved mystery that made you look twice.

I took a deep breath of the bay air—salt, the faint trace of eucalyptus riding the wind. Crisp and cool, anchoring me in the present. In yoga, they call it *pratyahara*—the art of withdrawing from distraction, turning inward. But no breath could pull me far enough from this reality.

Without a word, he stepped out, rounded the car, and opened the passenger door. A silent invitation. I slid into the seat. As he held the passenger door he looked through to say

"Good to see you, let's grab a coffee and catch up. Sounds good?"

I nodded. "Yes."

He firmly closed the passenger door.

He drove us down Gough Street toward Union, smoothly rolling into a right turn, casual but deliberate. No rush, no hesitation—just a confidence, like he had all the time in the world. The kind of man who didn't follow the rules—not because he had to break them, but they never applied to him in the first place.

The late-afternoon sun cut through the windshield, glinting off the rows of sleek boutiques and cafés lining Union Street. Effortless refinement—boutique fitness studios, wine bars with artistic signage, racks of dresses swaying in open doorways. People strolled past in designer sunglasses, holding matcha green tea lattes, chatting about their next pilates class, oblivious to the world inside the unmarked Ford.

Everything was curated—polished storefronts, pastel-painted Victorians, streets lined with perfectly pruned trees and flower boxes that never wilted. A place where the air smelled like fresh espresso and expensive perfume, where even the cracks in the sidewalk felt charming.

Inside the car, it was different.

The detective exhaled, shifting his grip on the steering wheel, his fingers tapping against it like he had somewhere to be. The moment he spotted a red curb in front of a fire hydrant, he cut the engine.

With a click, he unbuckled his seatbelt and turned to face me, his expression unreadable, just business.

"Rose—after a full investigation, the Deputy DA has closed your case. Insufficient evidence."

His voice was even, practiced. "Henry came in voluntarily, sat for questioning for an hour. Cooperated fully. Said it was consensual—on the pretext call, in person at SVU. No inconsistencies. No red flags."

A pause.

"We followed our department's orders. That's what matters."

I swallowed the bitter taste of a real-life nightmare and it was distinctively bitter. My eyes teared as I yearned for this reality to disappear.

"There wasn't enough evidence to move forward with criminal charges. Henry came in, answered questions, and cooperated. He seemed remorseful about the *misunderstanding* between you two."

The Detective continued.

"Seemed like a good guy—If he would have bought you roses and an airplane ticket to Paris would you still call it rape?"

Quietly I sat in the cop car's passenger seat as his words transformed into obscure glass. A thousand needles pierced into my mind. My face went numb as I tried to speak. What he said made me feel hopeless and stupid.

I couldn't tell if this was real.

Felt like I was slipping, like I was losing my mind.

"My friend said I could file a lawsuit against him," I murmured, my voice barely my own.

"I thought the six-hour forensic exam at the ER would prove what Henry did, wasn't that the whole point?"

"Rose—Don't file a lawsuit."

His voice was firm, measured.

"Those things don't end well."

"I've seen careers disintegrate over a single bad decision. One legal battle, one headline, and suddenly, doors start closing. Opportunities vanish."

He leaned in slightly, lowering his voice.

"You don't want to go down that road, trust me. No one wins in cases like these. And you definitely don't want your name attached to something like this—forever."

The beige interior of the undercover cop car's dashboard obfuscated into the cement sidewalk as the blue sky evaporated into a blur.

A blank stare overcame me as I sat in silence with my seat-belt on.

What I didn't know then was that law enforcement can 'clear' or administratively close a case in one of two ways: by arresting the suspect—or by invoking 'exceptional means,' a loophole wrapped in bureaucracy. A technicality. A magic trick.

It makes cases vanish, buries evidence, and lets offenders walk free—all without a trial, a conviction, or a single moment of public scrutiny. A legal disappearing act, signed, sealed, and protected by those in power.

They enjoy that power—the authority to rewrite reality, to *accidentally* misplace crucial evidence, to choose which facts see daylight and which are swallowed by the dark.

"Thank you, Detective, for doing your best. It would've meant a lot to me if he could go to jail..."

The words collapsed in my throat. Tears burned their way down my face, fast and merciless. The world tilted, edges folding into themselves, warping like a bad dream I couldn't wake from.

"It's a tough case to prove, kid."

Detective Viscari's voice cut through the static—like he was commenting on the weather. Like this was just another day, another case, another girl walking away empty-handed.

"I know you need to get to class soon," he added.

"How about we grab coffee at North Beach Café? I'll drop you off at the New Montgomery building. How does that sound?"

A truck could've hit me, and I wouldn't have noticed.

Like Sartre said, "*Existence precedes essence.*"

Maybe I didn't exist anymore—only a silhouette of who I had been. Life had become a broken mirror, throwing back a thousand fractured selves, none of them mine.

The Detective's voice fractured—blurred, digitized, eaten by the city's hum. My body felt detached, weightless, as if I weren't even in the undercover car anymore. A dream without edges, no waking. Or perhaps this was real, which made it crueler still.

Maybe the Detective's dissuasion was the only truth that mattered. Maybe the fight was already finished. I looked down at my Osprey—my laptop and class notebook tucked inside. My hands pressed against the fabric, numb. The edges bled into one another; nothing felt anchored anymore.

I hesitated for a beat. "Sounds good."

CHAPTER 10: KINGSLEY AND ROSE

Caught between two worlds, both real and unreal—Rose Visjonær dances through a San Francisco noir.

The invitation arrived in the mail, tucked inside a black envelope, its gold-embossed lettering shimmering like secrets. My roommate casually handed me the sleek envelope, not realizing it would mark the beginning of something unforgettable. I wasn't sure why I said yes—maybe it was her effortless charm, the daunting Adobe InDesign assignments, or something deeper—the undeniable urge to slip away from the weight of it all.

The Bently Reserve stood like a temple—a nod to classical Roman and Greek architectural styles, its stone-carved grandeur framed by monumental limestone columns, catching the shimmer of the city's fading light. Once the heart of federal currency and control, it had since transformed into an opulent chamber where socialites sipped champagne and made charitable contributions.

Alexis had invited me over to her Cow Hollow apartment, just a few blocks from mine.

"The Roaring Twenties—my favorite era," Alexis announced with excitement, handing me a gown with the *Retrofête* tags still on.

"You'll fit right in. Just don't start quoting Nietzsche over cocktails."

The gown was unlike anything I owned—a vision of 1920s Art Deco elegance, its sleek lines adorned with noir sequins that caught the light with subtle rebellion. The delicate silk viscose fringe trailed gracefully with every movement, swaying in a way that exuded grace and refinement, grounding me firmly in the present era with sharp, undeniable precision.

I slipped into the Violetta Dress as though I were stepping into a dream—an ethereal, Art Deco-inspired abstraction of a muse, a seamless blend of both the modern and the classical.

And it was unforgettable—for reasons I never could have predicted.

As Ella Fitzgerald's voice floated through the speakers near the entrance, velvet and haunting, I caught the line—*"That's why, darling, it's incredible... that someone so unforgettable thinks that I am unforgettable too."*

Inside, the marble floors gleamed beneath crystal chandeliers. The air buzzed with Gatsby-esque bravado—string quartets mingling with jazz, ethereal feathered headbands and elegant cigarette holders creating a surreal tapestry of decadence.

Something about the extravagance reminded me of that night at BIX—though this had a different kind of presence: more playful, more lighthearted. Beneath the glamour, I sensed the familiar undercurrent: power and philanthropy, wealth polished into performance.

I played a quick game of craps with Alexis and her friends at one of the large, rectangular, velvet-draped tables. Players gathered around the outer edge, while a stickman—or maybe a dealer—managed the dice with a long, polished stick.

I tossed the dice with quiet amusement, more intuition than focus. The room buzzed with champagne toasts and performative laughter, but my mind was elsewhere—probably magnetized by him, as if our encounter was designed long before I arrived

He was impossible not to notice, though he didn't seem to care if anyone did—a man in a crisp white tuxedo shirt, black bow tie, no jacket, as if he'd just stepped off the dance floor and into another frequency altogether. **Kingsley.**

He had the presence of someone written for another narrative entirely—refined, mythic—but with an edge, a bad boy essence just beneath the polish. Like trouble dressed in tailored silk. A Bond from another dimension, with a history you'd never quite be able to trace. But it was his eyes that stopped me—blue and pure, like they held a truth that hadn't been torn.

That's when we locked eyes.

Kingsley disarmed me with a smile.

There was something about him—clarity in a room full of pretense. He felt real in a way that made everything else disappear.

And then everything disappeared.

He began to move toward me and held out his hand. I slid mine into his—it felt both familiar and brand new. He led us onto the dance floor, where powerful lights beamed down upon us, casting us into a glow—dreamlike, electric, surreal.

Like a Tarantino film written just for me. And when the opening notes of Carmichael's *"Stardust"* drifted through the room, time collapsed—like we slipped into our own world entirely.

The music wrapped around our bodies, pulling us closer. Kingsley's hand rested lightly at my waist, his touch just enough to send a shiver through me. Everything was suspended. His trusting gaze never wavered as he held me, his movements effortless and playful—just to make me smile. His hand on my waist guided me safely with subtle precision, his fingers barely brushing the fabric of my dress, as though he was aware of every curve.

As we moved together, the music shifted—*"Stardust"* fading into the lively, sultry rhythm of Artie Shaw's *"Begin the Beguine,"* the tempo quickened, the atmosphere brightened, and suddenly, we were swept into a rhythm, dancing through the night with a serendipitous connection.

Kingsley's smile grew, the mischievous, playful edge sparkling in his eyes, and the dance felt lighter—like we were caught between two worlds, both real and unreal. Next he took my hand in his to guide us away. His lips were close as he sweet whispers meant only for my ears. I was mesmerized—*he was the lion to my lamb.*

As he led us toward a nearby table, two elegant, streamlined chairs awaited us. In the center, a large bouquet of dark crimson roses sat in a sleek, geometric Art Deco vase, their vibrant petals creating a striking image. Positioned in perfect symmetry, the bold, velvety petals of the roses swayed gently in the breeze from the open window. The sleek, white tablecloth was draped elegantly beneath, its smooth fabric accentuating the silver Art Deco-style sequins scattered across the surface, catching the soft glow of the surrounding light.

Kingsley pulled out one of the chairs.

"After that dance, you owe me!" His voice low and playful, but laced with something deeper—something dangerously intriguing.

"But for now, let's play a game. I know your name, but what's mine?"

He whispered into my ear, his cheek nearly touching mine. I could smell the peppermint on his breath, alluring me, while the space between us hummed with electric curiosity.

We looked deep into each other's eyes.

I almost laughed—but then caught myself to seriously consider his question.

Letting my gaze drift over him, then slowly traced the edge of his stark black bow tie with the tip of my finger.

"I love your…bow tie."

"That's not an answer!"

He teased, his eyes reflected the stunning blue lavender lights that shimmered above us.

"Alright," I sighed, a smile tugging at the corners of my mouth. "I know your name."

I paused again for effect, leaning in slightly.

"You're Kingsley."

I said confidently, letting his name remain on my *Rhode* Raspberry Lips.

He didn't respond immediately—just gazed at me, his eyes intense, as if I had unraveled something.

"*Say it again,*" he directed, his voice low and sensual, wrapped in velvet and heat.

My hands folded together, resting gently upon the noir black Art Deco dress, my heart bursting with adoration and fire. A gentle impulse surged through me as I whispered his name once more.

"Kingsley."

He swept me up from our seats, drawing us toward the dance floor and bright lights, guiding us towards the cascading velvet drape that majestically adorned the entire ballroom. He held me close to his chest, the crisp white tuxedo shirt against my skin.

I felt his beautiful heart beating—strong and steady.

Closing my eyes for a second, as if we had traveled into a dimension where space and time no longer mattered—a love that expanded across horizons, across vast distances and epochs.

"Here I have a gift for you."

Kingsley added, adjusting his stance with quiet integrity and honor. Standing at 6 foot 3, and with me barely reaching 5 foot 5 in stilettos, his height had a natural, effortless command. Like a magician, he swiftly moved his left arm from behind his back to reveal a perfect purple aura rose, its rich magenta blooms glowing in the light.

"What, where did you find that? Thank you—it's so different from the dark crimson roses that decorate the ballroom."

"I know your name," he replied, his tone enigmatic, as if he had discovered it through some secret means. "However I bet you don't know my favorite color."

"Blue."

I replied without thinking, reaching to touch the purple aura rose, its delicate petals soft beneath my fingertips.

"Incredible, how is it that you can guess so well?"

He paused, an amorous look in his deep ocean eyes. "You must be magical. Tonight you arrived from Venus on a Galactic spaceflight to dance with me?"

He smiled.

I laughed, a playful essence illuminated me.

"Venus? That's true, still adjusting to this planet."

The edge of the purple aura rose's exquisite and divine petals brushed against my fingers as Kingsley's gaze softened. He moved closer, his voice low.

"Rose, you've adjusted just fine."

He reassured, his voice taking on a more serious tone.

We stood there, in the middle of the dance floor, everything around us fading into the elaborate, glamorous 1920s roaring scene. The notes of Sweet Lorraine seemed to drift into a memory, replaced by the soft beating of my heart and the warmth of his presence protecting us.

The night seemed to suspend time, and all that mattered was us—intimate, electric, and filled with unspoken promise.

And then pow! Out of nowhere, a man practically launched himself beside us, full of glee, as if he'd been shot out of a cannon.

He was vibing high with energy, fueled by the atmosphere of the night. Dressed in a tuxedo, he resembled a jester more than anything else—his exuberance bouncing off the Bently's walls like a pinball.

"Good evening, lovely. I'm Houghs. I see you're getting cozy with my buddy here."

Houghs playfully nudged Kingsley on the back, his arm casually wrapping around his shoulder. His eyes glinted with mischief.

"So, Kingsley, still working that usual charm?" he teased, a smile tugging at his lips. "But I've got to ask—have you gotten the lady's number yet?"

Houghs pressed him further, his voice dripping with playful challenge.

"Come on, Kingsley! You're not really going to let her slip away, are you?"

Kingsley chuckled, his smile widening. He turned to me, his gaze locking with mine, steady and confident.

"I think that's a matter I'd like to settle right now," he said smoothly.

"May I?"

He asked as he reached for my hand, the warmth of his touch imprinting his signature upon me.

"Yes."

I unclasped my Retrofête chainmail purse, the delicate metallic catching the light as I slid out my Blackberry, the smooth surface cool against my fingertips. Kingsley took my phone with a confident smile and typed in his number. With a sly, almost knowing grin, he handed my Blackberry back to me. As he did, his phone began to ring from his tuxedo pocket, the familiar iPhone default ringtone cutting through the intimacy with contrast— so unexpectedly normal, it made me smile.

He brushed my blonde hair from my face, his touch lingering for a moment before he whispered, "You have my number, sweet Rose." His voice was soothing, with a quiet intensity that made my heart race. He kissed me softly on the cheek, his lips briefly tracing my high cheekbone.

Across the ballroom, leaning casually against a pillar, Houghs watched with a broad grin. Dressed in a tuxedo, his exuberance reminded me of a playful jester, bouncing between conversations and creative gestures.

"That's my boy," he said, chuckling to himself.

CHAPTER 11 : THE BLACK ARTS

Never attempt to win by force what can be won by deception.—Niccolò Machiavelli, The Prince

The psychologist's eyes sparkled with a hint of amusement as he gazed at the newspaper, his eyebrows slightly raised. "People are appalled by immoral acts, yet they're commonplace," he said, his tone conversational.

He flipped to a specific page in the San Francisco Chronicle, his fingers drumming lightly on the paper.

"I came across an article about your alma mater. *The Academy of Art University*, apparently they're accused of defrauding the federal government of hundreds of millions of dollars." He leaned back in his chair, steepling his hands with a contemplative expression.

"It says that the United States Supreme Court rejected the University's bid to dismiss the case, citing evidence that the school was using illegal enrollment tactics to recruit students who were unlikely to pay back their government-based subsidized loans."

The Psychologist leaned forward, his eyes narrowing slightly as he spoke.

"What year did you start?" he inquired, his brow furrowing in concentration.

"I started classes in 2010, but enrolled in 2009."

He nodded thoughtfully, his gaze drifting to the papers in the manila folder. He pulled out a few sheets, scanning them with a discerning eye. "Some recruiters claimed the university offered them incentive compensation schemes, promising raises up to $30,000 and Hawaiian vacations based on recruitment numbers." His tone turned slightly incredulous, his voice rising in pitch.

"You were recruited by an admissions rep whose recruitment numbers benefited from your enrollment." He looked up, his eyes locking onto mine with an intense gaze.

"Yes, and it was a miracle I graduated. I flunked classes, repeated them in summer school, and worked double-time to walk with my peers. The traumatic stress from the felony and subsequent police investigation hollowed out my focus and stained the quality of my work."

"I can see how that is so," the psychologist confirmed.

"Yes," I replied. "The city's largest private school operated less like an academy of learning and more like a factory—a financial engine fueled by government-backed student loans underwriting glossy degrees. It was artifice masquerading as art: brochures filled with saturated colors and polished typography, a Warholian repetition of promises mass-produced and sold as unique. Some of my peers thrived in the advertising world, but for me, the promise of a lucrative career remained elusive—like chasing the aura of a painting that, up close, reveals itself as print."

"Did you like your professors?"

"I was lucky to have professors like Mr. Roland Young or Dr. Shakespeare, who nurtured my creative intelligence. However other professors showed no mercy. Nevertheless Roland was incredible, he began his career with Louis Danziger and went on to flourish as a famous album cover designer. He previously taught at CalArts, Otis, UCLA, and Parsons. The Academy of Art University is where I met him, he was co-chair of the Advertising School. He had a gift for opening artists' minds to new perspectives. I miss him."

My thoughts circled through memories, I remember sitting in one of the Herman Miller Lounge Chairs in Roland Young's office, we'd discuss clever advertising strategies for Virgin Galactic. Occasionally I'd look out the floor-to-ceiling window view of the Bay Bridge. The University's School of Advertising was housed within a beautifully restored historic building at 60 Federal Street, which ran parallel to the I-80 corridor.

My psychologist's voice brought me back to the present moment, his eyes locking onto mine as he held up a newspaper article, snapping me out of my reverie.

"The university has profited over $1.5 billion in federal student loans and $171 million in federal student grants since 2006. Did you live in one of the university-owned buildings?"

"No. I lived in an apartment in the Marina–Cow Hollow with roommates. Not associated with the university."

"Did you get a job offer or have an internship during graduate school?"

"Yes—I started an internship with Louis Vuitton," I replied, a smile flickering across my face.

"I had the chance to work closely with managers, assisting in the travel bags and ready-to-wear departments. I thought it was so fun."

"I loved it," I added. "But during lunch breaks, I'd lose track of time completely. My mind drifted into daydreams—it was the only way I knew how to cope. A temporary escape from everything happening outside of work." I hesitated. "That was also when the Detective molested me."

The psychologist nodded, his expression steady, compassionate.

"An internship at Louis Vuitton is a dream opportunity. I want to make sure you feel safe and supported. Can you tell me more about what happened with the Detective?"

My gaze fell. Tears slipped down my cheeks—quiet, steady. I felt detached, observing the moment rather than inhabiting it—a familiar dissociative veil.

And then, without warning, a song echoed in my mind—Smashing Pumpkins. *Intoxicated with the madness, I'm in love with my sadness.*

The lyrics replayed in my mind. It captured what I couldn't say aloud: the comfort I found in music and art. Musicians like the Smashing Pumpkins are my refuge—a way to process emotions when words failed. Their songs resonated, offering understanding in moments when I felt alone.

"Yes," I said softly. "The internship was a dream come true. I was so excited to be there… but it was tainted. His abuse of authority left me with emotional scars. I started dissociating. Struggled to concentrate. I didn't feel safe in my own mind."

The psychologist leaned forward slightly, his voice a quiet anchor.
"Your mind would wander—and you'd lose track of time. I understand, Rose."

He paused, letting the silence hold us gently.

"Can you tell me, what year did you graduate?"

Another flashback hit, disarmed by the psychologist's compassion. It rose into existence, a supernatural phenomenon bursting forth with intensity, as if the past itself was clawing its way back into the present.

It's an encoded memory associated with a series of traumatic events. These memories are bound by the same parameters as my every-day memories. I felt the initial emotions experienced at the time of encoding as I re-experienced during my flashback episode.

I looked at him in awe.

"What are you seeing?" he inquired.

"I remember exactly what it felt like to walk across the radiant stage at the Graduation Ceremony inside the Cow Hollow Palace. I shook hands with Dr. Elisa Stephens — The president and granddaughter of the school's founder. Her elegant diamond earrings sparkled as she smiled softly and handed me my diploma. Sounds over the top maybe but the memory reminds me of multi-dimensional spacetime."

Dr. Elisa Stephens' elegant diamond earrings, a symbol of the intricate web of power and privilege. Like two glittering stars, the earrings shone brightly, refracting the light and casting a kaleidoscope of reflections.

Just as spacetime is warped by the presence of massive objects, the earrings seemed to distort the surrounding space, drawing attention to the woman who wore them - a woman whose family's legacy was built on the artistic ambitions of others, and whose institution had mastered the art of transforming creativity into capital.

"It was only a few minutes of time but it felt like an eternity. I had a loyalty to finish the MFA even though I struggled to complete classes. After I graduated, I realized that I had accrued almost 20 Federal Student Loans from the US Department of Education."

I continued to describe, "A private bank Nelnet convinced me to consolidate my loans via the Direct Consolidation Loan program. I was confused when I was trying to make this decision back in 2016 because I thought Nelnet was directly connected to the US Department of Education. They're making a lot of interest money off of me. I've accrued $200k + student loan debt; and now Nelnet is being sued for malpractice. All of this has felt so overwhelming."

"Rose— I found the *Forbes* article you referenced last week, titled *The Black Arts: The $800 Million Family Selling Art Degrees and False Hopes.*"

He said, leaning forward slightly, elbows resting on his knees, his fingers laced together in a deliberate, practiced pose.

He tilted his head just a bit, eyes narrowing with intent as he continued. "It says that four former employees are suing under the Federal False Claims Act, which awards triple damages to encourage whistleblowers to come forward if they believe the government is being defrauded. It could cost the school $450 million because there's evidence they used illegal tactics to enroll students from 2006 to 2010. *Serendipitously,* when you enrolled—right?"

His words landed with quiet weight, and he glanced sideways at me, watching my reaction.

"Yes," I said, keeping my voice even. "The nation's largest art school, and also one of the city's biggest property owners."

He leaned back, fingers tapping lightly against his knee, almost casually. "Where were you living during the time you were finishing up graduate school?"

"I lived in the Bush Street house with four other women from December 2011 to June 2012, and it was chaotic. One of them used to scream at me, spit at me, and lock Arielle Ivor's Pomeranian in my room so it would pee and poop on the floor. They blamed me for Arielle being sent to Langley Porter Neuropsychiatric Institute—because we were friends. The logic was flawed, but somehow persuasive in that household.

I liked it when she sang *Part of Your World* from *The Little Mermaid* to me in her operatic voice. Most of the time, I just tried not to be home."

"What kinds of self-care practices were you using during that time?"

"Yes. I practiced at the Bikram yoga studio in Nob Hill six days a week for months. Being in the 105-degree hot room, moving through the same set of asanas, helped release the tension."

He looked down, thinking carefully as he reviewed his notes.

"Did the detective spend time with you during that period?"

"Yes," I said. "He stayed in contact after the investigation closed—throughout grad school and for years after. I was often in a hyperactive state, and it never struck me as unusual. I naively assumed he was just an attentive, caring man checking in on me."

My mind raced, flickering through memories. He'd offer to swing by the Bush Street house, drive me around the city to talk. Real friendships felt unattainable then. I distrusted new people, kept my circle small. But the detective? He seemed trustworthy. Dependable. So I'd say yes, sliding into the passenger seat of his undercover cop car.

I remembered one time in particular—cruising down Hyde Street as he spoke about his day at work. It felt normal. Familiar. Like something that wouldn't hurt me.

"What kinds of conversations would you have with him?" the psychologist asked, his voice calm as I glanced around the therapy room, eyes resting on an assortment of green plants in soft light.

"Oh, all kinds," I replied. "He told me stories ranging from deeply personal to flat-out bragging—about his early years in vice, wild motorcycle days, or some career accomplishment he seemed proud of."

Another memory stirred.

We were parked outside the Clift Hotel on Geary Street, still in his undercover cop car. The hotel's façade loomed above us—majestic, timeless. Originally built for the Panama-Pacific International Exposition in 1915, it had the same haunting elegance as the Palace of the Legion of Honor. No surprise—they shared the same architects.

"My undercover cases can be fun," he said with a grin. "For example, I'm investigating high-end escorts who frequent the Clift. I'll be at the Prohibition-era Redwood Room, striking up conversations and sipping fine cocktails. The department's covering the hotel room. But more importantly, Miss Visjonær, I'd like to take you out for a celebratory dinner. I'm proud of you. All your hard work and dedication have paid off—you've reached a significant milestone."

"Thank you," I said, my voice steady, though I could feel the heat rise in my cheeks.

"How about a nice North Beach restaurant next week to celebrate? How does that sound?"

"I'm moving out of the Bush Street house and into my aunt's place in North Beach that week," I replied. "So that may work."

"Was it mid to late June when you had dinner with the detective?" the psychologist asked, jotting down another note.

"He took me to a woodfire pizzeria on Columbus Avenue. We split a Diavola pizza, the tomato burrata basil salad, prosecco, and red wine. Sat at the bar near the Fontana Vulcano oven, the heat rolling off the flames, the din of laughter and clinking glasses filling the space," I replied.

"Still remember the buzz of the crowd—people lost in their own conversations, their own lives. Completely unaware of the moment unfolding next to them."

"That's when he said it. The Detective leaned forward, , a satisfaction in his voice," I recalled.

"Rose, I'm on target to retire from the San Francisco Police Department within the next three years. Forty years in the city, and I'm finally ready for the next chapter. Private Investigations. Got my PI license from the Bureau of Security and Investigative Services. I'm well connected."

He let it sit there, like an **ace** played at the right moment—Deliberate.

"My work as a Veteran Inspector has paid off. I've got high-end clients lined up already. One even wants me to travel with them—private jet, full access. It's all set."

His tone was smooth. The kind of talk a man gives when he wants to project a certain image —powerful, untouchable.

During the drive back to my aunt's house, the Detective spoke with the ease of a man unburdened by consequence. "Thank you for joining me for dinner. I'm proud of you. You're smart, and I've always found you very attractive."

He paused, then his voice dipped, lower and more deliberate.

"As you know, I have a wife, but we don't have sex as much as we used to. I would love to have a romantic-sexual relationship with you. I want you to be my mistress. It could be a regular arrangement if you wanted it to be…"

I sat frozen in the passenger seat of his silver Mercedes-Benz coupé convertible, parked in front of my aunt's place. His words hung in the air, thick and heavy, like a confession without shame. A cool summer night breeze brushed against my face, but it did nothing to clear my head. Shock settled into my bones. Had I heard him correctly?

I glanced around, my gaze darting to the streetlights, the empty sidewalk, the world outside that somehow still felt normal. I had no idea what to say.

"Thank you, Detective, for the lovely dinner. It was a great evening. I'll think about it," I said, forcing my voice into something steady, something polite. Anything to end the conversation without confrontation. Anything to get out.

I pushed open the Mercedes door and stepped out, my pulse hammering as I moved toward the Victorian exterior. I didn't just walk—I leaped for the door, unlocked it in one motion, and jogged up the wooden stairs.

Inside, I collapsed onto the couch, breathless. My mind swirled, trying to make sense of what had just happened, trying to pretend it hadn't.

The house was empty. My aunt was on vacation. No one to talk to. No one to confirm that what I'd just heard was as disturbing as it felt.

I grabbed the remote and turned on Netflix, staring at the screen without watching. His voice echoed in my head, the casual arrogance of it.

His request had shaken me to my core. And yet, part of me—the part that wanted to forget, to pretend—kept trying to push it down.

"Rose—fawning is a trauma response. It's when someone develops people-pleasing behavior to avoid conflict and feel safe. In other words, it's a coping mechanism trauma survivors use to appease the offender," she explained, her tone calming.

I glanced around the peaceful therapy room, then turned to the window, letting my eyes settle on the quiet outline of the Marin County mountains.

"I've struggled to understand my reactions to his transgressions. I was in therapy with MSW Julie Robbins in the Marina constantly, but oddly, I'm not sure I ever told her the detective sexually abused me. Maybe I was protecting his reputation—or afraid of retaliation. When the perpetrator is a police officer, there's a real fear of backlash for speaking out."

The psychologist observed me carefully and responded, "Prior adverse experiences with authority figures—such as your initial report to the SFPD and subsequent interaction with the detective—can significantly impact a survivor's willingness to disclose. This pattern of institutional betrayal often contributes to delayed reporting and inhibited disclosure of critical information."

"The only way I knew how to cope was to block it out—to pretend it never happened," I said quietly.

The psychologist nodded slowly.

"Did you have other encounters like this with the detective?"

"Yes. Many."

A silence settled.

"There was another time in June 2012, just days before I left for a yoga retreat. He picked me up in his Mercedes—just like before."

CHAPTER 12: MAD MEN

He who seeks to deceive will always find someone who allows himself to be deceived.—A Machiavellian quote from *The Prince*, where Niccolò Machiavelli explores power, manipulation, and control.

We navigated Nob Hill, past the Fairmont, then descended into the Pacific Heights.

He loved reminiscing to me about his younger years—how, in his 20s and 30s, he would race his motorcycle up and down the city's steep hills, the engine roaring against the backdrop of San Francisco. How, at just 21, he had joined the police force, stepping into a world of authority and control.

The late afternoon sun hung low, casting long shadows across the hills, bathing the city in a golden glow. The streets, washed in amber light, felt timeless—unchanged by the decades of stories he carried. As I glanced over at him, caught up in his elaborate stories, I found myself wondering—*just how old was he?*

Not sure. Hmm. My guess? Somewhere around my dad's age.

He was sharply dressed, as if he'd just left an event—his light blue Boss shirt crisp, neatly tucked into tailored slacks, exuding effortless sophistication. Clubmaster Ray-Bans resting on his face, unreadable behind the lenses.

He drove effortlessly—the way men like him always do—casual, in control, as if the roads themselves bowed to his will. There was an ease to him, a quiet confidence that made every movement seem both instinctive and deliberate.

The detective's expression softened, his voice laced with unexpected warmth. "Let me tell you something, Rose. I've worked for everything I have—every last thing. Nothing came easy. And seeing you, after everything you've endured, standing here, finishing grad school... that's something to be proud of. And I am proud of you, Rose. Truly proud."

He paused, locking his sea-green eyes with mine.

A gaze that is unpredictable, shifting, and hard to pin down—like the ocean itself. It can carry a sense of depth, mystery, or quiet intensity, making it unclear whether his expression is inviting or dangerous.

He continued, "The dedication you put into your goal is exceptional."

There was a beat of silence, measured. Then, almost casually—"I'm feeling tired from the day. How about we watch a show or a movie together?"

The car slowed to a stop in front of my aunt's house on Chestnut Street in North Beach. The afternoon sun hung low, casting long shadows across the sidewalk. He shifted into park but didn't move to leave. Instead, he turned toward me, his sea-green eyes reflecting the warm light, unreadable. The quiet hum of the engine filled the space between us—a pause, an expectation, a pressure unspoken yet unmistakable.

A push—subtle enough to dismiss but firm enough to feel.

"We could go inside," he said, his tone easy, almost offhand. Then, without hesitation, he opened the driver's door and stepped out, coming around to mine.

The passenger door clicked open. An invitation. A test.

Before I could react, he extended a hand—not quite touching, but close enough to make refusal feel awkward. When I hesitated, he smiled, warm but insistent, his presence suddenly bigger than the space around me.

"Just for a little while," he said as if I'd already agreed.

Then, with quiet authority, he placed his hand briefly at the small of my back, a light, guiding touch—directing, not asking. A gesture just firm enough to be persuasive, yet fleeting enough to avoid objection.

The four-story Victorian building and dark wooden door emerged ahead, its worn steps leading to the front door. He walked beside me, close, but not too close—just enough to make it feel like he belonged there. Like this was inevitable.

I reached into my purse, but my keys slipped from my grip, clattering against the marble floor. I exhaled sharply, crouching to retrieve them, my hands colder than they should have been.

When I tried the lock, the key refused to turn. I jiggled it, twisted harder, but the door wouldn't budge.

"Here, let me," he said, stepping in closer.

His voice was reassuring, patient—but there was something else beneath it.

I hesitated, but before I could protest, he was already taking the keys from my hand. His fingers brushed against mine, deliberate and steady, before he slid the key into the lock with practiced ease. A twist, a quiet click, and the door creaked open.

He handed the keys back with a small smile, his palm lingering against mine just a second too long.

"See? Easy," he said, his voice smooth, coaxing. "After you."

Calculated. Patient. Never obvious.
Their power move is quiet, methodical—a slow tightening you don't feel until it's too late.
By the time you recognize the trap, you're already caught.

"Do you watch *Mad Men*?"

My mind started to race, but my body moved on autopilot—responding before I fully registered the question.

"I think I've heard of it."

It was *l'habitude*, as Maurice Merleau-Ponty might have put it: habit. The body acting before thought, before resistance. Muscle memory. Conditioned compliance.

The mind may rebel, but the body, shaped by repetition, follows patterns long established.
I was already engaging, already agreeing, already moving in the direction he wanted—before I had the chance to resist.

"It's about the advertising world in New York, right?"

"Yes. A critically acclaimed show," he said, drifting into the living room as if he belonged there.

He didn't pause at the threshold. Didn't wait for permission. It was subtle—a quiet assertion of presence, a seamless claim. With practiced ease, he crossed the room and lowered himself onto the plush pink sofa, its tufted velvet cushions yielding beneath his weight.

Above him, an ornate Victorian mirror hung on the wall—its gilded frame catching the soft chandelier glow, reflecting the room in delicate gold filigree.

A sense of fated belonging. A déjà vu I hadn't agreed to.

He gestured to the spot beside him on the couch. A silent invitation, wrapped in expectation.

"I watched an episode the other day at home and it reminded me of you," he said, his tone easy, assured. "The female lead—she's ambitious, determined. She wants to work her way up in a top ad agency, just like you."

I walked to the couch and sat next to him, just as he had subtly implied I should. It wasn't a command, not exactly—but it didn't have to be.

I was hardwired to comply, conditioned by a lifetime of unspoken rules. Authority wasn't just about orders; it was about presence, about expectation. Citizens obey law enforcement not just out of fear of consequence, but because we are taught to—because we're taught that defiance is wrong. That questioning power is dangerous. That saying *no* is an act of rebellion, even when it shouldn't be.

It was the kind of conditioning that kept society in line, the same quiet obedience that allowed tyranny to fester in plain sight. *People should not be afraid of their governments.*

Governments should be afraid of their people. But here I was, sinking into the couch beside him, proving that fear and obedience were deeply intertwined.

"It's set in the 1960s," he continued, his tone light and carefree. "How about we watch an episode?"

"Okay."

I reached for the remote resting on the glass coffee table and pressed the power button. Across the room, the black TV screen turned on, casting a faint glow into the dim space. I searched through the catalog of shows, the soft clicks of navigation filling the silence between us.

I found the *Mad Men* icon and clicked on it.

"What's her name in the show?"

He barely acknowledged the question, his response smooth, effortless—redirecting.

"The male lead," he said instead, "is this debonair ad executive."

Makes me wish I'd gotten into corporate advertising instead of law enforcement," he chuckled.

Then, with a smirk—"But then I wouldn't have met you."

The words hung in the air—deliberate, calculated. A casual remark laced with something more.

"Oh, it was Peggy Olson," he said, smirking slightly. "The talented copywriter who started as Don Draper's secretary."

His gaze lingered.

"She's ambitious, driven... and there's something about her—this quiet intensity, like she's just waiting to be unraveled."

I didn't have time to respond before he shifted, stretching out on the couch. The opening notes of *A Beautiful Mine* by RJD2 began to play—haunting, restrained, yet charged. The hypnotic rhythm slipped into the space between us like smoke curling under a door.

I fixed my gaze on the screen, trying to anchor myself in the flickering images—until something broke the stillness.

He leaned in and, without hesitation, kissed the side of my face.

Uninvited. Inevitable.

A heat surged through me—not quite anger, not yet, but the kindling of something raw and rising. Then his hand moved, slipping beneath my shirt. His palm met my skin—warm, deliberate. It started to curve around my breast.

He didn't ask.

I exhaled, not in relief, but in something tangled—resistance, disbelief. My mind raced, thoughts colliding too fast to catch.

"I'm not comfortable with this."

I shifted my shoulder, trying to pull away—to reclaim space that had never been his to take. But he stayed close, unmoved, as if my discomfort was merely a detail to manage, not a boundary to respect.

"Oh, I understand, Rose. I'll stop."

As if words alone could undo what had already been done. His tone was dismissive—meant to pacify, not acknowledge. But he didn't move his hand. Not right away. For a few lingering seconds, his fingers remained—pressing the moment into permanence.

Slow.
Deliberate.
Leisurely.

His hand slid downward, dragging across my stomach before finally withdrawing—not in retreat, but to adjust his pants. His belt buckle.

I froze.

My mind detached from my body, slipping somewhere distant. Unreachable. Another fear-induced paralysis. My amygdala—primal, instinctual—sounded the alarm, but my limbs refused to follow. My breath sat heavy in my chest, caged inside my ribs.

This was power in its rawest form—not loud, not forceful, but insidious.

The kind that disguises itself as familiarity, as entitlement.
Power, as Foucault wrote, isn't always wielded. It's embedded—woven into the structure of relationships, into the unspoken rules of who commands and who submits.

He had rewritten the script without my consent, reshaped my body into something not my own.
A space he could trespass.
An object he could maneuver.

And in that moment, as his hand retreated on his own terms, at his own pace, the violation was already complete— Not just in the act itself, but in the quiet certainty, that he knew, he could get away with it.

And then—he exhaled, relaxed against me, like nothing had happened. Like we were lovers. Like there had been no violation, no abuse of power, no silent war waged against my trust. He wanted me to believe this was normal. That his body against mine was something safe, something I'd invited.

I swallowed hard, disbelief fluttering sharp inside me, not like *butterflies* like blades.

It was the arrogance—the quiet, unshakable kind—that made him believe he could do anything. That his badge made him untouchable. That his wedding ring didn't matter. That breaking the law wasn't really breaking it—not when he was the one holding the gun and writing the report.

The betrayal was its own kind of violence. He was an undercover detective who claimed he worked hundreds of hours of overtime and worked day and night—a man sworn to uphold the law, to protect, to serve—using that authority not just to break the law, but to commit a crime against the very person he was assigned to safeguard.

There's a psychology to this. We're taught to obey officers. To comply. To trust. From childhood, we learn that disobedience has consequences—that when a cop speaks, you listen, or you risk trouble, punishment, or worse. The uniform commands obedience. The badge carries weight.

But a system built to protect had turned its gaze—shielding him instead.

It wasn't just his hands on me.
It was his authority.
His power.
Pressing down on me, making escape impossible.

The blind-maze game.
A psychological trap.

The game is the distortion of reality.
The cognitive dissonance created when what *should* happen is the opposite of what *is* happening.
It erodes perception.
Poisons trust.
Rewires the brain to doubt itself.
It breaks you down—*before you even know you're breaking.*

Fifteen minutes passed.
We watched *Mad Men*.

Then—his hand.
A slow descent down my thigh.
A slip beneath my yoga pants.
His fingers pressing against me.
Then inside. *Against my will.*

"Don't. I don't want to do this," I said, my voice cracking.

The words hurt to say. There was a sharp ache in my chest, as if speaking them carried weight my body wasn't ready to hold.

But he didn't stop. Not right away.
His hand lingered—fingers still pressing into me. The moment stretched, quiet and unbearable, defying my plea.

When he finally withdrew, it wasn't because I said no.
It was because he had decided he was done.

My body locked up.

Everything in me—my instincts, my reactions—froze. The reflex to resist never made it to my limbs. It was the involuntary freeze response, a survival mechanism I didn't choose.

He had crossed a line. He knew it.

And still, he leaned back casually into the couch, as if nothing had happened.

What he'd done wasn't just disturbing—it was a violation. Of trust. Of power.

Under *California Government Code § 945.9*, survivors of sexual assault by law enforcement officers are not bound by standard government claim filing requirements. That law exists for a reason. Because this happens.

Had he done it before? To other women who had passed through the Special Victims Unit —looking for help, and finding this?

A wave of nausea rose through me.

Henry. The Detective.

Two faces of the same betrayal.

Predators who never saw me as a person—only something to take.

"I *respect* you, Rose. I don't want to do anything you're not comfortable with."

A lie.

His voice was too smooth, too rehearsed—damage control dressed as sincerity. He wasn't offering respect; he was rewriting the moment, tilting the power back in his favor.

I turned away, fixating on the Victorian windows instead, where the late afternoon sun spilled through the blinds—golden, amber, indifferent.

"I am a discreet person," he added.

"I hope you know that you're special to me."

His green eyes locked onto mine, unshaken.

"I've got to go, but let's touch base after you're back from the yoga retreat."

The ease in his voice made my skin crawl.

I walked him to the front door, unlocking it with fingers that no longer felt like my own. He loomed over me—easily a foot taller—then pulled me into a slow, deliberate hug.

The closing scene. And just like that, he vanished. Leaving behind nothing but a void, an absence performed—a façade of departure.

A simulacrum, straight out of Baudrillard.

Puis, comme ça—il s'était évanoui, laissant derrière lui rien d'autre qu'un vide, une absence feinte, comme un simulacre à la Baudrillard.

CHAPTER 13: SAN FRANCISCO HUMAN RIGHTS COMMISSION

Our breath is connected to the air that every being breathes. By breathing consciously, we acknowledge our communion with all of life. —Sharon Gannon, Jivamulti Yoga Cofounder

The dark absurdity of life lured me into elaborate fantasies. One idea: stepping into the 24-hour FedEx Office and Print Center, churning out hundreds of copies—cover letters, résumés, corporate rejection emails, LinkedIn correspondences. Artifacts from a life I once believed in.

I imagined taking the four largest canvases I could find, arranging the evidence chronologically, gluing it down, then painting a massive red *X* over each one—an act of contemplation, destruction, and rebirth. The linework in my defiant red Xs would be raw, erratic, untamed—Basquiat-inspired, fierce and unrepentant. A visual requiem for lost illusions.

I spiraled into a trauma-induced mania—obsessed with culture, interdisciplinary art, and the psychology of museum curation. I dreamed of exhibiting at the Whitney Museum of American Art, imagining my name on a placard beneath a piece no one could ignore.

But reality tugged me in another direction. I threw myself into helping my boyfriend build his business—because I wasn't getting hired. He had just passed the CSLB (Contractors State Licensing Board) exam and had remodel jobs lined up in elegant Nob Hill homes. I pivoted, applying my skills in branding, design, and media to shape the company's marketing—willing his success to feel like my own.

The deeper I went, the more I immersed myself in business frameworks, attending SBA (Small Business Administration) workshops: *Intro to Accounting, Federal, State & Local Tax, Business Plan Development, Finance.*

RISE JUSTICE LABS

"Have you noticed the wave of activism after the MeToo movement?"

"Amanda Nguyen," I said instantly.

"She founded RISE, the nonprofit fighting for the civil rights of sexual assault survivors. She's incredible. Honestly, she inspires me—I even sent in a volunteer application to her organization."

I paused, then added, "Her 2016 Survivors' Bill of Rights changed everything. It forces law enforcement to properly handle, store, and test rape kits—actual legal accountability. It's already in place in New York, and they're pushing to expand it nationwide."

He flipped through his notebook slowly, eyes scanning his notes before looking back up.

"Are you familiar with activist journalism?"

I hesitated.

"Not sure if what I wrote on Medium.com qualifies as activist journalism—if that's what you're implying."

"Yes."

"I've come to see how our choices can shape not only national conversations, but global outcomes. We have a responsibility to make informed, ethical decisions—because if we don't, it's the next generation that pays the price."

I paused, taking a breath.

"I still remember reading about the outrage from Stanford's graduating class after the Santa Clara County Superior Court's ruling in the Brock Turner case. Their message— 'Protect Survivors, Not Rapists'—stayed with me. It gave me courage. It made me cry."

That was the moment something shifted.

"I wrote and published my first piece of journalism: *In Support of San Francisco Survivors of Sexual Assault: A Response to Emily Doe.* Then I created Medium.com/ ProtectSurvivors, hoping to create a space where other survivor-activists could contribute and be heard."

"Honestly, reclaiming my voice has been a slow process—denial and shame held me back for years."

"But Chanel Miller changed everything. She reclaimed her identity by publishing *Know My Name,* and her courage impacted me deeply. The way she spoke about the absurd scrutiny survivors face—socially, legally, personally—it was like she named something I had felt but couldn't articulate. I still remember the first time I read her victim impact statement on BuzzFeed. I couldn't stop shaking."

The psychologist nodded, thoughtful.

"It sounds like these individuals have been powerful and empowering role models for you."

"Absolutely," I said quietly.

He glanced at his notes, then looked up.

"That's excellent."

"I've been working on piecing together your timeline—can you help clarify a few key points? When did you first contact the police regarding your medical forensic kit and toxicology results? When was another significant encounter with the detective? And when did you begin volunteering to speak in support of the Human Rights Commission's legislation?"

I nodded slowly, the questions suspending in the air, pulling me into a memory.

FLASHBACK FEBRUARY 2017

It was a peaceful mid-afternoon, the kind of light that sharpens everything—the shadows stretching long across the pavement, the air crisp with just a hint of fog. I was walking down the steep incline of California Street, my Manduka yoga mat slung over one shoulder, the weight familiar against my back. The city's quiet hum buzzed in the distance, unremarkable, ordinary.

Then—a voice, cutting clean through the stillness.

"Hey, kid! Great to see you! You look great! Looks like we're neighbors!"

I froze mid-step. My muscles tensed before I even turned toward the sound.

There he was.

The Detective—leaning out the window of a red MINI Cooper, grinning like it was nothing. Too easy. Too knowing. As if this was just another casual run-in. As if he hadn't wrecked my life and left me to quietly assemble the pieces.

No. No way.

He was driving uphill, slow and deliberate. His tone was breezy, familiar—too familiar.

"I bought a three-bedroom flat up the street on Jones," he continued, voice smooth—too smooth, like this was just casual small talk. "Incredible views of the city from the top of Nob Hill. We want to remodel it. Doesn't your boyfriend do construction?"

I nodded, caught completely off guard—more than off guard.

"Yes, he does construction. We moved to Nob Hill last February so he'd be within walking distance of the remodel projects he's finishing up. I'll let him know."

A beat of silence. His eyes flickered—like he was reading something in my face.

A three-bedroom flat on Jones Street, in this part of the city? That wasn't just real estate —it was a fortune. I tried not to show it, but the thought flashed across my mind: *How does he afford that?*

Oh, right—he'd mentioned years ago that his wife worked for Sotheby's. And wasn't he planning to become a private investigator?

The details were hazy, but the question lingered.

"So," I asked casually, "are you still with the SFPD, or did you retire?"

"I retired in 2015," he said. "Now I'm a private investigator."

Something about the moment made my skin prickle. It was subtle—but unsettling. A barely perceptible shift in the air.

I had a class to get to.

I adjusted the strap on my shoulder and kept walking toward the bus stop. I was headed to a vinyasa class at Yoga Tree, but the city around me suddenly felt different—tilted, heavier. Like the air had thickened without warning.

I wanted to shake it off, to push the moment aside. But the past has a way of creeping in when you least expect it—slipping its fingers around your throat, tightening just enough to remind you it never really left.

CHAPTER 14: CALIFORNIA STREET

The most common way people give up their power is by thinking they don't have any. — Alice Walker

Unfortunately, victims in San Francisco who sought help were often met with intimidation, condescension, and accusations of dishonesty. I know—because I met them. Mockery and coercion into silence were used to control our stories. The system didn't just fail us—it chose not to test our forensic evidence, violated its duty to preserve evidence that could spoil if not tested right away, and obstructed our path to justice while our cases were still open. Beneath its progressive facade, San Francisco concealed a disturbing truth.

A reflection on the disorder—a haunting echo of abuse and power imbalance. This theme resonated throughout the narrative, adding weight without overwhelming it. In long, searching conversations with survivor-activists, we began to unravel complex threads. What emerged was staggering: a pattern far more widespread than we'd imagined, revealing hundreds—possibly thousands—of victims.

Their forensic medical kits, collected at Zuckerberg San Francisco General Hospital's ER, were discarded. Authorities refused to submit the request forms in time for the SFPD crime lab to process them, allowing toxicology evidence to spoil. As a result, their cases were dismissed for "lack of evidence." But the truth was that evidence had been erased.

Each revelation peeled back another layer of a wound that refused to heal. The deeper we dug, the more disturbing it became—a slow-motion disaster hiding in plain sight. Pandora's box had cracked open.

While researching, we came across multiple *SFGate* and *SF Chronicle* articles about another survivor-activist in the city—Augustine. I sent her a message on social media.

It took a year for her to see the message. But when she did, she replied: *"Rose, I would love to connect with you. Do you know if your kit and toxicology samples were actually tested?"*

Her question stopped me in my tracks.

I searched my memory, trying to recall even the smallest confirmation that the Detective had ever told me my forensic exam kit had been tested. No record. No follow-up.

Blindly, naively—I assumed a veteran cop would follow protocol. That the toxicology report and DNA findings from the ER would be in the file sent to the DA for fair review. But assumptions can be dangerous. I was about to learn just how much had been deliberately kept from me.

What if he never even submitted the request to the Crime Lab?

"I don't know if it was tested. I'll ask. Thank you—I'd never even thought of this before,"

I told her, the realization crashing over me like a wave.

The Detective had taken me to the Crime Lab during the investigation and told me the kit was going to be tested.

Augustine replied immediately. "You need to follow up with the SFPD. Request a copy of the Incident Report, the SF General Hospital forensic exam, and the toxicology results. Find out if they were ever processed—if a DNA profile was made. There are thousands that never were. I support you. Message me if you have questions."

"I emailed you a sequence and timeline of my events. A lawyer can help fill in all the details of SFPD coercing and intimidating you. I'm still in litigation—it'll take years."

Her words hit me hard.

Augustine and I had both been silenced. A UCLA graduate and playwright, she used her experience to expose the failures of the criminal justice system. We were both raped in the same year. We both followed every instruction: underwent the six-hour forensic exam, reported the felony drug-facilitated sexual assault, and cooperated with a flawed SFPD investigation.

Yet neither of us was ever told what happened to our forensic evidence.

Augustine found out the truth—her kit and toxicology samples were never tested during the investigation. After two years, the evidence had spoiled. In January 2016, she filed a federal civil rights lawsuit against the San Francisco Police Department, stating: "They denied me equal protection by failing to properly investigate my case and failing to test the rape kit taken at the hospital."

The realization stayed with me. I had never questioned the detective, the process, the badge. I assumed the system worked. During the four month investigation, I believed my kit had been tested because the Detective told me it was being tested. I would never imagine that he would *misrepresent* that?

But now, I wasn't sure of anything.

The idea of requesting the records felt overwhelming.

How had I never thought to ask?

Was it fear? Conditioning? Obedience disguised as trust?

I placed my faith in the SFPD, in the detective's words—in the illusion that someone, anyone, was doing their job. But maybe no one had been.

Later that day I submitted the SFPD Request Form—just as Augustine had advised.

Her advocacy pushed local law enforcement to finally confront long-standing delays in forensic testing. In response, new rules now require police to send evidence to the Crime Lab within five days of collection.

WTF

And in that same month—August 2017—just weeks after my conversation with Augustine, the Detective spotted me in the neighborhood and waved me down.

"Rose, hi! Got a minute?"

His tone was casual, easy—like we were old friends.

"You should come see the new place—top of Nob Hill near Grace Cathedral. You'll love the view."

I froze mid-step. A jolt of unease shot through me—sharp and immediate.

My eyes flicked to California Street, scanning the familiar slope as if it might anchor me, giving me something solid to hold onto. The late afternoon light stretched long shadows across the steep incline, catching the glint of the cable car tracks embedded in the pavement. A faint clang of a trolley bell echoed in the distance, haunting and hollow against the quiet stillness that often settled at the top of Nob Hill. Ornate facades lined the street—grand pre-war buildings, tall arched windows, and wrought iron balconies—silent witnesses to lives unfolding behind closed doors.

The weight of his presence settled in before I even turned to face him.

I turned to meet his gaze.

"What?"

"I'm almost moved in," he said, as if we were picking up an old conversation.

"It's a process—gonna take a few more weeks. Finding space for my wife's clothes has been a challenge."

He chuckled lightly, then pivoted without missing a beat.

"I'd like to meet your boyfriend—see some of his remodel work. Is he still over at the Comstock?"

"Yah he's wrapping up the last remodel—ready to be done," I answered.

"Good to hear. Maybe next week we can all meet up. I'll buy you coffee if you're around. Have a great weekend, Rose."

"Thanks, you too," I replied, turning toward my apartment, trying to shake the feeling that he always managed to appear when I least expected him.

And a few days later, there he was again—California Street, as if he'd never left.

"Rose," he called out.

"Are you two free to check out the condo this week?"

He paused, shifting his stance with that easy confidence—a practiced kind of charm that masked more than it revealed. Something about his presence always reminded me of Bruce Willis in *Unbreakable* —quiet, watchful, unknowable.

"Or if you've got time now, you could just run up with me and take a look?"

His voice was smooth, inviting—like this was nothing more than a casual favor. Disarming, almost friendly.

"My wife and I are still considering Baytech Construction for the remodel. Nob Hill's a whole different world from where we were near Seacliff—big change, but a good one."

I hesitated, adjusting the strap on my shoulder. Something in the way he said it—soft, persuasive, strategically harmless—made me pause.

"That's fine… you mean take a few photos for him to check out?"

"That'd be great," he said, watching me carefully. His expression was unreadable, but his tone didn't waver. Controlled. Intentional.

I nodded slowly, still trying to place the strange current running beneath the conversation. It should've been simple. Just a condo. Just a remodel. But it didn't feel simple. It felt like something else entirely.

"Alright. He's still tied up at Comstock, but I can stop by. The condo's near Grace Cathedral, right?"

"Yeah, just up the street."

He smiled, that same effortless ease. "If you want, we can see it now?"

I glanced at my iPhone, unsure. Every instinct in me wanted to delay. But the moment kept moving forward, and I found myself caught in its momentum.

"Sure," I said quietly. "I finished teaching yoga, so I've got some time."

"That would be great," he said cheerfully, motioning for me to follow as a cool summer breeze swept through us.

"Okay, I can do that. I'll check it out. Your new condo is near Grace Cathedral?"

"Yes—if you'd like, we can walk there now?"

"Sure. I taught this morning, so I've got some free time," I replied, glancing toward the iconic Episcopal church, its grandeur echoing Notre Dame in Paris.

"Our condo's just next door, on the same side of the street," he added. "I'm proud of my Italian heritage. Did you know the central entrance is a replica of the *Porta del Paradiso* — Doors of Paradise—crafted by a great Florentine sculptor?"

"Wow, I had no idea. That's amazing."

"Bronze—90% 10% tin. Sixteen feet high, four inches thick. One ton. Each panel shows Old Testament scenes with detailed flora," he said, his voice gliding effortlessly into lecture mode as we turned onto Jones Street.

Grace Cathedral majestically towered above us, stoic and still. I tilted my head upward, catching the glint of one stained-glass gospel window—but it was harder to stay present than it should've been. My body felt unusually alert. My steps are more measured. I wasn't sure if it was awe or instinct.

"You won't see the doors from the condo," he continued, "but you'll have a clear view of the Gothic edifice from the kitchen window. And if you look down, you'll see the labyrinth in the courtyard."

His voice was still warm, still polished. But something in it felt over-rehearsed, like a script he'd delivered before.

At the Art Deco building, a doorman greeted us, and we stepped inside. The elevator doors closed behind us with a soft chime. Inside the golden cab, I stood slightly back— not out of politeness, but something else. On the fifth floor, the hallway was quiet. Only two units. No sound, no footsteps. A hush that felt almost staged.

He gestured toward the first large door, pulled out his keys, and opened it. I followed slowly, hesitating at the threshold.

Inside, he flipped on the lights. A white glass sconce flickered to life, casting a soft glow across freshly painted walls. The scent of solvents still hung in the air—sharp, chemical, unfinished. Something in my body registered it as a warning.

I stepped into the great room. The herringbone floor was exquisite, the geometric grain pulling the eye outward into the expansive, empty space. But as I moved through it, my body tensed without explanation—shoulders tight, breath shallow, heart pacing faster than the moment seemed to warrant.

"Rose—take a look at the view. I'd like to remodel the kitchen and both bathrooms," he said, gliding from room to room with a sense of ownership that felt performative—like a presentation meant to impress, but also to disarm.

I drifted toward the corner window—two walls of glass forming a sharp angle. Light poured in, illuminating everything, yet it didn't feel warm. Just exposed. Below, I saw the labyrinth in the garden of Grace Cathedral.

Unlike a maze, it has one path—unicursal. No tricks, no wrong turns. Just a journey: Purgation—Releasing. Illumination—Receiving. Union—Returning.

A strange irony. The space below was designed to guide people inward. But here, in this stark, echoing room, I felt farther from myself.

"Out this window," he called from behind me, "you can see the Golden Gate in the distance."

DARK DÉJÀ VU

You never really remember the beginning of a dream, do you? You always wind up right in the middle of what's going on. —Inception, Christopher Nolan

His voice echoed off the walls—an acoustics trick, but it landed in my chest with weight. I turned toward the second window, watching clouds slip through the Golden Gate, drifting like specters—beautiful, majestic, untouchable.

But something about it—this view, this moment—felt oddly familiar.

A surreal vision as if I'd stepped into Dalí's the *Persistence of Memory* painting long before I arrived. A story written for me, but not by me.

The condo was still and echoing, every footstep magnified by the emptiness of the space. The polished wood floors reflected the late afternoon light in fractured streaks, and the silence hung heavy—thicker than it should've been.

I followed him toward the kitchen, where a sleek island jutted out beneath recessed lights. Two barstools stood on one side, like placeholders in a scene already rehearsed.

"You could picture guests here," he said, motioning toward the chairs. "This space is perfect for entertaining."

I nodded absently, the strap of my crossbody camera bag resting against my hip. I was still in my yoga clothes—Lululemon leggings, a white athletic zip-up hoodie. My body felt soft, relaxed from earlier movement, but tension had begun to crawl back beneath my skin.

Then came that eerie sensation—the *dark déjà vu* I'd felt before, but never quite like this.

A chilling familiarity settled over me, as if I'd stepped into some distorted echo of the past. Being alone with him again, in a quiet, empty space—just the two of us—it felt like the past was folding in on itself.

Why did I let myself be alone with him again?

I tried to dismiss the feeling, to rationalize it away, but it stayed—low, insistent, coiling somewhere deep in my gut.

He moved closer.

Too close.

His hand brushed past mine, then lingered on the curve of my lower back.

I shifted sideways, subtly, but the space between us didn't grow.

"You've got such a calm presence," he said quietly. "Grounded. Even in a city like this."

I didn't respond.

Then, without warning, his hand slid around my waist—fingers pressing into my side. I felt his palm move lower, cupping me through the fabric of my yoga pants. I froze.

A hollow ringing filled my ears. The world tilted slightly, like I was watching it from outside myself.

His other hand came up—unzipping my jacket halfway, fingers slipping inside the collar, grazing the skin beneath.

"You're a little tense," he said, almost teasing—light, coaxing, like he was commenting on something innocent.

His voice was soft, his tone feigning tenderness, but beneath it was something far more calculated. As if this were nothing more than a gentle observation—not an intrusion.

Then his hand moved—cupping my breast firmly, as if testing the boundaries of my silence.

His fingers pressed in, deliberate and slow.

His other hand slid lower, tracing the line of my waist, then over the curve of my hips— casual, practiced, as if he'd done it a hundred times before. He didn't ask.

I wanted to say something—anything—but my mouth wouldn't form words.

My body locked.

And then, without warning, a fragment of literature surfaced—unbidden, surreal. A line from *The Lover* by Marguerite Duras: *"Very early in my life it was already too late."*

Not because this moment resembled her plot, not out of some false equivalency—but because Duras had captured a feeling I now knew in my own body: the eerie detachment, the folding of time, the way a woman's body can become the setting for someone else's narrative.

It wasn't a comparison of consent. It was a psychological echo—a haunting parallel in tone, not content. Only now, I wasn't reading it from the safety of a page. I was inside it.

A trolley bell rang faintly outside, a chime against the stillness.

The city went on, indifferent.

A rush came over me.

I pulled back sharply, stepping away from him like the floor had burned beneath my feet.

"I—I have to go," I said, my voice brittle but firm.

I grabbed the strap of my crossbody bag like a lifeline and turned toward the door.

He didn't try to stop me.

I moved quickly down the hall, toward the elevator, my pulse hammering in my ears. The air felt tighter with every step, like the walls were closing in behind me. Inside the elevator, I pressed the button with a shaking hand and stared straight ahead, trying to hold myself together as the golden doors slid shut.

Only when I stepped out onto the street did I exhale, like I'd been holding my breath the entire time. The breeze hit my face, cool and sharp, but it couldn't wipe away the heat still crawling under my skin.

A sleek Tesla Model S rolled past, windows down.

That song—*As the Rush Comes*—drifted from the speakers, faint but unmistakable.

'Traveling somewhere... could be anywhere... We drift deeper into the sound...'

I ran past the stone façade of Grace Cathedral, its gothic arches stark against the blue sky.

At the corner, the traffic light turned green, its glow spreading across the city pavement like a stage cue. I sprinted across the street toward the Big Four at the Huntington Hotel on California and Taylor, its heavy wooden doors swinging open as patrons spilled out into the cold air. It felt cinematic.

I kept running, my steps echoing toward the Masonic—the Grand Lodge of California Freemasons—its massive façade watching over me from across the street. From the sidewalk below, the San Francisco Masonic Auditorium rose in sharp concrete angles, its modernist design catching the daylight.

Across the front stretched a bas-relief by Emile Norman, *Fraternal March of Mankind*—figures carved in strict geometry, workers frozen mid-stride, tools raised in permanent gesture, symbols of labor and Masonry locked into the wall itself.

The sheer scale pressed down, but in that instant the figures felt alive, towering above like guardians, as if the building had turned its gaze toward me—protecting me as I ran. I bolted downhill toward 1233 California, fingers shaking as I buzzed the black gate. When it clicked open, I raced up three flights of stairs and quickly unlocked my apartment door.

I dropped my bag on the couch, collapsed beside it, and let the tears fall—fast, unstoppable. My chest heaved as I curled into the cushions; the room tilted around me. I stayed there until my breath slowed.

My sense of safety had been shattered, and I found myself searching for an anchor. Maybe seeing the Masonic façade as protective was my mind projecting a need for guardianship. A momentary substitute for the protection the Halls of Justice and the Detective denied me.

Through the tears one image stayed: the Masonic—an echo of *liberté, égalité, fraternité* —an architectural promise of order and strength. In that moment, I held onto the hope that power might protect rather than betray.

My thoughts kept racing as I sat on the couch, so I opened my journal and began to write. Eventually, I would tell Andrew—my boyfriend—when he came home from the Comstock penthouse remodel. I didn't know how to explain it yet.

CHAPTER 15: SERGEANT VERSCHWÖRER

Wenn ihr's nicht fühlt, ihr werdet's nicht erjagen, Wenn es nicht aus der Seele dringt, Und mit urkräftigem Behagen, Die Herzen aller Hörer zwingt.
— Faust, lines 534–538, Johann Wolfgang von Goethe

Sergeant Verschwörer—Sergeant V, as she preferred—protected the Blue Code like scripture, unwavering in her allegiance. Part of the boys club, to her loyalty, was about preservation. Preserving power. Preserving the system. Justice wasn't blind. It was performative—a construct. A stage, as Michel Foucault might say, not built to serve truth, but to maintain control.

In August 2017, I requested a copy of my kit's DNA and toxicology results, along with the incident report. A few weeks later, Sergeant Verschwörer from the Special Victims Unit left a voicemail. I still have the recording—sharp, clinical, and deeply unsettling:

> Rose, I have reviewed the Detective's investigation. Yes, your rape kit was forensically analyzed, and DNA was developed in the summer of 2016. I'm not certain which month.

She paused—short, deliberate—before continuing:

> You did a pretext call with the suspect. And the suspect, Mr. Henry, didn't make statements that corroborated that it wasn't consensual sex. The naked pictures he provided of you were included in the case file. The Detective presented the case to the DA, and the DA completely discharged the case. You had multiple opportunities to leave the suspect's condo. You did not. I don't see how we could move forward on this. You can give me a call, but hopefully that answers your questions

Her voicemail left me shaken—and deeply confused. What does: "The *DNA was developed in 2016*" even mean?

The phrase felt deliberately vague. Hollow. Like a placeholder masquerading as truth. A bureaucratic shield, not a real answer. If it had been processed in 2016, why was I never informed?

And if it hadn't been—what exactly was I supposed to believe now? It contradicted everything I'd been told. The Detective walked me to the SFPD Crime Lab, down a sterile hallway, reassuring me in confidence: *This is where your rape kit is being tested. Thanks for doing it right away.*

I took that moment as a promise of transparency. Now it felt like theater, a carefully staged illusion. And then, just like that, the Detective appeared again.
I had just finished Bikram Yoga at Nob Hill. For some reason, the same 26 postures in a room heated to 105 degrees—provided comfort.

My attempt at rebalancing my nervous system. I always felt on edge. I wanted to reclaim some sense of control. I was completely disarmed, bundled in a sweatshirt and sweatpants after this yoga class and as I stood in the produce aisle, feeling grounded for the first time that day. I heard his voice as he approached me in the grocery store.

"How's your mom?"

He always started conversations that way, as if he knew her well. But he didn't. It wasn't just small talk—it was a quirk, a tic in his manner that always unsettled me.

For two minutes, it was almost normal. *Almost.*

Then the conversation shifted.

"Do you remember that special night in North Beach? I'd like to do that again."

I froze.

He was bringing it up again—the proposition that had once terrified me. The night he asked me to have sex with him. To be his mistress.

I couldn't process it at the time and tried to pretend it hadn't happened.

And now, here he was! Bringing it back to life like it was some harmless, shared moment. A chill ran down my spine. The store aisles blurred. My voice came out flat, almost robotic.

"Thanks for taking me out to dinner to celebrate my graduation."

When I stepped outside, the unease lingered—swirling ike fog off the bay. Maybe I wasn't meant to live in San Francisco. His new condo, these so-called chance encounters —none of it felt random anymore.

Fast forward to May 2018: I stood inside San Francisco City Hall, speaking before 200 people and nine City Supervisors. I shared my experience working with the police, testifying in support of Supervisor Hillary Ronen's legislation to establish the SHARP Office within the Human Rights Commission. The initiative aimed to improve the city's response to victims of violence and increase accountability when city agencies fail survivors.

Supervisor Ronen underscored the gravity of the crisis: *"City Departments are failing to keep San Franciscans safe from sexual violence. City employees are blaming victims and denying survivors their right to an objective investigation."*

Another activist underscored the urgency of SHARP, calling it a much-needed watchdog: *"It will bring more responsibility and transparency to rape investigations in this city. SHARP will help oversee the SFPD, Victim Advocates, the DA's Office, and other systems. It's a light at the end of the tunnel—it sends a message, and it's a real step toward change."*

In September 2018, Mayor London Breed signed the SHARP legislation into law, establishing new oversight and a clearer path for survivors to access services and advocate for their rights. The following month, encouraged by the women I met at City Hall and guided by Supervisor Ronen's advice, I filed a report with the Department of Police Accountability (DPA).

I completed a one-hour recorded interview with a Senior Investigator, during which I stated that the detective had coerced and sexually assaulted me, violating the trust meant to exist between law enforcement and a survivor.

The guidebook Donna gave me underscored how far the system had to go. "The Police Executive Research Forum began to research these issues in 2011, when we convened a national meeting of police chiefs and leaders of women's and crime victims' organizations to discuss problems and solutions. Our larger goal was to identify best practices that all law enforcement agencies can adopt in order to provide sexual assault victims with the help and the respect they need while improving investigations and bringing more perpetrators to justice. One key recommendation is that police departments should adopt and incorporate "trauma-informed" practices into their response to sexual assault. This involves recognizing the symptoms of trauma and its prevalence, and understanding how those symptoms can affect an individual who has experienced trauma. The trauma of sexual assault can affect a victim's memory and behavior in unique ways, both during and after the crime occurs. Police officers must understand these dynamics in order to respond appropriately to sexual assault victims, It is one of the worst types of crimes, so it requires the best efforts of law enforcement agencies to investigate it thoroughly, prevent new crimes, and treat victims with respect and compassion."

— PhD Chuck, *Wexler Executive Guidebook: Practical Approaches for Strengthening Law Enforcement's Response to Sexual Assault*, May 2018

CHAPTER 16: CITY HALL SURVIVORS MEETUP GROUP IN THE MISSION

There is no greater tyranny than that which is perpetrated under the shield of the law and in the name of justice.— Montesquieu

March 16, 2019 – 4:00 PM, After months of correspondence and planning with the survivor-led activist group, we were finally going to meet in person. I arrived in San Francisco a few hours early and parked in the Mission District. I hadn't been to the city in over a year, so I wandered for a bit and eventually found myself inside *Borderlands Books: Mysteries and Supernatural.* I spent a quiet stretch of time reading, letting the calm of the bookstore settle me.

As our meeting time approached, I purchased a copy of *The Girl with the Dragon Tattoo,* then stepped back outside and headed south. I turned into a narrow alleyway in the Mission—its walls alive with vivid murals, painted across garage doors, gates, and the exteriors of buildings. A warm spring breeze moved through the alley, and I noticed the creamy white blossoms of Southern Magnolia trees drifting gently in the air.

I checked Google Maps on my iPhone to confirm the address. The number "66" matched the Victorian house ahead.

After being buzzed in at the gate, I climbed a steep, vertical set of stairs to the top-floor condominium. The front door was already open. I stepped into a bright kitchen with high ceilings and warm wood floors.

At the kitchen table sat two familiar faces—Redell Griffiths and Nola Bailey—women I had met the year before at City Hall, while we were advocating for the SHARP legislation. Two newer members of our group, Chloe Tsang and Heather Van de Berg, were sharing their stories. They spoke candidly about the bias and institutional coldness they encountered when reporting their drug-facilitated sexual assaults to the police. Their frustration and disbelief mirrored what so many of us had already experienced.

We all shared the same reality—we had been victim-blamed, coerced, bullied, and denied transparency in our own cases. The detectives and the Special Victims Unit, the very people tasked with investigating these crimes, had worked against us instead of for us.

As the conversation unraveled, one thing became clearer with each passing minute: nothing had changed within the SVU. Not in years.

Chloe Tsang spoke first, her frustration barely contained.

"I reported the felony to the SFPD a year ago. This city has an atrocious track record when it comes to prosecuting rapists and domestic violence perpetrators. And beyond that, I've seen firsthand how San Francisco's justice system outright <u>violates</u> California state law—denying victims access to their own police reports, delaying crucial information about their rape kits, making it impossible to move forward."

"I want to get a restraining order against my assailant, yet they make it an uphill battle. So I have to ask—what is their plan to actually make this city safer for women? When do offenders face real consequences?"

Heather Van de Berg shook her head. "My choice for San Francisco District Attorney is Chesa Boudin. Maybe he'll actually do something about violent crimes against women."

"The whole process is infuriating. The SFPD treated me like I was the criminal—not my rapist. A few months ago, they even threatened to arrest *me* instead of my perpetrator, just to shut me up and make me go away. Our cases should not be ignored by Assistant District Attorney O'Conner. This can't keep happening. Something has to change."

"Hopefully the new District Attorney Chesa Boudin will fight the inequality we're drowning in. This city needs to wake up. We make up half its population, yet its justice system treats us like we're disposable."

Chloe's expression darkened as Heather spoke. She looked disturbed—more than that, she looked furious. She reached for her notebook, flipping through her notes with quick precision. There was something unwavering about her—a kind of strength that refused to be shaken, even by the weight of what we were discussing.

She met our eyes and said, "Yes—serious action needs to be taken to hold the SFPD accountable for how they treat rape victims."

"I believe in respecting the law, but the way the SVU flexes their authority over emotionally traumatized victims instead of actually investigating and prosecuting assailants? It's horrifying. It's sick."

Across from me, Redell Griffiths—who had stood before the City Supervisors last year, demanding accountability—nodded.

"I hear you. The dismissive, condescending attitude, the refusal to take our cases seriously—it's an all-too-common trait of the SVU and SFPD detectives."

She leaned back, crossing her arms.

"Nola, Rose, Michelle, and I testified before the Board of Supervisors about how city agencies have mishandled our cases. We've been mistreated and discarded by the very people who are supposed to help us. And we're not alone."

She assured us, "That's why I've been doing advocacy work—consulting victims, helping them navigate this system. Because I know it now. I've lived it. And I won my civil lawsuit against the man who raped me—someone I once worked with. It was a DFSA crime."

She paused. "People think justice means a trial, a conviction, a sense of closure. But too often, that's a myth. At best, we're left with a consolation prize for the trauma we endured."

Heather Van de Berg, who had been hand-washing dishes at the kitchen sink behind Redell, suddenly stopped. The sound of running water filled the silence as she turned, a stunned expression across her face.

She dried her hands quickly, pulled out a chair, and sat down at the table. "The criminal justice system is actively hostile toward civil suits filed by rape survivors. Outsiders might find that surprising, but we don't. We've lived it."

She glanced at Hanna. "It's incredible that you won your case."

Then, shifting uncomfortably, she exhaled. "I finally got a copy of my toxicology report from the SFPD. But the way they treated me…" She trailed off, shaking her head. "They were so dismissive, so outright hostile. It's like my medical forensic results didn't even matter to them. This process is unbelievable."

Redell sat in thought for a moment before nodding.

"Thank you. It's crucial that we push for a greater sociocultural investment in the rehabilitation of survivors—on a global scale, yes, but here in the City, too. Change starts with awareness."

Heather, visibly uneasy, poured herself a vodka drink before speaking.

"Exactly. That's why I've been working on visuals for a social media campaign. I illustrated some myself and printed them out at home." She set down her glass. "Let me grab my binder."

Chloe turned to Redell, her curiosity piqued. "I noticed in our emails—you really know law enforcement and the judicial process. How did you learn all this?"

Redell didn't hesitate.

"I have a Bachelor's in Criminal Justice, so I had the tools to process the injustice with an informed perspective. I also understand how, in court, the prejudicial effect of evidence often outweighs its actual probative value."

She leaned forward.

"One of the biggest problems? Jurors don't trust accusers in rape cases. Their cognition is wired for heuristics—it's a mental shortcut, a way to process information quickly, but it's flawed. In the courtroom, jurors are confronted with fact patterns that don't make sense, where someone's behavior appears irrational. And instead of analyzing the complexities, they latch onto the easiest explanation: that the victim is lying or exaggerating for selfish reasons."

She exhaled sharply. "That's why a civil case is such a rude awakening. It's not just about presenting the truth—it's about confronting the biases baked into the system."

We were all at different points in our journeys, which kept the conversation flowing easily. Two hours in, I pulled out my phone and played the voicemail Sergeant Verschwörer had left me. I needed their perspective—was I overthinking it?

As the message played on speakerphone, I watched their expressions shift: confusion, then skepticism.

"Play that again," someone said.

At the worn picnic-style kitchen table, Nola Bailey—who had stood at City Hall last year under the alias *Jane Doe*—turned to me.

"Rose," she said carefully, "this voicemail is vague."

"Like, deliberately vague. The Sergeant doesn't say when your rape kit was tested. It almost sounds like it sat for six years. But it's hard to tell—it could just be a really awkward message. You need to call SVU, request a meeting, and ask for your medical records. In writing."

Her words hit like a jolt. Why hadn't I thought of that?

I scheduled a meeting with a sergeant at the Special Victims Unit in the Hall of Justice.

CHAPTER 17: MARCH 2019 - SPECIAL VICTIMS UNIT

Throughout history it has been the inaction of those who could have acted; the indifference of those who should have known better; the silence of the voice of justice when it mattered the most; that has made it possible for evil to triumph — Haile Selassie (*qädamawi haylä səllasé*)

28 MARCH 2019 — 2PM I entered the lobby of the Hall of Justice building 40-minutes before the scheduled meeting. I took the elevators to the 5th floor and walked into the Special Victims Unit towards the administrator who sat behind what seemed to be bulletproof glass from the 1960s. As I shifted my tote bag gently around my shoulder I nervously said, "Hi — I'm here early but I have a 2PM meeting with Sargent Verschwörer. I'm Rose Visjonær."

The administrator curiously gazed at me through the glass and replied, "Yes, take a seat she will be back from break shortly." She pointed towards the back of the room so I nodded and said, "Thank you." So I turned around and quickly sat into an awkward forest-green plastic cushion love-seat. I placed my bag next to me, took out my iPhone to play music while I scanned my notes. 30-minutes later two female Sargents walked through the door.

One of the Sargents announced, "You must be Rose — Nice to meet you — I am Sergeant Verschwörer or Sergeant V and this is my partner Sargent Stokes." I shook hands with the two female Sergeants and followed them into a nondescript conference room.

It was obvious to me that Sergeant Verschwörer was the highest-ranking officer in the room and had been in the SFPD for decades. She wore navy-blue slacks with a heavy tactical police belt and badge with her button down navy-blue blouse. While her partner was younger and had a more feminine nature to her subtle expressions.

The light gray shade of paint on the walls made everything seem more vacuous and empty. The air smelt like old tattered books. As I walked towards a metal office chair at the large conference table, the two Sergeants took their seat across from me while I felt my heart race in my chest. There was a brief silence as we organized our things on the table to prepare for our discussion. I noticed how the Sargent placed a silver audio-recorder in front of her.

My mind raced a bit as I questioned why there were two Sergeants in the room instead of just the one I had correspondence with —perhaps it was for liability reasons.

I took a breath and began.

"Thank you for meeting with me today. I need clarity on something—was my rape kit from San Francisco General Hospital ER ever tested? *I don't know,* the Detective alleged that it was being tested by the Crime Lab during the investigation, but I don't know the truth? Given the serious nature of that six-hour procedure this is strange. I need to know the rape kit's toxicology."

Heather Van de Berg and I had gone over this the night before.

Drafting pages of questions. I had my notebook open, pen ready, treating the meeting like an assignment—something I could approach methodically, so I wouldn't get swallowed by the weight of it.

The Sergeant folded her hands and replied, "I know when you had the forensic exam done. The 'kit' was kept and booked into evidence once the Inspector closed the investigation. But the criminal element wasn't whether or not sex happened—" she paused, choosing her words carefully, "the suspect said it was consensual."

She continued, "The 'kit' wasn't the focus of the Detective's investigation. If he wanted it tested, he would've needed to request it via form. The 'kit' was not tested until 2016. By that time, the District Attorney's Office had fully reviewed the case. They declined to proceed with any criminal charges. There wasn't enough evidence in the file to corroborate that it was a non-consensual act."

Her words rang in my ears. The 'kit' wasn't tested until 2016.

"Interesting," I said, my voice sharper than before. "Why wasn't it tested until then?"

This was the first time I was hearing any of this. The first time I realized just how deep the negligence ran. Betrayal hit me like a slow, sinking weight. They had left me in the dark on purpose.

HARD KNOCK LIFE FOR US

She glanced at the seizable beige police folder in front of the metal table. It was the police case-file which contained classified documents, medical forms and photographs about the crime that happened to me — which seemed to be forbidden to see.

For a flicker of a moment, my mind retreated to a childhood memory of watching *Annie* (1982), Annie and the orphans stomping across the screen, singing about the "hard knock life." Their chorus of defiance against a world stacked against them suddenly felt too close, as if their voices echoed across into this sterile room.

The Sargent carefully answered. "The Inspector never requested for the medical forensic exam or 'rape kit' to be tested during the investigation. Again it wasn't a question if sex happened. Rose— you said that you had sex with him and Henry said he had sex with you."

I shook my head as she continued to explain the distortion.

"So finding his DNA inside you or on you or his sperm on your clothing wasn't a question — Does that make sense to you?"

A cold silence followed. A sense of doom crept in. Her tone was devoid of empathy, but the grotesque clarity of her words made my body tremble. Now she's telling me DNA is meaningless? That because the assailant's profile is finally logged in the City's Crime Lab database, I'm supposed to forget everything?

It was mind-numbing. Surreal. The kind of betrayal I didn't think could be real.

"No," I said, my voice sharp. "That doesn't make sense."

"I was in pain. I reported what happened—to the ER doctors, to the nurses during the forensic exam, and to the two patrol officers later that day. And now, nine years later, I'm sitting in the SVU office, learning the Detective deceived me. The kit and the toxicology weren't even analyzed in time—when that was the key evidence."

There was a brief silence as a feeling of impending doom creeped into my mind.

Her tone was emotionless and empty — yet the graphic and unpalatable visual that her words illustrated caused me to tremble. Now she is telling me that DNA is insignificant evidence? Is she implying that because his DNA was finally logged into the City's Crime Lab Database she wants me to forget about it?

The medical forensic exam and toxicology report are crucial tools for documenting assault and identifying repeat offenders or solving cold cases. Did she forget that? Her words were unsettling. I'd read in the *San Francisco Chronicle*that Assistant Chief Schmitt, who oversees the SFPD Crime Lab, said, "The rape kits are the most valuable piece of evidence in these cases and we support this 72-hour collection."

The Sergeant insisted, "The Inspector discussed this with you thoroughly. You did a pretext call with Henry, but it didn't provide insight. You declined a second call. When questioned, Henry claimed it was consensual."

It was remarkable how much credibility was given to Henry's account.

Effortlessly, she handed him the power—the authority to define the narrative. His version of events, not mine, determined whether the SFPD Crime Lab would even analyze my rape kit and toxicology. Six hours in the ER didn't matter. What mattered was the word of a wealthy socialite.

The fluorescent lights above buzzed and cracked softly, a dull soundtrack to my unraveling. I kept my focus on her voice as she recounted what Henry told the Detective at the SVU Office years ago.

She added, sternly and without hesitation, "Henry never recalled you saying no. He also provided the Inspector with several nude photos he took of you that night—before the sex. So the DA closed the case."

Her biased perspective felt like an obliteration of my soul. I dismissed it, steadying myself, and replied, "I screamed NO. I fought him. My head slammed against the wall."

A nightmarish shiver ran down my spine as I closed my eyes. I could picture them—inside the privacy of the Detective's Office—speaking in hushed tones, a quiet exchange 'between men' to make sure the incident was swept under the rug, left without a trace. That implicit agreement was likely why the Detective never submitted my toxicology samples or forensic kit to the Crime Lab—though he misled me into believing he had.

Speculatively, I could see another layer: Henry's photos of me—passed along like currency—may have piqued the Detective's curiosity. The betrayal wasn't just institutional—it was personal.

<u>REFLECTION</u>

Absence of evidence is not evidence of absence.—Carl Sagan, *The Demon-Haunted World*

The Sergeant, the Detective and the District Attorney concluded that there was no proof of 'non consent' because the criminal suspect said it was 'consensual' — Both the police and the DA's Office took a false statement and accepted it as the truth. As a result I became curious about what fallacies are commonly used in arguments.

The absence of evidence is not proof that 'non consent' was not given.

The Detective chose to not include the medical forensic exam and toxicology report to the District Attorney for a fair evaluation and decision. He did not include important evidence which would have corroborated my account that this was a drug facilitated sexual assault (DFSA) crime.

Their argument exemplifies the Appeal to Ignorance Fallacy also known as '*argumentum ad ignorantiam*' because the Sergeant assumed that Henry's statement must be true because it wasn't proven false by the Detective's incomplete investigation.

"The photos that he took — mean that the crime did NOT happen? He was calculated. Fought him off many times, screamed NO into his face and my head hit hard against the wall. How long are these photographs kept in the case-file?" I asked.

With an eerie inflection the Sargent answered, "They will always be kept."

I thought for a moment and asked, "Who has seen Henry's photos?"

She replied, "The Inspector, the District Attorney, the Lieutenant and myself." So I asked, "May I see the photos he took... or see the police case-file?"

She responded with a misdirection, "No — You would need to go to our Legal Department to try and get them because we don't give out items from the case-file. It's against unit orders. Our Legal Department is here on the fifth floor across the hall. Use the <u>black phone</u> on the wall adjacent to their office to call them."

Puzzled by her ominous or sinister 'black phone' answer to get information that technically belongs to me since it happened to me — I decided to ask an obvious question, "Are Henry's photos confidential and a part of the police case-file?"

Sergeant replied, "Yes — The photos are evidence and a part of the case-file. Once the gentleman spoke with the Inspector at the SVU to provide his statement they came in as a part of Evidentiary Purposes."

"The Inspector conducted the interview here and it gives the gentleman the opportunity to provide information concerning the offense," she added.

"The photos were nothing more than a con man's confidence trick. He took advantage of me, and I believe I'm not the only one. By taking those photos while I was drugged and unable to consent, he committed a serious violation of the law."

There was silence.

So I asked, "Could I get a copy of the toxicology report, or any other tests that were done? They took blood and urine samples at the ER — I'd like the results emailed to me."

The Sargent answered, "No — I cannot give you that information."

"You can go to the SFGH Medical Records Office or the UCSF Trauma Recovery Center where you've been seen to request a copy. I'm not allowed to give that to you."

"I had been in shock when I called my school from the ER during the exam. I told my professor, *I'm missing class because I was raped last night.* So why weren't my witnesses ever interviewed? They could have corroborated what happened."

The sergeant replied, "I can't go into the details of the inspector's investigation. You said the assault happened at this gentleman's home—you went to dinner with him, you consented to go back to his place in Cow Hollow. And unfortunately, everything that happened after that, no one else saw. Unless one of those witnesses was actually present at the scene, their statements wouldn't be considered probative."

My eyes began to water as tears fell down my face.

"When a woman enters a man's home, she's at risk of being disbelieved and blamed by the police? The Detective needed relevant information to make a fair decision."

There was a brief silence.

The Sergeant, who usually remained quiet, subtly adjusted her posture, becoming more attentive.

"When Henry was questioned at the SVU, was it recorded? How long was the interview?"

Her response seemed rehearsed.

"Yes, it was recorded by the inspector at our office and included in the case file. He always conducted lengthy interviews and provided a detailed chronological summary as part of the investigation."

I checked my notes and asked, "Why was the case dismissed?"

"The inspector presented the case to the DA, as I mentioned," she replied. "After reviewing the statements and evidence, the DA didn't believe there was enough corroborative evidence to prove it wasn't consensual. Taking a sexual assault case to court is difficult—it's hard to prove beyond a reasonable doubt."

I reflected, "Why would I undergo a six-hour invasive exam, take seven medications at the ER, and go to UCSF for eleven months of counseling if I wasn't a victim of a crime recognized by the state of California?"

Her eyes flickered, and she said softly, "I understand."

But what did she understand?

That truth, as Foucault warned, is not simply uncovered—it is produced, sanctioned, and policed by institutions. That law, as Aristotle said, is reason without passion, but in practice becomes passionless reason—indifferent to suffering, committed only to its own procedures.

"This is mind-numbing. I remember the Detective showing me photos of 'real victims' while we sat in his undercover car. He always suggested a reason to meet up. He handed me black-and-white photos of beaten women—bloodied, unconscious. He said the DA only prosecutes cases like those," I gasped.

"He said that I wasn't an example of a 'real rape victim' and he warned me the DA will not prosecute cases like mine — this gave me nightmares."

Sergeant Verschwörer nervously shifted the case-file papers on the table in front of her.

In shock she questioned, "Who showed you this?"

"The Detective did."

She scrutinized, "This is hard for me to believe."

"What is? That he would show me crime scene pictures — Well he did — The Detective did many things that were uncomfortable. For instance when he told me the DA closed the investigation he asked me — If Henry would have bought you roses and an airplane ticket to Paris would you still call it rape? — He made me feel stupid."

As a few tears streamed down my cheek, I gently brushed them away. I asked, "It was upsetting that he earned my trust and then said that to me—was he testing me? Was he trying to shame me, or just hoping to silence me? In that same conversation, the Detective mentioned that the District Attorney closed the case due to insufficient evidence."

I took a deep breath and continued.

"His behavior was unprofessional, so I filed a complaint with your Office of Accountability. I had a 1-hour recorded phone conversation in October 2018, after working with City Supervisor Hillary Ronen and other survivors. What's the follow-up on something like that?"

Sergeant V responded, "This is the first time I've heard of the complaint."

"Oh—if the case is closed, why can't I have a copy of the medical forensic exam 'rape kit' or the toxicology report? Do I need a lawyer to subpoena it?"

Sergeant V replied, "The case file is part of a Police Investigation. Our Legal Department decides what we can release. The DA's Office declined the case, and our Unit Orders mandate that we cannot release information while it's still considered an Investigative File."

"Why did a survivor I know receive her toxicology report and learn what drugs were in her blood?"

"I'll gladly give you the toxicology results once I receive them. For some reason, it's not in the police case file, and I'm not sure why. I'm still waiting to get the report, but everything else is here," she replied as she looked through the case file.

I reflected on her response.

"The Detective mishandled this case—abusing power, showing negligence, and misconduct throughout the investigation. If my 'kit' and toxicology samples weren't included in the case file for a fair DA review, the Managing DA now needs to file charges. I want to prosecute."

In my view, the suspect is a serial rapist. Henry was calculated, and I'm sure he's exploited other women. *S.1197 — 109th Congress (2005-2006) (Sec. 1005) eliminates the statute of limitations tolling for sexual abuse cases when DNA testing implicates someone in a felony.*

She replied, "The Inspector took all the necessary steps. His DNA was found and analyzed by our Crime Lab. The rape kit was positive, but unfortunately, there's nothing more we can do to move forward with criminal charges."

I had to questioned her.

"In your voicemail, you mentioned that my failure to leave the condo after the crime indicated consent?"

The Sergeant quickly corrected.

"No—I didn't say that."

"I left a voicemail in August 2017 to inform you about your forensic results. My department asked me to contact you regarding the case-file requested."

The room felt stark.

We sat at a long, rectangular table—two Sergeants on one side, me on the other. Between us lay the silver police-issue voice recorder, its small red light unblinking, and the police case file that lay open in front of them, its edges catching the light like a blade, a silent reminder of everything withheld, never once offered for me to see.

I paused, reassured by the fact that I had saved her voicemail as a record.

Gathering my binder and notebook, I kept my voice steady.

"Thank you, Sergeant."

"I will head to the Legal Department now to request a copy of my forensic medical kit. Use the black phone on the wall, right?"

The phrase echoed in my mind—the *black phone in the Legal Department* sounded surreal, as if lifted from a Kafka parable, less a tool of justice than a reminder of a system warped beyond recognition.

<u>GOOGLE SEARCH</u>

In a time of deceit, telling the truth is a revolutionary act.— George Orwell

As I gathered my things to leave, the Sergeant's voice sliced through the silence.

"Sorry this investigation left a *bad taste* in your mouth," she said the words laced just shy of mockery.

She didn't wait for a response. "I'll be honest with you—he was a very thorough investigator. I worked with him for many years, and I'm sad to hear that this was your perspective."

A pause.

"I reviewed your file. He did a great job."

Self-assured. Unbothered. The blue wall holds firm.

I studied her for a moment, listening to what she wasn't saying. This was the 'Blue Wall of Silence' in action—a seamless, well-rehearsed defense to protect one of their own. I had seen this before. He could have done anything, and she would have still said the same thing.

I already knew more than she thought I did. Before this meeting, I had Googled his name. The results were… revealing.

Multiple articles from San Francisco Chronicle, SFGate. The allegations stacked like bricks.

Fraudulent involvement in multimillion-dollar sports betting operations. Investigated for the murder of his own partner. And yet, here she was—calm, defending him as if he were a saint. I got the cream of the crop.

Her dismissiveness only pushed me further. I saw how deep her loyalty ran.

"Interesting."

"How old is he now?" I questioned.

The Sergeant hesitated.

"Did he serve four or five decades with the SFPD?"

She blinked, caught off guard.

Then with a measured breath, she answered, "I am not sure."

The two sergeants exchanged glances before their eyes settled back on me.

"After I graduated from the Academy of Art University with a Master's—which, honestly, felt like a miracle given how the investigation and the distress wreaked havoc on my life—the Detective kept in contact with me. Friendly. Like nothing ever happened."

Sergeant Verschwörer let out a low, almost agreeable hum. "Mmhmm." Her voice carried a forced lightness, like she wanted me to keep talking, to keep feeding the narrative they were already constructing.

I continued, "He asked to take me out for a celebratory graduation dinner in June of 2012. At first I didn't think anything of it. But now it's one of the reasons many — Why I've been concerned that the Detective interfered with the quality of the investigation."

Sergeant Verschwörer who seemed content sat back in her chair and the SVU Sergeant who never spoke shifted her demeanor into curiosity.

"A year after the investigation was closed the Detective requested many times if I would have sex with him and be his <u>mistress</u>. He told me that it would be a regular arrangement if I felt comfortable. This horrified me."

The grayish-white walls of the SVU conference room seemed to glisten as my eyes watered. The two Sergeants gazed at me expressionlessly. I was standing up from the table and I felt light-headed. I could not believe that I was admitting this to them — I knew they were the least likely of all people to believe me.

So I continued, "Not until I started to work with the other San Francisco survivor-activists, last May, did I admit this to anyone. For years I felt incredible shame about his requests — He was the Detective that investigated a crime that happened to me — He abused his power — and he was my father's age."

Humiliation burned through me. Denial is powerful.

"I clung to the idea that he was an *Honorable Officer*, that he had conducted a fair, impartial investigation. Because if I let go of that—if I admitted the truth—then the entire case wasn't just flawed. It was just a performance."

It was a joke. A performance designed to fail me from the start.

And now, the illusion was breaking. I was beginning to see it for what it really was.

Caught within a *stratagem.*

I had believed—blindly, naively—that the Veteran Detective followed an *ethical code of conduct* as an officer. In hindsight, that meant nothing to him.

He saw my vulnerabilities and used them to his advantage.

So I did what I had to—I rejected the memories, buried them, prayed they weren't real.

Dissociation became my refuge. But silence has a cost. The more I tried to erase what happened, the more my body rebelled—impulsive, hyperactive, hyper-vigilant.

And beneath it all, an unshakable truth settled like stone: If I told anyone what he had done—what he had *asked* of me—no one would believe me. The police hadn't believed me when I reported the felony Henry committed. So why would they believe me about the Detective?

The quiet Sergeant looked momentarily stunned. Sergeant V, on the other hand, barely flinched—skeptical, disbelieving, already deciding what *not* to hear.

My body trembled, an involuntary response to the weight of it all. I felt utterly alone. How many times had I screamed for help, only for my words to vanish into silence? But I couldn't stay silent. My heart pounded.

"Isn't his job to protect victims? To put criminals in jail?"

My voice wavered, but I pushed forward.

"The Detective did the exact opposite."

"And years later, after everything, after I thought I'd put distance between us—I moved to Nob Hill. And somehow, he found me again. In 2017, he stopped me on the street. Like it was nothing. He told me he had just bought a three-bedroom condo. "

"Two blocks from me. Jones and Sacramento. He knew exactly where I lived. California and Jones. Just a few minutes' walk. And then, so casually—like we were catching up— he asked if my boyfriend did high-end remodels. Like that was why he stopped me.He did something so inappropriate I can't even bring myself to say it right now.," I added.

The memory claws at the back of my mind.

"Then he found me again. Grocery shopping. We stood near the checkout, fluorescent lights buzzing overhead. The mundane setting, the normalcy of it, made it worse. The Detective hinted—so confidently—that we should 'hang out soon.' It was creepy and still haunts me. It made me uncomfortable. Eventually we had to move out of the City...."

The Detective never showed the slightest trace of remorse. Was he a sociopath? Or just exceptionally incompetent?

In hindsight, I see it clearly—the four-month SFPD 'criminal investigation' was an absurd charade. A joke. A pantomime of justice. A dehumanizing experience that eroded my self-worth. I was in denial for so long that I couldn't even see how the larger consequences infected my daily life.

But now, for the first time, I see it for what it is.

The Detective didn't overlook evidence—he buried it.

The toxicology samples. The forensic exam. He never authorized the crime lab analysis. The truth was locked away before it ever had a chance to be seen. Had the District Attorney received that evidence, it would have corroborated my account. It would have changed everything.

Cui bono? Who benefited? Not justice. Not me. The suspect did.

This wasn't negligence. This was an obstruction. A deliberate act—an exercise in *mauvaise foi.*

In French existentialist philosophy, *mauvaise foi*—bad faith—is the lie we tell ourselves to justify our actions, the illusion of powerlessness when we hold all the power.

The Detective wasn't just complicit; he was an architect of the cover-up, disguising his choices as inevitabilities. Justice wasn't blind. It was looking the other way—because he made sure of it

He had coerced me while simultaneously pretending to be a *friend*. A man who spanned four decades in law enforcement. A man who, ipso facto, had likely violated his Police Officer's Oath *many* times before.

There's a concept in French existentialism—that *mauvaise foi* isn't just lying to others, but lying to oneself. Pretending you are powerless when you hold all the power. Convincing yourself that what you're doing isn't a choice. The Detective didn't just *betray* justice. He *embodied* mauvaise foi.

And the entire system enabled him to do it.

After the meeting, I walked out of the conference room, my body moving before my mind caught up. Through the hallway, past the cold walls, to the Legal Department—just as Sergeant V had instructed. I picked up the black phone on the wall. An automatic ring.

A voice on the other end. A buzz. Then the answer I already knew was coming:

"No. You cannot have a copy of your medical forensic exam or toxicology screens. It's part of the investigative file."

I shook my head. Of course. Sergeant V's advice had been useless—and she had known that all along the bureaucratic red tape was designed to demoralize. To exhaust. To make you give up.

I needed to be somewhere that felt real. Somewhere that wasn't decaying from the inside.

I walked straight out of the Hall of Justice and headed to the Yoga Tree in the Castro. I arrived an hour early for the 6:15PM Advanced Vinyasa class with teacher M. Morford. The air smelled of eucalyptus incense, very peaceful. I sank into the red vintage waiting room chair near the changing room and closed my eyes.

CHAPTER 18: SEROLOGY, SECRECY, AND MEDICAL RECORDS

In every culture, blood means life. Without it, there's no being.—Guillermo del Toro

November 1, 2019, marked a turning point. That morning — the day after my favorite holiday — I arrived at Zuckerberg San Francisco General Hospital and Trauma Center (ZSFGH) to collect my medical records. At 8:00 a.m. I met with the office manager in Records and took the documents into my hands. As I read, one crucial detail stood out: serology tests had been performed during the six-hour emergency visit, corroborating my account.

Serology—the science of blood analysis, the immune system's response to pathogens and foreign substances. Multiple tests. Multiple confirmations: Blood Alcohol Concentration levels; PHL Chlamydia TMA (urine); PHL Gonorrhoeae TMA (urine); Syphilis RPR; Human Immunodeficiency Virus 1/2 (HIV-1/2) Antibody Test.

Blood was both a biological truth and a mythic symbol — and it was all there.

Evidence that my blood had been drawn for laboratory analysis. Evidence that could have been used for toxicology testing. Evidence that existed — and then vanished. Because no one requested timely analysis, it wasn't preserved.

Destroyed by inaction. And for nearly a decade, no one told me.

On March 28, 2019, during a conversation with Sergeant V at the Special Victims Unit, I heard something for the first time:

The medical forensic kit wasn't the main evidence the Inspector focused on — he would have needed to request the analysis via form. The Inspector never requested for the kit to be tested by the Crime Lab during the investigation.

Later she added:

I will gladly give you the results of your toxicology once I receive it. It was not in the file, and I do not know why not — I am still waiting to receive the report.

So casual. So dismissive. No big deal. Just someone's life. Just someone's safety. Just blood reduced to paperwork — then left to expire, as if truth itself had a shelf life. As I pieced the puzzle together, gathering fragments between March and November 2019, a question began to haunt me:

Were the SFPD — and my assailant — lucky it took me nine years to figure this out?

That morning, the Medical Records Manager urged me to visit the UCSF Trauma Recovery Center. I followed her instructions, clutching my disclosure form, needing a doctor's signature.

They placed me in a private conference room with a counselor. We talked. I cried. She listened. She understood why I was doing this—why I was investigating my own case. She understood the weight of it. The silence of it. The oppression that comes when the system buries truth and leaves you to exhume it alone.

Now that I have a Doctor's signature I am hopeful that I'll receive the CALEMA 923 from the SFGH ER Medical Records Department. It is the standard 'Forensic Medical Report Form' required by the state of California. It is used by the emergency room Doctors and Nurses conducting medical/evidentiary examinations and collecting evidence for the (SAFE) Evidence Collection Kit submitted to the crime laboratory. Should have. But I didn't.

5 NOVEMBER 2019

I received a callback from a Health Sciences Clinical Professor and physician at the UCSF Trauma Recovery Center. She had reached out to discuss the process for obtaining additional medical records—specifically, my toxicology report and mental health documentation.

The UCSF TRC Doctor explained: *Rose—technically, one of the records you're requesting is just a lab test. But it's considered the property of law enforcement— specifically the Inspectors and Sergeants in the Special Victims Unit. The 'rape kit' DNA findings and toxicology report are in their custody. They are the only ones who can release that information. Still, you have the right to it.*

She paused, then added: *I've been doing this work for a decade... and San Francisco survivors, like yourself, often face what we call 'secondary victimization' when dealing with law enforcement. Their attitudes are something you shouldn't have to deal with—and yet, so many of you do. Not only were you raped, but now you're forced to endure a complicated and demoralizing process to access the truth. The very system designed to protect and support survivors ends up causing more harm. We need to change that—and what you're doing now, Rose, is part of that change. I'm very impressed. You've had to become a detective to figure this out. And now, you're uncovering the truth. That matters. There's real power in that.*

Around the same time, in the eleventh hour before the election, the San Francisco Police Officers Association launched a $669,867 media blitz targeting public defender and progressive judicial reform candidate Chesa Boudin, who was running for District Attorney.

Boudin's campaign platform explicitly supported the prosecution of sexual assault cases —a notable stance in a city where rape prosecutions have long lagged behind the crisis-level volume of reported assaults.

8 NOVEMBER 2019

I made three phone calls: I left a voicemail with my advocate at SFPD. I called both the Office Manager at the Medical Records Department and I called the Doctor at UCSF TRC. I had conversations about records and how I needed to sign more forms.

22 NOVEMBER 2019

Last Wednesday, November 13th, I drove to San Francisco to sign a new 'medical release form' regarding the 'sensitive information request'. The Office Manager, Penélope Nguyen, had said to me that the UCSF Doctor wanted more signatures from me. So today I called the ZSFGH Medical Records to check on the status of the recent request with my signatures to make sure the UCSF Doctor had got them.

Medical Records Office Manager Penélope answers, "Hi nice to hear from you. Did the UCSF TRC Doctor give you a call? We've been busy."

"I bet no the Doctor didn't call me so you sent over the fax or email?"

Penélope responded, "Yes I did. In her email back to me, she said it looks great and she is making a statement and 'hospital discharge summary'. I thought she called you to let you know about the update." I replied, "The Doctor is doing a summary?"

"Rose – Looks like she emailed me back on the 17th. I emailed her your request form on the 13th. The Doctor is working on the 'medical record summary'. She will email me and then the records will be available for you to pick-up here at our office."

"Sounds great, I will come into the office when it's ready. Thank you for your help," I said.

"Yes it was good that you came in-person to sign them. Thank you so now we are just waiting on UCSF TRC and the Doctor. If you want you can call them today to check on it."

"I will. Last week you said that in my 'confidential medical records file' there wasn't a standard document, the 923 form... Why do you think that is? You said that normally there is a document that it happened in the hospital records," I asked.

"Yes—*Normally* we have the Cal EMA 923," Penélope responded.

"Do you think because the SFPD waited 6 years to analyze the kit — that is why Zuckerberg SFGH Medical Records Department wouldn't have a copy of it?"

"No — The emergency room doctor or a SAFE nurse examiner did it that day. So the '923 Form' is supposed to be in your medical chart here. For us everything we do in the ER we keep a record of it. Then we put it in storage. If we call it back and order it we get it. Whenever it's not in the 'confidential medical chart' — we take that into serious consideration and we notice that we don't have it," Penélope detailed.

I replied, "During the early stages of the investigation the Detective said the SFPD Crime Lab was analyzing my rape kit and toxicology samples. In reality — it wasn't tested for 6 years and then I didn't know that until recently. It's a puzzle. It seems like the evidence was tampered with on purpose to protect the suspect."

She replied, "Yes—Do you have a lawyer?"

"I've found out a lot on my own and I want one."

She replied, "It will be a faster process if you get one."

"Because a lawyer can subpoena the police—to get a copy of the 923 form?"

She nodded. "Yes and I don't know the exact legal process at SFPD, but whatever they have, it can be subpoenaed. The lawyer can help you with that."

I reflected aloud, "The SVU Sergeant told me a DNA profile was created on the suspect."

"Rose, SFPD has the forensic medical exam kit, the specimens, and the CalEMA 923 form. But we always keep documentation here, too. Your exam was done in this ER with our doctors, so we should have it—without question. But... it's not here."

I looked at her, grateful. "You've helped me so much these past few months. Thank you."

"Of course. Give TRC a call and remind them you're still waiting. Hopefully you can reach them before the holiday, but I'm not sure how long it will take the doctor to finish the summary."

CHAPTER 19: AUGUST 2019 - INTERROGATION

I wanted you to see what real courage is, instead of getting the idea that courage is a man with a gun in his hand. It's when you know you're licked before you begin but you begin anyway and you see it through no matter what. You rarely win, but sometimes you do. — Atticus Finch, To Kill a Mockingbird

The Managing District Attorney of the Preliminary Hearing Unit, Maddox O'Conner, entered the conference room with Sophia Belrose, the Victim Services Advocate from SFPD. We were inside the San Francisco District Attorney's Office at the Hall of Justice Courthouse.

I had read that the Hall of Justice—designed by Weihe, Frick & Kruse and built between 1958 and 1960—was a granite-clad, austere structure housing the Sheriff's Department, County Jail, Coroner's Office, District Attorney's Office, and various municipal courts. It felt as cold and monolithic as the system it upheld.

DA O'Conner wore a gray suit, a tie, and rectangular glasses. Professional. Composed. I stood to shake his hand.

"Nice to meet you. Thank you, Mr. O'Conner, for taking the time to speak with me today —it means a lot," I said, settling into my chair across from him.

Sophia spoke first, gently steering the conversation.
"I think she wants to understand why the case wasn't charged back in 2010."

O'Conner nodded, folding his hands.
"Okay. This case was originally reviewed by one of my colleagues—before I was heading the unit. I've read his notes and gone over the initial report myself. He concluded at the time that it wasn't a provable case. And I have to agree."

He paused, then clarified:
"In order to charge a criminal case, we have to provide evidence sufficient to convince all twelve jurors, unanimously, beyond a reasonable doubt. Without that, we cannot ethically file charges."

He leaned back slightly, then added,
"What complicates this is a case law precedent—*People v. Mayberry*, oddly enough. It stands for the proposition that if the suspect honestly and reasonably believes the victim was consenting, then he lacks the criminal intent required for conviction. In other words, without intent, there is no crime. That's what makes the so-called *Mayberry* defense so difficult to overcome in sexual assault cases."

The DA described as he sat back comfortably in his chair.

I knew he was throwing me off guard and his strategy is commonly used. It involves referencing a higher authority, policy or law to deflect the person raising a complaint.

He referenced The People v. Brooker T. Mayberry, Supreme Court of California, September 1975, [15 Cal. 3d 144] as if it were a profound law when he could've referenced the 'consent defense' so I asked another question.

"What constitutes a complete and thorough police investigation?"

"Everything they did — They investigated him and got statements from him and they did a pretext phone call," he replied.

Sophia Belrose interjected, "Do you remember doing the pretext call?" I replied, "Yes very clearly so."

The DA continued, "Statements that they got from you as well. That is basically what it comes down to and obviously there are no other independent witnesses — it was just the two of you in the circumstances of what happened at his place." I felt intimidated. I didn't mention to the DA how I had three individuals who were able to corroborate my statements.

I changed the subject and asked, "What is the standard protocol for a Detective working with a victim who goes to the ER for the forensic exam and blood draw for the toxicology — Does the Detective include those records/tests in the case-file before he hands it over to the District Attorney?

Managing District Attorney Maddox O'Conner explained, "Usually we have the medical forensic 'kit' and toxicology report within the file. It's given to the DA — I don't know what happened to yours — The DA's Office will typically get those exam results before a 'charging decision' is made. They're important because we want to know if there was forensic physical evidence that corroborates the victim's complaint. We want to know if it was a forced or violent or alcohol and drug facilitated act."

I questioned, "If the Detective withholds incriminating evidence from the file, can the SFPD still close it?"

The dismissal of the crime benefits the perpetrator — The Detective's actions, giving an incomplete case-file to the DA, demonstrate that he was hiding corroborative evidence, my physical injuries and the DFSA-findings, that would have been damaging to the perpetrator. I think he may have done this intentionally so that the DA would decline the case. The SFPD were able to declare the case resolved through what is known as an "exceptional clearance".

The DA replied, "He didn't withhold evidence — *Alright*."

"I have the medical records here."

I flipped through the binder, the pages neatly ordered by date, and said, "This is the Medical Screening Exam Record from Zuckerberg San Francisco General Hospital. It documents multiple injuries—several of which are noted on February 23, 2010, the date of the crime."

I looked up, steady. "The records list: *head trauma, traumatic injury, abdominal pain,* and *burning.*"

O'Conner raised an eyebrow. "You're saying he hit you in the head?"

"I'm not saying he hit me in the head," I said calmly.

"Well—how do you account for the head trauma?"

"He pushed me back forcefully, multiple times. My head hit the wall. I resisted, I yelled *no*—again and again. He didn't stop."

There was a moment of silence.

Then Sophia's voice cut in—light, but marked with caution. "Hold on—we want to be very careful about discussing any new facts, because they're part of an ongoing police investigation."

"Wait—can you repeat that?" I asked, caught off guard.

She turned to me gently, choosing her words. "Rose—we have to be careful with any new details that don't already appear in the case file or original police report. Anything new needs to go through the proper channels—through the criminal investigation first."

She paused. "Were these medical records provided to the detective back then?"

I clarified, "He did not request these records. When I spoke with the Sergeant a few months ago, I understood for the 1st time that he withheld evidence and the case was negligently handled. The 'kit' and toxicology samples were not tested by the SFPD Crime Lab because of the Detective's judgement call."

"You found this out when you met with her at the SVU Office?" Sophia questioned.

I confirmed, "Yes — I was deceived for years and he withheld incriminating evidence from the file. Was the Detective protecting the rapist? It seems that way!"

"Why would he lie about having my toxicology tested by the Crime Lab? He betrayed me. And, I literally just found this out during the meeting with the Sargent."

The DA pretended to be incognizant of what was said.

"Hold on — I got a bit lost there. In terms of the SART Nurse at the SFGH Trauma Recovery Center, where you go into to do the forensic examination those tests don't go anywhere else. They go to the police. Next our office receives them so it's not like those tests go to a different Crime Lab or forensic analyst — All right."

He continued to gaslight me.

"Maybe I misheard you but the Detective wouldn't send your medical exams to anyone other than our Crime Lab — Usually we receive the samples used for the toxicology report and those would have been sent to our analyst and they'd determine what, if anything, was in your system and if there were illegal drugs or alcohol that would be tested."

Next he returned to the consent issue.

"In this case, there was no question about 'who done it'—which is typically the reason our Crime Lab runs DNA swabs from a rape kit. When the police don't know who the perpetrator is, we run the tests to establish identity. But Henry never denied having sex with you. Quite the contrary—Mr. Henry describes having numerous sexual encounters with you that evening. You spent the night at his place. That wouldn't have been an issue."

That wouldn't have been an issue.

"I told the Detective I felt drugged," I shot back. "I described my symptoms. The dizziness. The confusion. The inability to leave Henry's condo. And yet, here you are, blaming me for staying the night."

His expression remained unreadable.

"Henry made me a drink after we left BIX. He asked me to take art model photos for him. And before that, he had been grooming me."

Grooming. The calculated manipulation is designed to gain a victim's trust, to lower their guard, to set the trap.

The DA gave me an uncanny look—because he had already seen the photos.

I let the silence stretch, then continued, my voice unwavering.

"I was a college figure model. I modeled for painting classes. He tricked me into taking photographs. I was disoriented, physically weak, while at his home. And those same photos? He handed them to the Detective as proof that it was 'consensual sex.'"

I leaned forward.

"I pushed him off me. I yelled NO in his face. He violently forced himself on me. And yet —you take his word over mine. Fascinating."

The DA said nothing.

Sophia, the advocate, broke the tension with a vague, practiced line: "This is a sexual assault case that is difficult to prove. We have survivors who go through different motions when reporting to law enforcement. They all feel different things."

I stared at her. I felt like I was the one on trial.

"I have medical records here to corroborate my account. Why would a woman go to the ER to do the invasive 6 hour forensic medical exam rape kit and report the crime if it didn't happen?"

Sophia vindicated.

"I wasn't implying that and sense that you're getting frustrated. The police do a good job of maintaining order and making sure everyone follows the rules. It comes down to how these cases are reviewed. When the District Attorney or Detective are analyzing these sexual assault cases it's very fact-based. It's not like we think something didn't happen to you — Unfortunately we're unable to prosecute the suspect due to the law."

I shivered and replied, "These assault cases are not analyzed based on fact-based evidence. Look at how my case was mishandled. The Detective's investigation was discriminatory and deeply biased. So disturbing to hear you reiterate, what Henry said to the Detective just a second ago, Henry drugged and raped me. He used intimidation and violence to rape me twice and you're taking his side."

The DA calmly replied, "No — I have to deal with what the facts are from what the Police tell us — In the initial report the Dispatch Officers took — it says that the victim didn't want to put anyone in jail. She was reluctant to call the police in the first place. She didn't feel comfortable pressing charges against Henry because he was a nice guy."

"I didn't say that."

The DA challenged me, "Well — It's in the intake report."

I elaborated, "Victims undergo a great deal of fear for coming forward and I said that yes I do want him to go to jail. I was traumatized and disoriented after what I had gone through."

Sophia gently looked over at me and replied, "I'm aware that assault survivors go through many different emotions and it is a challenge."

I added, "Honestly, I was terrified when the two patrol officers came to my apartment late at night, less than 19-hrs after I was assaulted, to take the SFPD intake report. Probably made it seem not as bad as it really was out of fear."

Sophia said, "Maddox totally understands and that is not how he meant to come across ."

"A nice guy? Henry is an insidious and calculated predator who acts charming. The Detective tampered with evidence by concealing and withholding it. I discovered this in March when Sergeant V told me."

The DA redirected the conversation and asked, "The ER where you said that you sought treatment is apart of the San Francisco General Rape Treatment Center (RTC). I do not have a copy of your 'tox screen' here in this folder. Do you have it?"

Sophia reflected on the DA's question and replied, "That isn't released to the survivors."

"I've asked many times if I could get a copy of my toxicology report."

"*Oh* — sounds like you've got information about the Tox Exam that I do not," the Deputy DA replied.

"The Sergeant didn't want to give it to me. She said it's against her unit's orders."

Sophia asked gently, "Rose—did she explain to you what the findings were?"

"She said she didn't have the toxicology report in her case file," I replied. "And she told me she couldn't release confidential information."

The DA followed up. "Did she tell you there was an adulterating substance in your tox report?"

I shook my head. "No. She said she didn't even have a copy of it. According to her, the SFPD Crime Lab didn't test the rape kit until six years after the assault. That's what the Sergeant told me. And that's why she said the tox report wasn't included in her file."

At the time, the department policy was to test kits within a week.

The DA nodded slowly. "Originally, this wasn't her case. But I'll talk to the Sergeant. I have to work with the facts, just like my predecessor did. I assume the forensic medical exam was collected and evaluated during the investigation. And I assume they had the toxicology report—but I can't confirm, because I don't have the full case file."

I kept my voice steady.

"All the medical records and findings need to be included. This was mishandled—negligently. He should have documented everything: the interviews with my best friend, the SART nurse, the UCSF TRC counselor, the ER doctor. All of it."

The DA paused, then gave the familiar dodge.

"We have to focus on what's admissible in court. What you told them might be considered hearsay—which is generally not allowed. So, not everything you said would count as evidence."

A silence hung for a beat before I asked, "What exactly does hearsay mean?"

The DA leaned back, clinical.

"For example, if I go into court and say, *Well, Sophie told me the following,* that's hearsay. It's a statement made outside of court that's being offered to prove the truth of what Sophie said. As the attorney, I can't introduce that into evidence. There are exceptions, but what you're describing wouldn't be admissible."

But I had already done the research. I knew the rule. Medical reports are admissible. And I remembered that call—still in the ER, trembling as I phoned my professor and co-director, telling her I'd been raped. That fell under a clear exception: excited utterance.

"I want to move forward with the prosecution. I want the crime-scene evidence that was withheld included in the file. What he did was a felony. And we have the evidence—it's all in the ER records: traumatic vaginal injury, head trauma, abdominal pain. The doctor's reports are compelling—far more compelling than any vague claim of consensual sex."

The DA responded—measured, but dismissive. "I've seen plenty of RTC reports, but I haven't reviewed your forensic exam. As for the trauma you mentioned—headaches, abdominal pain—those aren't what we'd classify as 'observable injuries.'"

His tone stayed clinical. "You also described burning and vaginal pain, but I'm not sure any trauma was documented. In sexual assault cases, sometimes there aren't physical signs. They would've looked for abrasions or lacerations. I'm speaking speculatively, of course—but based on what I have, my predecessor didn't believe it was a provable case."

What he didn't say: the forensic exam and toxicology weren't tested until six years after the assault. How could it ever be *provable* when the evidence was left to be destroyed?

Under California Penal Code § 680, victims have the right to know within 30 days whether a kit was tested and the results disclosed. The statute exists to prevent precisely this—what Michel Foucault called *bureaucratic forgetting.*

A silence not born of absence, but of control. A silence that doesn't merely delay justice, it defines it out of reach.

CHAPTER 20: THE TOX SCREEN WASN'T TESTED RIGHT AWAY

"I had injuries. The Detective showed me what the police consider the *real victims*—mutilated, bloody women—and told me I wasn't one of them."

O'Conner sidestepped the Detective's procedural violations, saying, "These cases vary—from violent assaults to rape by intoxication to rape of an unconscious woman. In the latter cases, there may not be physical evidence."

I pushed back. "I was dizzy, detached from my body—waking nightmares. I told the Detective I'd been drugged; it's documented in my four-page Narrative. These are symptoms of drug-facilitated rape. Why wasn't my toxicology included in the file?"

He replied, "I don't know what's in the Toxicology Report. If it's just alcohol, that's not a Date Rape Drug. I don't have your report, so I can't say."

But isn't it the DA's job to know? Alcohol is the most commonly used date rape drug—that's basic knowledge. It felt like he was twisting facts to excuse a failed investigation.

I said, "Then how does anyone get toxicology results? My exams were ignored for six years. The Detective told me it was being tested, but toxicological evidence expires if not analyzed immediately. Did he delay it to protect the assailant?"

The DA paused.

"I accept what you're saying—the tox screen wasn't tested right away."

Amazed to hear him confirm my theory, I added, "You're right, it wasn't. The Sergeant said it wasn't tested until the summer of 2016 because, during our meeting, she explained that the Detective didn't consider the medical forensic exam or toxicology samples important evidence. He ignored protocol and never requested the toxicology analysis."

The DA looked visibly startled.

"Okay, I'll check with the Sergeant. So, you're saying the toxicology screen wasn't done until 2016? You're not saying the forensic medical exam—the rape kit—wasn't examined until then, are you?"

"Yes," I said, holding his gaze.

"That's exactly what I'm saying. According to Sergeant V, the kit wasn't tested until 2016—six years after the assault. She told me the Detective never submitted the request form during the original investigation. He drove me to the Hall of Justice, walked me into the Crime Lab, and misled me—telling me my kit and toxicology were already being tested."

The DA shifted focus, pivoting to the DNA results—despite previously stressing the importance of toxicology.

"I'll check with the Sergeant about the tox screen and see if anything's noted in the 923 form. But again, this isn't a case of *who* did it—it's about *what* happened. Rape or consensual sex."

"It was rape," I said firmly. "Which is a felony."

He nodded, but his tone cooled.

"I understand that's your position. But I have to look at the evidence objectively. I want to be on your side—but I'm not your attorney, and I'm not his. I have an ethical duty to only file charges I believe can be proven beyond a reasonable doubt. And based on what I've seen, I don't disagree with my predecessor."

"Who was your predecessor?"

"Gascon."

"Is it a violation for a Detective to share confidential information about other cases? Or is it just unethical—or illegal—for him to lie to a victim about the status of her forensic exams during an active investigation?"

California law provides explicit protections for survivors and demands integrity in criminal investigations. Penal Code § 680 guarantees a victim's right to know whether their rape kit has been tested and to receive timely updates. Penal Code § 135 makes it a crime to willfully conceal or withhold evidence that should be disclosed, including forensic reports. Penal Code § 118.1 imposes criminal liability on peace officers who knowingly make false statements in official reports.

If a detective tells a victim her kit was submitted for testing when it wasn't—and delays that testing for years—that isn't just misconduct. It may constitute a direct violation of state law.

PECULIAR

Language is also a political instrument, means, and proof of power.—James Baldwin

Deputy DA O'Conner leaned back in his chair, arms crossed, his expression unreadable.

"No—I'm not here to prosecute the Detective. I'm here to look at your case, and quite frankly, there are a lot of things that are peculiar about it."

Peculiar. The word rang in my ears, sharp and deliberate—an echo of warning.

"Like what?"

I asked, my voice measured. He didn't answer. Instead, he pivoted, his focus turning to me.

"Did you go to his house voluntarily?"

I blinked. He's going to do this.

"He picked me up from my apartment. Drove us to the restaurant. Then he drove me to his condo, where he entrapped me," I said, slow, controlled.

Maddox didn't even hesitate.

"Did you go to his house voluntarily?"

"He drugged me. And going to his home does NOT give him the right to rape me."

A pause. A flicker of something in his eyes—like he hadn't expected me to say it outright.

"Of course not," he said, a beat too late.

Sophia jumped in, her tone soft, practiced.

"Of course not—we're going to take this one step at a time."

The tension in the room thickened, surrounding us like the fog rolling off the bay.

Sophia's voice dropped, shifting to something pacifying.

"I understand, and I want us to be mindful of how you might feel. We need to review what happened that night, but these answers might not be beneficial to your healing. What I do want to focus on is getting your questions answered. Maddox's intention is not to make you feel bad, and I see that you are frustrated with the criminal justice system and how these cases are prosecuted—is that a fair assessment?"

How so? I was the one being interrogated as if I was the criminal on trial.

SERIAL PREDATOR?

"It was negligence," I asserted.

A pause.

My voice steady despite the frustration tightening in my chest. "The Detective never spoke to the bartender at BIX about the alcohol we consumed while sitting at the bar for over two hours. He never looked into whether Henry had taken other women there under the same circumstances."

Sophia nodded, her expression carefully neutral.

"We can't speak to the Detective's investigation, but Maddox will follow up with the Sergeant about the toxicology report. We'll get an answer on that, don't worry. I want you to feel empowered and get closure. My role is to guide and facilitate this conversation, to make sure you leave here feeling empowered."

"It was rigged from the start."

The Deputy DA gazed at me.

I'll do as Sophia said—I'll check with the Sergeant, see if there's anything suspicious in the report, like a 'date rape drug.' That could be significant."

Sophia pivoted. "Rose, I know you've had concerns about the Detective after the investigation was closed. You'll need to follow up with the Department of Police Accountability. Did you ever speak with an investigator from the Department of Stalking?"

I studied their faces, searching for any sign of weakness in their scripted responses. "In April, an Inspector called me right after I spoke with the Sergeant. But they'll play the same game—'he-said-she-said,' deflecting responsibility, dragging it out until it fades away. It's not worth it. In October 2018, I did a recorded interview with someone from the Department of Police Accountability, and there was no follow-up. Why?"

Sophia hesitated.

"I'm not sure. Did you mention this to the Sergeant in March?"

"Yes. She said it was the first time she'd heard about the complaint. The justice system isn't designed to protect us—it's designed to protect criminals. A detective can mishandle evidence, submit an incomplete investigation to the DA, and act inappropriately."

The victim services advocate quickly interjected, "I don't think the Inspector mishandled the evidence. Mr. Maddox will speak to the Sergeant about your toxicology report, and we'll get the answers."

I took a deep breath.

"The Detective was a predator investigating another predator."

I looked them both in the eyes. "If a victim tells the truth and seeks help from the authorities, we're met with disbelief, intimidation, and even lies. I've been told there's 'no proof' and 'no corroborative evidence,' when it's the SFPD's own negligence that kept the evidence from being tested in the first place."

Sophia's tone softened, carefully composed. "I understand that this has been frustrating."

BLESSED BY THE SFPD

Sophia steered the conversation gently. "Rose—I remember when we spoke on the phone, you told me about your work with the Human Rights Commission and the new Office of Sexual Harassment and Assault Response Prevention (SHARP). You stood alongside Supervisor Hillary Ronen and the activists to push for real change. That was huge. It will impact survivors for years to come. You did that. That was your voice. And you are strong."

I exhaled. "Yeah—I spoke at City Hall, in front of 200 people, about the injustices we face. Meanwhile, all Henry had to do was sit back and lie. *'Oh yeah, I banged her a couple times. She loved it. Look at these hot photos I took—aren't they great? I don't remember her screaming NO, or fighting me off, or that I drugged her. It was consensual, baby.'*

"And the Detective? He favored him. Helped him. Probably *deliberately* buried my forensic exams so the Crime Lab never even got them. What an asshole. It's sick. It really is." My voice shook. "Henry committed a felony, and he's getting away with it. He's done it before."

Sophia and the DA exchanged uneasy glances. She hesitated, then said, "I see that you're upset. Let's take a few minutes to go over your options."

My chest tightened. My vision blurred. "It wasn't just some 'misunderstanding.' It was calculated. He *knew* exactly what he was doing. If you met him, you'd think he was charming. It's a façade. A cover for what he really is."

Sophia's voice softened. "I know this is difficult, but we have to be fair."

My stomach twisted. "Fair? He exploited me. *Then* the Detective preyed on me *after* the investigation was closed. This isn't just injustice—it's terror. It's sick."

Sophia nodded, glancing at the DA before standing. "I know this is overwhelming. I'm going to step out for a moment, grab a couple of things. Maddox and I will go over the next steps."

She gave me a reassuring smile, but it didn't reach her eyes. Then she left the room, the tension lingering in the air long after the door clicked shut.

"What I will do now is see if the Sergeant is at the SVU Office and if I can retrieve a copy of the toxicology report," the DA said. With that, he and Sophia left the room.

So I shut my eyes as the tears rolled quickly down my face.

THE HIPPA PRIVACY RULE

Sophia reappeared and said, "I found you a stress ball," placing it in front of me. "Not sure if you're a tactile person, but it might help with tension."

She sat down and exhaled. "I know this is difficult to hear. It's not always what you want or what our Victim Services Office wants, but within the criminal justice system, there are ethical obligations we have to follow. I want to help you get your questions answered."

She hesitated before continuing. "Maddox went to check with Sergeant V. She might not be in the SVU office today, but we're looking into it. What do you think would be the most helpful steps moving forward?"

I met her gaze.

"Today, the DA implied that even though I went to Zuckerberg SFGH, underwent a six-hour forensic exam, and have an ER report documenting violent physical injuries, he still doesn't think it'll hold up in court. That's absurd. Also, the police withheld evidence, and that's why the DA couldn't make a fair decision. I want to prosecute."

Sophia kept her tone even. "He has to consider all angles. I know it's hard to hear, but a DA has to anticipate every possible defense strategy. Going to trial means subjecting a survivor to cross-examination. A defense attorney's job is to create doubt."

I clenched my jaw. "The only reason there's doubt is because the police made sure there would be."

Silence hung between us.

Sophia sighed. "We work within the laws and standards we have. We can't change that overnight. If a case goes to trial, there's always the possibility that a survivor will have to face a grueling cross-examination."

I replied, "They'll try to make us feel like garbage."

Sophia nodded. "Yes. I looked into the Executive Guidebook: Practical Approaches for Strengthening Law Enforcement's Response to Sexual Assault, the one you mentioned. I found it on Amazon, and I'll buy it. Each case I work on is unique. I want to hold onto the uniqueness of your case, not just follow others' accounts."

The DA stepped back into the room. "Sorry for the delay. I went up to the SVU, but the Sergeant isn't in today. I got her cell number, though, and I left a voicemail about the case —specifically the medical forensic 'kit' and toxicology. As soon as I hear back, I'll let Sophie know, and she'll update you."

Look, I'm sorry, Rose. I know we had to meet under these circumstances. I'm not trying to mislead you about what's going on or the likelihood of what we can do. I wasn't informed of the details you've described today. As soon as I find out from the Sergeant what she's got, I'll review that as well."

Sophie nodded. "Maddox and I talk all the time. I'll get back to you as soon as he calls me with an update."

"Thank you for your time today, Mr. O'Conner."

The DA gave a small nod. "Take care."

Sophia turned toward me, her expression soft yet firm. "It's challenging for survivors to go through this process, so it's important to recognize that healing and the investigation are separate. They're not contingent upon one another. I want you to feel empowered, no matter the outcome. What happens in this case won't change what you've been through. I want you to have the tools to work through this. As a system, we have to be transparent about the process. What Maddox was explaining—if the information he gets from the Sergeant doesn't help the case, he doesn't want to mislead you about the likelihood of it moving forward."

I paused, taking in her words, then replied, "I see. But the ER medical screening exam that details the traumatic injury, the forensic exam 'kit', the toxicology, and the 11 months at UCSF Trauma Recovery Center—none of that is enough corroborative evidence to bring criminal charges?"

Sophia shifted slightly. "When you mention the UCSF Trauma Recovery Center, you're referring to your therapy there?"

"Yes," I said.

Her voice remained steady and rehearsed. "Mental health records are confidential and can't be used in court due to HIPAA privacy laws. Those conversations remain private and wouldn't be considered as evidence."

I stared at her, processing the misinformation. While confidentiality is vital for clinical psychologists, the HIPAA Privacy Rule exists to protect health information, not to render it untouchable. A client and their therapist can release records if needed. A lawyer can subpoena medical and psychological records, and a therapist can testify in court.

Sophia either didn't know that—or didn't want me to.

I nodded, deciding not to argue. There was no point.

"Thank you for scheduling this meeting."

Sophia offered me a practiced smile.

"Of course. And remember, no matter what happens—you are a survivor. You are a survivor."

Her words rang hollow. *A prepackaged consolation prize.* We stepped out of the DA's Office together, heels clicking against the dark green tile as we moved toward the elevators. The long hallway felt even longer under the weight of what hadn't been said.

"Take care," she said as we reached the doors. "I'll talk to you soon."

The massive silver doors of the 1960s-era elevator opened, and I nodded. "Yes, thank you."

I pressed the button, and the heavy doors slid open again. I stepped through the passage, and they shut behind me.

Moments later, they re-opened as I stepped into the bustling lobby of the Hall of Justice. I passed by a few City Public Defenders and uniformed SFPD Officers, feeling the weight of each step as I pushed against the heavy exterior glass door. The door swung open, and I emerged onto the gray cement steps. I paused for a moment, breathing in the cool Bay breeze, and looked up at the indigo-blue sky.

CHAPTER 21: SERGEANT VERSCHWÖRER, MANAGING ATTORNEY O'CONNER

He who passively accepts evil is as much involved in it as he who helps to perpetrate it. He who accepts evil without protesting against it is really cooperating with it. — Dr. Martin Luther King, Jr.

In preparation for this meeting, I spent time listening to Dr. King's speeches, drawing strength from his unwavering pursuit of justice. He fought for equal protection under the law—something I've realized is still not fully extended to victims of sex crimes. Only 0.05% of cases reported to San Francisco law enforcement result in prosecution. I uncovered why.

On December 19, 2019, at 1:30 PM, SFPD Victim Services Advocate Sophia Belrose entered the secure waiting room of the District Attorney's Office at the Hall of Justice. I stood to greet her and shook her hand. After grabbing my black Osprey backpack, I followed her down a dim, olive-green hallway. As we walked, she spoke with careful precision.

"The purpose of today's meeting is to get some of your questions answered and to discuss the DA's decision. Some of what you hear may be difficult—triggering, even. If you need to stop, we'll stop."

She opened the door.

Inside, Managing District Attorney Maddox O'Conner and SVU Sergeant Verschwörer were already seated. I stepped in, lowered myself into the modern armchair across from them, and met their gaze.

"Thank you for meeting with me and taking time out of your schedule," I began. "It means a lot. I've been researching this case because the Detective mishandled the investigation. He left out critical evidence. First, I want to ask—Is my four-page narrative in the case file?"

The Sergeant barely looked up.

"I would imagine if you wrote a statement, it would be included as part of the evidence."

I studied her. This time, she wore an oversized gray hoodie—a stark contrast to the polished formal attire she'd worn at our last meeting. The shift felt intentional. Or maybe just tired. Either way, the message was clear: this wasn't a courtroom. It wasn't even a negotiation.

It was containment.

Sophia, seated beside me in a crisp white turtleneck and delicate gold necklaces, interjected, "Typically, anything you submit in writing is in the case file."

"It's a typed document," I clarified. "The Detective asked me to write it."

The Sergeant flipped through the case file.

"Yes—it's right here. It's all here," she said with forced certainty.

"Do you have a copy of the CALEMA-923 form in the case file?"

They exchanged a brief glance before responding in unison.

"Yes."

"Rose—just to be clear, you were shown all of this when you met with me and my partner, Sergeant Stokes. We showed you everything in the case file."

Her words hit like a slap—*brazenly false*, and delivered within the first few minutes of the meeting. I steadied myself, voice low but resolute.

"No, Sergeant. You never showed me the case file. You only had it in front of you at the meeting."

I paused, the question rising like smoke.

Who benefits from her lie?

I could feel the facade she imposed—a flimsy veil of legitimacy, crafted to shield a broken judicial system and a compromised SVU unit. It wasn't just falsehood; it was performance. The undertones of manipulation were unmistakable. And I knew—if anyone benefited from her lie, it was them: the very institutions with a vested interest in keeping the truth buried.

The SFPD wasn't just negligent—it was fraudulent. A hoax draped in the trappings of law, sworn to protect victims but weaponized to safeguard offenders. They didn't uphold justice. They contorted it, twisting statutes into shields for misconduct.

The Sergeant remained unfazed. Robotic.

"No—we showed it to you. We gave you the option to look through it and review it. I told you that you couldn't have copies because it's evidence. We're the custodian of records. I can't give you evidentiary items—that's part of my case file. But we did give you the opportunity to review it that day."

"No, you didn't give me the option to review the case file, kit or Henry's photos!"

Sophia interrupted on purpose, "this happened earlier this year, in March, during your meeting?"

The Sergeant confirmed, "Yes."

"The Detective took me to the Crime Lab in the basement just days after the crime. He told me they would analyze my 'rape kit' and toxicology samples. So why didn't that happen? Why did he lie?"

Please add some clarity to this: "Your forensic medical examination rape kit was tested," the Sergeant answered.

"Yes. Six years later it was analyzed by the SFPD Crime Lab."

"Why would the Detective lie during the investigation that it was being tested?"

Silence.

"He deceived me. Cops, especially detectives, should not deceive victims. This was so shocking—I didn't know until I spoke with you, Sargent Verschwörer, that the Detective did not submit the basic request form to have it analyzed by the Crime Lab during an active investigation."

Evidence had effectively sat on a shelf for years, unattended, until it was eventually processed as part of a broader backlog clearance effort.

Sophia interjected.

"We will take this one step at a time."

The Sergeant nodded.

"Thank you, Ms. Belrose. Correct me if I'm wrong, Mr. DA, but the sexual assault forensic medical examination you had at the ER is more helpful when the suspect is unknown, or when it's a question of an 'intimate encounter' rather than in this case. You said you had 'sexual relations' with him, and Mr. Henry was identified. He said it was consensual sex, so analyzing the kit wouldn't have mattered," the sergeant asserted.

"No — I was raped and in pain analyzing the kit does matter, he may be a repeat offender and he used drugs on me. I opened my old *Apple* computer last week and found the Narrative I wrote for the Detective — Six different criminal offenses were committed during the felony. I had blocked-out the memory that he had committed forcible sodomy."

With an alarmed look on her face, Sophia abruptly interrupted, "It's important we take this one-step at a time — Your original question was about the analysis of the 'kit' toxicology and why a decision was made. So let's focus on that."

I wanted to hold the SFPD accountable for their wrongdoings so I announced, "I want the SFPD to be on the side of law and order — The Detective should not lie to a victim about evidence being tested during the early stages of the investigation. It's unethical — This is not a joke."

The sergeant I used to spell retorted, "Well — You're not letting me finish."

Like clockwork every time I made a statement that they didn't want to hear, Sophia redirected the conversation, "It's important that we do not talk over each other."

I asserted, "There is no excuse for a Detective to behave that way."

Sophia interrupted again, "You need to take a step back — You're asking us to speak about something we didn't work on and about something that was said but it wasn't said by us. Sounds like you have questions about the evidence that was collected and we are here to answer those questions. Take a deep breath and let's go forward."

The DA looked at me and asked, "I would like clarification — What did you think was going to be tested?"

"The physical evidentiary exam and the blood and urine samples," I answered.

The DA answered, "The San Francisco General Hospital SART Nurse and Doctor did a full-examination and interview. From what I've got here — there were no findings or observed injuries and no redness and no swelling. That is the principle thing the examiners look for. They would also take swabs for DNA. The urine and blood tests are for the toxicology report — You'd have to consent to that being done. My understanding is that you didn't consent."

"Yes — I did consent."

"Let me finish," he said.

"In cases with an 'unknown suspect,' DNA is used to identify the perpetrator. But in your case, that wasn't necessary. Mr. Henry never denied being 'intimate' with you, just that it was 'forced.' So, getting his DNA from you wouldn't change anything."

I shot back, "Fascinating. The Detective told me if the suspect hurt anyone else, my case would be reopened. The DNA testing matters. These exams can also identify repeat offenders."

The DA nodded, flipping through the CAL EMA 923 report. "I was concerned about the injuries, but I didn't see any observable ones. In our last meeting, you mentioned 'head trauma,' 'abdominal pain,' and 'burning,' but none of that was in the report."

I placed three folders on the desk and replied, "I've compiled these for you—the 'medical screening exam' records and serology tests, including the blood draw and urine sample. If the Detective had actually submitted them to the Crime Lab, they could've been used for toxicology."

The DA adjusted his glasses.

"Can I see that? And which part shows that rape occurred?"

handed him the purple folder—medical records, tests, HIPAA privacy law, the California 'Fresh Complaint' doctrine, the DFSA-Crime handbook, a sample of the CALEMA 923-form, and my two-page report on 'SFPD malfeasance and wrongdoing.'

"Here's the evidence," I said, pushing the folder toward him.

"I consented to the blood draw; these are the serology tests. The doctor reported intoxication. The Detective failed to submit these to the Crime Lab for toxicology, despite what he told me. The medical exams also show 'head trauma,' 'abdominal pain,' 'burning,' and 'suicidal tendencies.'"

I paused, then continued.

"I made this folder for you. The 923 form and toxicology report are police property—and since they weren't tested for six years, some of the evidence has deteriorated. It was destroyed."

I flipped through the pages within the folder.

"I went back to the same ER two days later. It says I was 'suicidal,' had 'vaginal burning,' 'fevers,' and couldn't concentrate. These are my outpatient records from the UCSF Trauma Recovery Center."

"The Detective never interviewed my witnesses—Kristy Eichlier, my closest friend at the time; my professor, whom I called from the ER to say I'd been raped and was terrified; or the SART doctors and counselor who saw me that night. They all would've spoken up. But he never asked. He wrote it off as 'he said, she said' and withheld the very evidence that disproved that narrative."

The DA brushed past it, unfazed.

"The Detective didn't withhold evidence," she announced. "Alright—We usually get the CAL EMA 923-form from the SART examiner to assess for signs of assault, and we have that in the case file."

"Then why is it documented in the ER medical screening?" I asked.

The DA deflected. "Maybe you told them—but not the SART Nurse. If you had, it would be in the CALEMA 923 report."

I was skeptical. "Why do only the police have a copy of the CALEMA 923?"

Those medical exams documented my injuries—key evidence for prosecution. The Detective withheld them, blocking a fact-based charging decision.

"Was he protecting the assailant?" I asked.

There was a pause. Then the Deputy DA questioned.

"When did you go to the ER?"

"Within a few hours of the rape."

"When did you report to the police?"

"I was at the ER first. The officers came to my apartment at 8 PM."

He frowned. "Then you were taken to the San Francisco General ER?"

"No — It was the ER first and then the officers came to my apartment."

He said, "The timeline is confusing—when exactly did the ER visit happen?"

"Rape happened at 2 AM. I went to the ER at 10 AM and spent six hours there. Police took my report that night at 8 PM."

The DA asked, "That morning—was it the ER here in San Francisco?"

"Yes," I replied. "The San Francisco General Hospital ER."

He paused, then repeated, "So that morning when you went to the ER—it was the one here in San Francisco?"

"Yes. The San Francisco General Hospital ER."

"Did you get the rape treatment then?"

"Yes."

He nodded slightly.

"So the earliest meeting you had with medical professionals was during the RTC examination?"

"Yes. That's when I first spoke with the SART nurse, the ER doctor, and the on-call UCSF TRC counselor."

The repetition wasn't accidental. It was a strategic form of circular questioning—designed to subtly erode the credibility of my consistent testimony. Though my answers were corroborated by medical records and protected under California Evidence Code § 1035.4, he continued to frame my responses as ambiguous, despite their factual clarity.

Instead of assessing my statements based on evidentiary standards, he distorted the inquiry into a credibility test, forcing me to repeatedly re-establish what was already documented.

This wasn't a pursuit of truth. It was an undue burden—shifting the weight of proof onto the victim. I wasn't just being asked to recall facts. I was being asked to relive, revalidate, and requalify my own trauma to satisfy a presumption of doubt. In that moment, I understood: the real issue wasn't memory. It was power. And the players in the system wield repetition like a weapon—to wear you down until even reality resembles hearsay.

DECONSTRUCTION

The Party told you to reject the evidence of your eyes and ears. It was their final, most essential command. —George Orwell, *1984*

The DA liked to play the devil's advocate.

"You didn't complain of any physical injuries during the exam."

I pushed back. "Then why are those injuries recorded in the ER medical screening?"

He leaned back. "I don't know—you'd have to explain that to me."

I lifted the folders I'd organized and held up the ER reports. "These were filled out by the ER doctor or SART nurse. This wasn't a different exam—why are you suggesting otherwise?"

He scrutinized the records. "When you reported the assault, you didn't mention head injuries or abdominal pain. They would've documented that. So you must've gone to a different ER later."

I was stunned. He was accusing me of falsifying records—implying I visited a second ER to manipulate evidence. I hadn't. I was terrified after the rape and went straight to San Francisco General. His distortion wasn't confusion—it was a tactic to undermine me.

Maybe he thought he was playing defense attorney in a courtroom. But this wasn't a trial. He was a Managing DA—and his job was to uphold justice, not weaponize doubt.

This kind of gaslighting from those entrusted to enforce the law is exactly why so many survivors stay silent. Reporting a felony shouldn't come with this kind of dehumanization.

"Mr. O'Connor—we're talking about the same ER. San Francisco General Hospital," I said, trying to ground the conversation.

Sophia jumped in, "There's the Rape Treatment Center and then there's the ER, correct?"

I paused. Were they truly confused—or pretending to be?

Was this genuine misunderstanding, or strategic doubt? After all, Sophia had said she'd worked as a Victim Services Advocate for ten years, and he'd been a Managing DA for thirty. I couldn't shake the feeling: they were gaslighting me.

"I'm still confused," the DA added, deflecting.

"There's nothing to be confused about," I replied firmly. "All these medical records are from the ER at San Francisco General Hospital—specifically, the RTC."

The room grew tense. They weren't just questioning me—they were asserting control by casting doubt on my memory, subtly rewriting the timeline, insisting things happened differently. It was classic psychological manipulation. Denying these records, or implying I went to a "different ER," conveniently allowed them to sidestep the medical evidence that could implicate Henry.

I glanced at Sophia. Her posture was poised—legs crossed, hands gently folded in a resting prayer on her thigh. She looked back at me calmly and explained, "We're just trying to clarify—did you go to a different ER, or were these exams recorded after you visited the RTC? We want to understand the timeline. Thank you for preparing the folders."

She smiled. I returned it, holding back my frustration.

"No problem," I replied.

"It's the same ER and SART nurse, so these medical exams must be included in the case file for a fair decision. I had physical injuries. Ms. Belrose—you told me HIPAA prevents medical records from being used in prosecution, but that's not true. I included the rule in the folders I prepared," I said firmly.

Sophia dismissed my point with a patronizing smile.
"I just want you to get some answers—and find closure for your mental health."

It felt like institutional gaslighting: deflect from the evidence, reframe the issue as emotional, and shift blame onto the survivor.

I stayed composed.

"Okay. I also included a copy of *People v. Brown* (1994)—the California Supreme Court's 'fresh complaint' doctrine. It clearly states that when a victim reports the assault shortly after it occurs, that statement is admissible. You've repeatedly told me it's inadmissible."

The DA cut in, sternly. "No—it's hearsay."

"It's not hearsay," I replied.

He doubled down. "Yes, it is."

Then, softening his tone just enough to reassert control, he added, "It's up to the court whether to allow it. It's not substantive evidence. It doesn't corroborate. Judges may consider it, but it's not a formal exception to hearsay—it just isn't, all right?"

I reflected on his words—condescending and an explicit contradiction.

What he was really saying was that it's up to the court—not him—to decide if the evidence is admissible. But that doesn't make it inadmissible by default. A more experienced sexual assault prosecutor might see it differently. A motion could be filed, and the evidence presented in court.

I held the statute in my hand and read aloud:
"The 'Fresh Complaint' doctrine allows testimony from someone the victim confided in shortly after the assault to corroborate her in-court testimony. While there's no statutory authority, California courts have long recognized its admissibility when the disclosure is made to someone the victim would naturally turn to for protection or advice."

The DA insisted, "It is not admitted for the truth of the matter — It's just to show that you made the complaint therefore it doesn't corroborate your account. There are exceptions to the rule against hearsay."

"An excited utterance is a legal exception to hearsay." The DA agreed with me, "That is correct."

"Yes — An example of an 'excited utterance' was when I had called my best friend Kristy Eichlier at 6AM shortly after the 3AM crime."

"Again — That just means you made the complaint," the DA replied.

I continued, "The 1975 'Mayberry Defense' you mentioned last time—something I had to look up—isn't applicable here. Henry entrapped me from the start. He insisted on driving because we were neighbors. I was 25, naive, with only two prior sexual partners. This wasn't a date—I told him I had a boyfriend.

Weeks earlier, he said he wanted to talk about career goals and life as a CEO in San Francisco. He used superficial charm to gain trust. In my Narrative, I describe how he ordered multiple strong drinks—whiskey, cognac, a wine tasting—far too much alcohol. He claimed to be a regular at BIX and said everything was fine.

The 'Mayberry Defense' doesn't apply. He's a predator. He committed a felony. He's a serial rapist."

The DA sounded annoyed, "That isn't what Mayberry stands for."

His mistake of fact was alarming. Legally, it means claiming such a deep misunderstanding of the situation that criminal intent is absent. In rape cases, it often means the accused *thought* there was consent—even when there wasn't.

I told police multiple times that Henry got me extremely intoxicated—and I believe he drugged me. The night felt calculated. Yet the SFPD repeatedly ignored this.

I pushed back: "The *Mayberry* defense claims a rapist avoids criminal intent if he *reasonably* believes there was consent. But I didn't have the capacity to consent. That's what they keep missing."

The DA's face tightened with disapproval.
Stubborn—just as I expected.

I held my ground. "I'm not a liar. I wouldn't go through all this if it weren't true. He's done this before—this was a calculated crime. The photos prove it. I'm not asking for sympathy. I'm asking for justice. For equal protection under the law."

After a brief pause, I asked, "Do you know what the Detective said when he told me the DA had closed the case?"

They stared back blankly.

"He said, 'If he had bought you roses and a plane ticket to Paris, would you still call it rape?'"

The words still burned. He betrayed me—and I was silenced. His comments were mind-numbing. I started failing classes. My work fell apart.

Sophia stepped in, deflecting. "I think we need to take a step back—we're here to respect one another."

I added, "So not only did the Detective withhold evidence, like the toxicology report, from the file he also hit on me when the case was closed. He sexually coerced and intimidated me. He requested many times that I should be his 'Mistress' and that I should have sex with him on a regular basis — A 40-yr Veteran Detective asked a victim of the crime he represented to do this?"

As the Sargent leaned back into her chair, she shook her head in disbelief.

Sophia responded, "Sounds like there is an unresolved anger."

"He mishandled the case—clear misconduct, negligence, and abuse of authority."

The Sargent shook her head again as she crossed her arms along her chest. Sophia wanted to redirect the conversation so she replied, "What I want us to focus on is the evidence that we have — I understand you are angry about it."

I declared, "Imagine if you were raped and next preyed upon by the Detective you believed was there to protect you."

Sophia said, "We are here to help you. The Sargent, ADA O'Connor and I are here to answer your questions. It's important to not take out this anger that is displaced out on us. It diverts the purpose of our conversation."

As I looked at the three of them, I wondered how many others had been hurt by the SFPD's inefficiency and dishonesty. "Thanks, but I feel the Detective's mishandling is why they're not cooperating."

Sophia responded, "New SFPD training and trauma-informed approaches are being implemented. I'm sorry this happened to you, but we're doing what we can. I don't want your healing to depend on what you can't control. We have to follow the law in these cases."

I countered, "The Detective withheld evidence. This case shouldn't be dismissed—I have the ER exams and the UCSF TRC Mental Health Summary from December 2019. This is strong corroborative evidence to prosecute."

Sophia continued, "Today we've been discussing one side. A defense attorney will find flaws in the testimony, as O'Conner and the Sergeant have explained. Charging the case would be a disservice to you. We believe we can't meet the burden of proof, and you'd face a Maddox-examination in court."

I saw through her attempt to use fear. "I understand, but we still have the burden of proof. We have the Doctors, Nurses, TRC psychologists, my Professor, and friends who will testify. We have everything we need to move forward—except your cooperation. This is a DFSA crime, unlawful restraint, and he's done this to other women."

There was a pause in the conversation.

I looked around and after a minute or so I asked, "No?"

"He's a serial rapist — It would be doing the community a disservice to not put him in jail."

"I was hoping that during this conversation, you'd be able to see things from our perspective," Sophia shot back at me, her words were measured, but there was an edge to them—a quiet reprimand.

"We have a 30-year District Attorney here, someone who knows what happens in court. Legal arguments supersede my knowledge. But I've been with the Victim Services Division for ten years. I sit in that courtroom all the time. I see what happens. I see how survivors are cMaddox-examined, how brutal it can be."

She exhaled, eyes narrowing.

"I've had victims scream, break down, have panic attacks on the stand. It's a disservice to them. To you. This is a loss you have to grieve. And half the time we've been sitting here, I think we've triggered you."

She leaned forward slightly, voice cooling.

"We are not here to make things worse."

The DA nodded.

"I agree with Ms. Belrose, we're not here to make things worse. Unfortunately, the answers we have to your questions might not be what you want to hear. I wish I could offer something that would ease your pain. The Doctors and SART Nurses you mentioned can't testify that you were raped. They can only testify that you said you were, but that's hearsay and not admissible."

He minimized my stance, continuing, "The friend you made the 'Fresh Complaint' to—that's considered an 'Excited Utterance.' She can testify that you said it, but it's not proof that rape happened. The nude photographs Mr. Henry took are part of the case file."

I responded, "I thought a nurse or a doctor's medical assessment was admissible?"

The DA interrupted, "A jury would hear Mr. Henry say he invited you to his place to watch Netflix. He'd say he asked if you'd feel comfortable taking off your pants, and you agreed."

"He tricked me into thinking it was for *art model* photos. He conned me—he entrapped me. Why are you saying the photos prove it wasn't rape? He put something in my drink."

"We have no evidence of that," the DA said flatly.

"Right. No evidence, because the Detective never submitted the request for toxicology. My blood and urine could've been tested. Why did the Detective lie about that?"

The DA ignored my question, shifting the blame. "This isn't about the Detective. What I'm saying is that it wouldn't sound non-consensual to a jury. You took your pants off, watched a movie in your underwear—it seems consensual. He performed oral sex on you, and after a couple of minutes, you said you weren't consenting."

I leaned forward.

"No. I kicked him away immediately. He ejaculated in me within three minutes. That's what you're misunderstanding. Did I let him perform oral sex for a couple of minutes? No."

I paused, my hands trembling as I clutched the ER reports.

"You're constructing a false narrative. Consent isn't measured in minutes. Consent isn't implied by a movie playing in the background. And the absence of toxicology isn't absence of truth—it's absence of diligence. As Kant warned, treating people as means rather than ends corrupts the very foundation of justice. Isn't that exactly what you're doing here—reducing me to evidence you find convenient, dismissing what doesn't fit the script?"

The DA responded, "What Ms. Belrose is getting at is that the Defense will argue the 'Mayberry Defense.' It states that if the perpetrator 'honestly and reasonably believes' the victim consented, he can't be guilty of the crime."

"That's ridiculous."

"He entrapped me. I fought him off. He threw his weight on top of me and raped me. I screamed. How could any man 'honestly and reasonably believe' that I consented? You'd have to be delusional. The 'Mayberry Defense' is dangerous—it would strip any victim of their power to seek justice."

The DA antagonized.

"Did he forcefully take your pants off?"

I retorted.

"No — He tricked me into thinking this was about art model pictures."

The DA continued.

The DA asked, "He didn't forcibly undress you and make you pose nude, did he?"

"No — He spiked my drink with drugs and alcohol, leaving me incapable of giving valid consent."

He pressed, "You did it, and you weren't unconscious, right?"

"I wasn't unconscious, that still doesn't give him the right to rape me."

Sophia interjected, "We're not blaming you. The DA is just explaining what the defense would argue if this went to trial. We don't support that outdated idea that this is somehow your fault. Don't be so hard on yourself."

"That's exactly right," the DA confirmed, leaning back.

Sophia hesitated, then added, "What I'm sensing is that you need to forgive yourself for the decision you made that night. I know the 'mistake of fact' Mayberry defense isn't something you want to hear, but I don't want you to carry the weight of self-blame."

"Maybe. But by the SFPD's standards, they view this as 'consensual sex' because I took my pants off for art model photos I was tricked into doing. Then I was blamed by the Detective and Sergeant for not leaving his condo—even after I told them I'd been drugged."

"No—don't misunderstand," Sophia said quickly. "You're assuming the SFPD sees this as consensual. What we're trying to determine is whether we can prove to a jury that it wasn't."

Silence settled over the room. Then the Sergeant spoke, her voice steady, rehearsed. "The Detective conducted a thorough investigation. He absolutely presented the facts of this case to the ADA at the time. He worked hard and wanted to move it forward. But the ADA declined. The way evidence was processed back then was different. Things have changed. We manage these cases differently now. The Detective did fight for you. There just wasn't enough evidence to proceed."

She denied what I already knew: the Detective was the reason there was no evidence. It was a textbook *Appeal to Authority Fallacy*—she claimed something was true simply because someone in authority said it, though those "authorities" were the ones who failed me.

The Detective. The Assailant. The Blue Wall of Silence, all closing in, protecting the SFPD's wrongdoing, discouraging me from asking the right questions.

The Sergeant's tone softened, almost sympathetic.

"What ADA O'Conner explained is that a judge won't say, 'Yes, this was sexual assault.' Neither I nor the Detective ever claimed it wasn't consensual. But what we can prove in court is another story. Sometimes I go home frustrated because we can't prove it. I'm sure Ms. Belrose and the ADA feel the same way."

Sophia nodded, almost instinctively.

FALSE DILEMMA FALLACY

Those who can make you believe absurdities can make you commit atrocities.— Voltaire

The DA adjusted his glasses, then spoke, his voice measured. "I supervise all areas of criminal prosecution. The men who commit these crimes? They're the worst of the worst. Worse than murderers, honestly. I've had cases where I absolutely believed the victim. But if I don't have enough evidence to prove it beyond a reasonable doubt, I can't file charges. I cannot sign a complaint."

A cold wave swept over me.

"How about the head trauma and injuries documented in my medical exam from that night?" I shot back. "Or the UCSF Trauma Recovery Center's outpatient mental health records?"

The DA studied me, eyes narrowing over his glasses, but his expression remained unreadable.

"I understand," he said calmly. "But the emotional impact? That's not surprising. And it doesn't prove what happened."

The words hit me like a dull thud. Dismissal, disguised as reason. Bureaucracy masking as objectivity.

Every time I brought up evidence—medical exams, expert diagnoses—he dismissed it. Accusations of me going to a "different ER," when I hadn't. Why was all of this being brushed aside? Why was everything I presented met with such indifference?

"I went to the ER for a six-hour forensic exam," I pressed, my voice sharp. "And then to UCSF TRC for twelve months! Why is that being ignored?"

The DA barely reacted. *"I understand. I get it."*

The deceptive nature of the conversation made me feel like I was sinking—drowning in a warped version of reality, like I had stumbled too deep into the matrix. My fingers tightened around my notebook as I forced myself to focus, to push forward.

"This protected health information gives individuals our rights," I stated, my voice firm. *"It allows disclosure to prevent serious threats to the safety of an individual or the public. I can report the PHI in the courtroom—to criminally prosecute. That's what I want to do."*

For a fraction of a second, the DA's expression remained composed, but something flickered in his eyes—something unreadable.

"You're saying the ER doctor can come into court and say, 'Yes, she was raped'? Well, that's not going to be admissible. It's considered hearsay. Unfortunately, these crimes don't happen in front of people, so they're challenging to prove."

The DA's statement is a textbook example of a false dilemma fallacy, presenting the prosecution of sexual assault as an either/or scenario: either the crime happens in front of an audience, or it is nearly impossible to prove. This ignores the vast spectrum of forensic, circumstantial, and testimonial evidence that can corroborate a survivor's account.

He also misapplies the legal concept of hearsay. Medical professionals do not simply echo a patient's words; they offer expert analysis grounded in physical evidence, trauma indicators, and toxicology reports. Their findings are clinical, not anecdotal.

This argument—the idea that medical testimony is inadmissible or insufficient—is designed to make conviction appear unattainable. It subtly shifts the burden of proof onto the survivor, ignoring the investigative failures that created the evidentiary gap in the first place. It sustains a systemic bias that protects perpetrators—a worldview in which, if rape isn't witnessed by a third party, it might as well not have happened at all.

I sat with his statement, turning it over in my mind. Countless crimes happen without an audience. No one sees the first punch thrown in a domestic violence case. No one watches a hacker siphon money from a stranger's bank account. A hitman doesn't leave witnesses. What proves the crime is the aftermath—the body, the weapon, the evidence. Not a crowd of spectators. But when it comes to rape, the absence of witnesses is somehow exonerating?

"So, what I've learned," I said slowly, measuring my words, "is that it's easy for the suspect to get away with rape."

I never imagined myself saying something so stark, so absolute. But it was statistically true. The numbers didn't lie. And the only way to change them was to dismantle the very mechanisms that kept them in place—the 1975 Supreme Court of California's *Mayberry Criminal Defense*, the rigid exclusion of *excited utterances* and *hearsay* that, in any other case, would be deemed valid. The rules were designed to protect the accused. The system, as always, had its priorities.

Sophia's voice softened, coaxing.

"No, it's not—don't let that be the takeaway. You've done activism for the community, raised awareness, stood up for other survivors. Focus on that. On empowerment. You've been brave. And you will have helped a lot of women. *As you know, 95% of survivors are women.*"

Her words had the polished tone of reassurance, but they left a hollow space where resolution should have been.

"You're overthinking this — The best thing you can do is not give him any thought!" Sophia asserted.

Puzzled by her dismissive response I reached for my Nalgene water bottle and thought to myself 'are you kidding me? Could it be any more obvious that she is protecting the SFPD?' This has been a nerve-wrecking experience and she just wants me to shut-up, go away and forget that it happened because that would be more convenient for them.

"Rose — It's giving him the power back. You're here at the District Attorney's Office to reclaim your power and I want you to see you to start 2020 fresh — I don't want you thinking about this. We are all human and you shouldn't be so hard on yourself. Think about the courage it took to report to the police and the guts it takes to be here today — We are here to support you."

"Really?"

There was a pause as my feelings of optimism or hope for justice vanished.

The Managing District Attorney looked at me with a calm yet stern expression. So I asked, "Mr O'Conner when we met in August—You said, 'there was something peculiar about this case' and I wondered what you meant?"

The DA looked at me and shook his head and replied, "I don't remember saying that so I have no idea — There isn't anything peculiar about this case per-se."

I listened to him and next I inquired, "It really stood-out to me that you said that! You don't remember?"

Sophia redirected the conversation with a light-hearted remark, "He calls me peculiar all the time." She giggled as the DA shifted the papers in his folder. I observed them and realized they wanted to discontinue the conversation.

<u>SHREDDER</u>

The past was erased, the erasure was forgotten, the lie became the truth.—George Orwell, *1984*

I placed my hand on the three folders and announced, "I made these for you — They document the felonies committed, the police misconduct, the unethical actions done that violate my rights and some of the missing medical records — like the serology tests that you claim I didn't consent to doing."

The fluorescent office lights in the ADA's office flickered. A small distraction, but it didn't break my focus.

"I was concerned the Sergeant did not have a copy of the toxicology results. The SFGH Office Manager said she didn't have one, and I didn't know if the Detective had messed with it. Typically—hospital medical records, law enforcement, and the crime lab will all have a record of it."

Sergeant V cut in swiftly. "We have it—we will always have it."

No explanation. No documentation. Just a statement meant to sound definitive enough to end the conversation.

Sophia quickly chimed in, layering the misdirection with praise.

"They have it—Look how knowledgeable you've become about the process."

I knew what was happening. Instead of directly addressing whether the toxicology report had been withheld or tampered with, they gave vague assurances—designed to sound like answers without actually answering anything.

Then came the pivot.

The Sergeant leaned forward, adopting a more personal tone. "All the women—like yourself—who have been in that horrible position and voiced their opinion as public awareness are enforcing citywide changes. You are one within the group of survivors that spoke for legislative change. Don't forget what you've done and how that now provides resources for others who are in your shoes—I'm not sure if that makes it any better."

A classic tactic: placation disguised as validation. They weren't addressing the injustice; they were reframing it. A subtle way of saying: *Be satisfied with what you've done. Stop pushing for answers.*

"Yes—Sergeant, it's true, that is the positive. Thank you. Supervisor Ronen proposed the new legislation for the new human rights committee, and she asked me to speak at the City Hall conference."

Sophia urged, her voice soft, almost coaxing. "Hold onto those empowering moments."

I knew exactly what they were doing. The sudden shift from institutional failure to empowerment was meant to steer me away from pressing further. To make me feel acknowledged, while discouraging me from demanding accountability.

Because the truth was simple: they didn't want me asking any more questions.

I replied, "It's been a puzzle and I have a general question — In 2016 the Federal Government gave millions of dollars to Crime Labs around the country to enable them to catch up on 'rape kit backlog' Did San Francisco receive funding from the State and Federal Government to do this?

The DA vaguely replied, "We are caught up." Next the Sargent added, "We started to do that in 2014 — We're one of the 1st and largest US City Police Departments that has caught-up with our 'rape kit' analysis for the last 2-yrs now."

Sophia and the DA confirmed, "Yes."

There was another long pause. I pressed for clarity.

"So, the Detective withheld evidence. He let the toxicology spoil because he never submitted the request form to the crime lab. Maybe you got the 923 form—but not the rape kit, not the Tox Screen. And the charging decision was made without any of that?"

The Sergeant said, "For whatever reason—no toxicology testing was submitted to the crime lab by the Nurse Practitioner. I've explained this before, but it's still unclear. The Medical Examiner's Office never received the samples. The RTC told me that if they did take those samples, *you may have declined the tests that day*."

I responded firmly, "I consented. The blood draw is standard protocol."

I paused, then added, "In November, I got an official copy of those tests from the OM at Medical Records. The samples existed. They could have been used for toxicology. They just never were."

"If you alluded to a *change of mind* about the blood draw analysis during the forensic medical examination, the SART Nurse would have followed your directions. It's your call, your body—obviously, they're not going to do something you haven't consented to."

Was she really fabricating a *women's rights* statement to throw me off—invoking "choice" only when it absolved the Detective of his duty?

Henry never had my consent. And the Detective's duty wasn't optional: he was required to submit the request form to the crime lab so my kit could be tested while the investigation was still active. He didn't.

Sophia jumped in, her voice syrupy with reassurance.

"Yes—the nurses won't do anything you don't want them to do."

I locked eyes with them, letting the weight of their hypocrisy settle.

"Unlike Henry."

Their faces went blank, as if I'd just pointed out an inconvenient typo in their carefully rehearsed script.

"I signed off on the exams. So why are we playing this little game—pretending the Detective's negligence is somehow my fault?"

I could feel the tactic: wear me down, push me toward surrender.

The tactic wasn't aimed at me alone—it was designed to make us all surrender. To wear us down until compliance feels inevitable. This is institutional betrayal at its core: a system that relies on exhaustion, coercion disguised as procedure. The system counts on it. It always has.

The irony wasn't lost on me—Sergeant V feigning concern about my consent for a routine ER blood draw, but not for the drug-facilitated assault itself. And the contradiction was glaring: back in March, she admitted the Detective didn't think the six-hour forensic exam was "important." That's why no toxicology report exists—because he never submitted the Crime Lab Request Form.

And then came the final contradiction. Back in March, Sergeant V herself admitted the Detective didn't think the six-hour forensic exam was "important." That's why no toxicology report exists—because he never submitted the Crime Lab Request Form.

This wasn't an oversight. It was a decision. His decision.

They dodge accountability for the so-called 'missing' corroborative evidence by pointing fingers—at the ER nurses, at me. And somehow, the CAL EMA 923-form is conveniently absent from the hospital's medical records. When I asked the OM about it, she seemed alarmed. "Do you have a lawyer?" she asked. Because apparently, the only copy of the 923-form is in SFPD's possession.

Sophia redirected the conversation, "Focus on the positives and empowerment — The work you've accomplished as an activist has brought change. Do you have plans over the weekend?"

I replied, "I do."

She answered, "Great — I want you to leave this negativity and the terrible memory behind in this room Rose."

A surge of energy rose from within, my eyes filled with tears yet met their gazes.

"I wouldn't have spent weeks preparing these folders, gathering legal references, if this felony hadn't happened. I included the Federal Rules of Evidence on Exceptions to the Rule Against Hearsay, the HIPAA Privacy Rule, and others."

placed my hand on the three folders and announced,
"I made these for you — They document the felonies committed, the police misconduct, the unethical actions that violate my rights, and some of the missing medical records — like the serology tests you claim I didn't consent to doing."

The fluorescent office lights in the ADA's office flickered. A small distraction, but it didn't break my focus.

"I was concerned the Sergeant did not have a copy of the toxicology results. The SFGH Office Manager said she didn't have one, and I didn't know if the Detective had tampered with it. Typically—hospital medical records, law enforcement, and the crime lab will all have a record of it."

Sergeant V cut in swiftly. "We have it—we will always have it."

I froze, her words slicing the air like a blade. *Shredder.* Not the machine in the corner office, but the villain from my childhood—the armored nemesis in *Teenage Mutant Ninja Turtles,* master of destruction, always lurking in the shadows. For a moment, the line between comic book villain and institutional power blurred. The same menace.

Victims who report to law enforcement often become victims of the blue code too. The SFPD and DA's Office won't hold their own accountable—it's an unspoken rule, an unbreakable pact. They listened, sure. But the moment I presented facts that threatened their narrative, they dug in.

The *blue shield of silence* is real. And yet, they still let perpetrators frame the dialogue.

I eyed Sophia, skeptical. She offered a soothing smile. "Rose—I want to do a quick mental health check-in before you go. The Sergeant and ADA O'Conner have another meeting."

The DA meticulously arranged his briefcase, the Sergeant already halfway to the door. Then, as if on cue, she turned back, extending her hand.

"Do you want me to make this folder part of the case-file?"

"Yes."

The word left my lips, steady—but inside, I wondered if I had just handed truth to the shredder in disguise.

Straightaway, she tucked my work into the police case file—a beige portfolio thick with omissions.

The DA adjusted his coat.

The Sergeant smiled, confidently.

"Best of luck to you."

I held my ground, offering a tight nod.

"Take care."

And just like that, they were gone.

I left the office, moving quickly through the seemingly endless hallways, then stepped into the silver 1960s elevator and rode it down to the lobby. Past the police officers, through the heavy doors—I was out. Exhausted. Exhilarated. Outside the Hall of Justice, I slipped in my AirPods, queued up TOOL—enigmatic, dark, defiant—and ran.

CHAPTER 22: MARCH 2020 – THE PANDEMIC

During California's COVID-19 lockdown, I saw an opening. With professionals working remotely, I reached out to Aaron Berdychiv, an associate attorney at an international firm in San Francisco. I knew he'd be home—and I needed his insight.

By protocol, both San Francisco General Hospital and SFPD should have copies of my forensic exam. But when I requested the records from a Sergeant at the Special Victims Unit, she refused—claiming she couldn't release them. I told Aaron. He listened, clearly unsettled. "This process is…" he muttered, trailing off in frustration. Sensing something was off, he drafted a simple, strategic email to the DA's Victim Services Division to test their response.

SUBJECT: CALEMA 923-FORM

Good Morning,

I hope you are all staying healthy during this difficult time. I am an attorney trying to point a self represented friend in the right direction. She suffered a sexual assault several years ago, and she would like to receive copies of all record of the testing that went on following her reporting of the assault. Specifically, this is in reference to the CALEMA 923. She has not been able to get a copy of it. Would she need to serve a subpoena on the SFPD Custodian of records? Or is there another, less obstructive way to help get the records she needs relating to the horrific events that happened to her. She has had to go to numerous offices and medical centers to piece things together, and it is quite frustrating to see that victims cannot get straight answers - especially in light of the current understanding as to how sexual assault has been treated in this country.

Thank you for your assistance.

Best Regards,
Aaron Berdychiv

On March 30, 2020, Aaron received a reply from the District Attorney's Office—ironically written by my Victim Services Advocate, who didn't realize he had emailed on my behalf.

RE: CALEMA 923-FORM

Dear Mr Berdychiv,

I hope this finds you well. I am in receipt of your email and understand that you are asking for the procedure to request the CALEMA-923 form which is the documentation of the sexual assault forensic exam. Through my experience this form is considered a law enforcement form and part of the investigative file through the police department, and is not distributed outside of law enforcement. However, under CA AB 1312 Victims Rights which was amended 2017-2018 it does highlight that victims must be informed of the following:

Whether or not the evidence is analyzed within 120 days of your assault, Whether or not a DNA profile of your assailant was developed from the evidence, Whether or not the DNA profile of your assailant has been entered into the law enforcement database, Whether or not the DNA profile of your assailant matches a DNA profile contained in the law enforcement database. Full text of CA AB 1312 Victims Rights can be retrieved by clicking the weblink: http://leginfo.legislature.ca.gov/faces/billTextClient.xhtml?bill

In your email, you mentioned the assault occurred several years ago. I recommend first confirming the status of the rape kit. While this isn't the same as accessing the documents, it may help your friend in their healing process. If you provide a police report number, I can contact SFPD to identify a point of contact and share that information with you. Please note: an SFPD representative will need to speak directly with the victim. If you'd like to proceed with serving a subpoena to SFPD Legal, their number is (415) 777-9994. Let me know if you'd like me to follow up with a sergeant—just send the report number. I hope this is helpful, and I look forward to hearing from you.

Best Regards,
Sophia Belrose
Pronouns: she/her/hers
Victim/Witness Advocate/ Team Lead-Sex Assault/Human Trafficking Unit
Office of District Attorney Chesa Boudin
working remotely may have limited capacity to respond or assist

CHAPTER 23: REBIRTH

The courage to confront evil and turn it by the dint of will into something applicable to the development of our evolution, individually and collectively, is exciting and honorable
— Maya Angelou

Recovery begins with an instinct—an urgent pull to reclaim, to self-preserve, to *fight back*. Reporting the crime took courage. What followed was a gauntlet: working with law enforcement meant enduring peri-traumatic dehumanization, humiliation, and re-victimization. But I dove in anyway. I demanded answers. I researched every detail of the investigation, trying to understand where it all went wrong.

Every time I sought justice, I collided with the *Blue Code*—an unspoken allegiance that shields the system from accountability. The SFPD didn't just mishandle my case; they buried it. Obstructed it. Twisted reality to protect their own.

And the personal cost? My voice—*literally*. I developed a psychogenic disorder, my body manifesting what the system had drilled into me: *your words are meaningless*. My voice trembled, weakened, as if coerced into submission.

But I lost more than my voice. I lost my sense of self—eroded by a system that manipulated, coerced, and gaslit me at every turn. A system that expected me to disappear. To endure. To stay silent in the face of injustice.

Recovery isn't just about healing—it's about survival. It demands perseverance, an unrelenting will to rise above the weight of institutional betrayal. I had moved to San Francisco to build my future—to earn my Master's degree, to launch my career, to work my way up to becoming a powerful and successful art director. Instead, I found myself unraveling the very system I had once believed in.

There's an intelligence—an intuitive, *sixth sense*—that enriches our lives, if we're paying attention. And I had to pay attention. Self-examination wasn't just a practice; it was my lifeline. If I wanted to reclaim myself, I had to confront the unconscious material I had absorbed—strip it down, analyze it, *understand* it. To live truthfully, to live *fully*, is to pursue the realization of one's true potential.

This led me to psychology. To the works of Abraham Maslow, Carl Jung, the existentialists.

Jung's teachings, in particular, struck a nerve. He argued that to heal, we must first understand the unconscious forces shaping our reality—only then can we change the future. But knowledge is a double-edged sword. The more I learned, the more I *felt*—elation, devastation, the crushing weight of truth.

So what comes from enduring adversity? Life tested me. It betrayed me. Heartbroken, I attempted suicide more than once. I didn't know how to navigate the PTSD, the hypervigilance, the erratic thoughts tearing through my mind like a storm. I needed a role model—someone who embodied the kind of unshakable strength I longed for.

Beatrix Kiddo. The Warrior Heroine of *Kill Bill.*

She was adrenalized for justice. She moved like the world depended on it. And maybe, in some ways, it did. Watching her, something in me shifted. I stopped fearing risk. This transformation—this rebirth—wasn't born out of hope, but *self-preservation.* It's a tale of redemption and responsibility, twisted and bittersweet in its own way. But here's the tricky part—compassion. *Self-care?* Yah, right. I'd rather have a double shot of clase azul tequila.

Too much had been stripped from me. Only my intellect withstood the storm—so I buried it like a diamond, sharp and untouchable, and pretended I knew nothing.

The emotional wounds lingered. Like eight million needles piercing straight through my heart. I fell into a self-destructive rhythm, a cycle I couldn't break. I would binge-drink until I blacked out, trying to numb the pain, but it only fractured me further. It was a self-inflicted wound, a temporary escape that only created a new set of problems.

Alcohol rewired my brain, silencing the parts of me that remembered, that analyzed, that wanted to understand. The hippocampus—the seat of memory, of learning, of rational thought—dulled under its influence. But the pain never truly disappeared. It just bled into something else.

Then came the mania. A reckless, hyper-energetic spiral that felt better than sadness, better than doubt. I preferred chaos over quiet. I would rather burn through life at full speed than sit still long enough to feel the weight of what had been done to me. But acting out came at a cost—I lost friendships. I was misunderstood, dismissed. People walked away, leaving behind nothing but the hollow phrase, *Good luck.* I came to associate those two words with abandonment, with pain.

Metamorphosis is inevitable after tragedy. It breaks you or it remakes you. *If you let it.* It can forge willpower, strength, wisdom—but only if you choose to see it that way. Perspective is everything. It dictates choices, sets off butterfly effects that ripple through the rest of your life.

For me, this metamorphosis led to an obsession with justice and law. But years ago, I was naïve. I thought justice was *simple.* That if I reported a crime, it would be taken seriously. That evidence meant something. That a perpetrator would face consequences.

Kafka wrote, *"He found himself transformed in his bed into a monstrous vermin."* I thought reporting the crime would bring justice, but instead, I became the problem. The accused. The inconvenience. I wasn't transformed into something monstrous—but the system made me feel as if I had.

The kind of person who intellectualizes their problems—who dissects them, who analyzes them in search of understanding—is often someone trying to impose order on chaos. This is a defense mechanism known as *intellectualization,* a cognitive strategy used to detach from overwhelming emotions by focusing on logic, reason, and abstract thought. It's a way to regain control. A survival instinct.

For trauma survivors, intellectualization becomes a fortress—a way to process what happened without being consumed by the raw, unbearable weight of emotion. It's a form of self-preservation, a way to stay functional when reality feels incomprehensible. Sigmund Freud identified intellectualization as a defense mechanism that distances an individual from distress, preventing emotional flooding. Cognitive-behavioral psychologists recognize it as a coping strategy often employed by those with high analytical tendencies—people who seek answers, who refuse to be lost in the abyss of their own suffering.

For me, intellectualizing my trauma became second nature. Emotion was too painful, too unwieldy, so I converted my experiences into ideas. I reflected, I analyzed, I tried to understand. It was easier to study history, law, psychology—anything that could provide structure—than to sit with the unbearable truth.

And what did I learn?

Reporting the crime wasn't difficult—it was devastating. It was numbing. A battle against a system rigged against the victim. Now, I understand why so many choose silence over the crushing weight of disbelief. The process is designed to exhaust you, to make you question yourself until you surrender.

But I refuse.

Perseverance in the face of deception is necessary. When the establishment builds a false narrative, you must resist the temptation to accept it. Sometimes, the only player left on the battlefield is you. And you have to believe in yourself, even when no one else does.

To understand the present, we must unearth the past—history is our greatest teacher. It exposes mankind's fallibility, the way jurisdictions will conceal their own weaknesses. Truth is not always what we are told; it is what survives scrutiny. What we accept as fact today may one day be revealed as an illusion. That is why we must always examine, cMaddox-examine, and question.

For survivors, trauma is rarely a single event. It compounds. It follows you. Repeated violations, systemic failures, ongoing psychological damage—it all accumulates, leaving behind an insidious kind of pain. The kind that doesn't just fade with time. The kind that burrows into your choices, your relationships, your self-worth. It manifests in ways we don't always see at first: depression, anxiety, complex PTSD, addiction, self-destruction.

And so, I reflect. I analyze. I intellectualize. Because understanding is the only weapon I have left.

Your path forward will never be without obstacles. But true transformation—deep, lasting evolution—requires consciousness, perseverance, and the willingness to grow beyond what you once believed possible. The goal of an evolved life is self-actualization: to transcend tragedy, to break through perceived limitations, to become the fullest expression of who you are.

Close your eyes. What do you want? You must see it first—hold the vision in your mind before you can take the steps to make it real. But here's the truth: your worth is not defined by institutions, by validation, or by how others perceive you. I made that mistake too many times—constructing my reality on acceptance and rejection, mistaking someone else's judgment for truth.

Purpose is greater than perception. It is cultivated through focus, discipline, and resilience. If you are willing to confront the deepest parts of yourself—to illuminate the hidden corridors of your mind—you will reclaim, redefine, and reinvent your reality.

But of course, there are days I forget this. Days when I lose myself. What creates that drift? Maybe it's the delicate tension between control and surrender—the push and pull of order and chaos, the state of flow.

What I do know is this: I've become hyper-aware of the subconscious programming I adopted in response to trauma. The survival mechanisms. The illusions. The parts of myself I buried. I wanted to understand my shadow—the unseen forces that shape me, the hidden self Carl Jung spoke of.

This journey—to recover, to rise above the fractures of the past—has been brutal. But it is necessary. True power comes from self-knowledge. To influence anything—your life, society, existence itself—you must first understand it.

A person is only as free as their mind allows. When people operate in a state of enforced ignorance—clinging to illusions that preserve the status quo—the shadow only grows stronger. Every aspect of the unconscious self that remains unexamined, untransformed, becomes an obstacle, a silent force impeding progress.

There is nothing more terrifying than confronting the deepest, most hidden corners of the psyche. But there is also nothing more rewarding. Recovery is not a static destination—it is a dynamic process, rooted in psychotherapy, introspection, and relentless self-examination.

I have been examining the limitations of the mind, studying the systems that keep us trapped. True transformation begins with radical honesty—with the willingness to admit where change is needed, to acknowledge the places inside ourselves that must shift.

A HEALING BODY AWARENESS EXERCISE

Self-Reflection (svadhyaya) is a tool, not only to access where we've been, but where we're going! There are techniques from many traditions and disciplines on how to do this. Here is one formula that I found that works:

1. How is my breath? Is it short, hurried, deep, slow, erratic, grounded? Before we can use our body/mind to reflect on our lives, we need to fuel it with oxygen.

2. How is my body? What am I feeling and where? Do certain events seem to trigger areas of my body? Is the sensation of pain or pleasure influencing my choices? What is my gut telling me about what my heart is telling me? Intelligence only gives the illusion it lives in the mind, the body is also wildly intelligent, listen to it.

3. Can I accept what is happening right now? Before we can change, evolve, or impact a situation, we have to meet it just as it is.

4. What do I need or want? At the root of all action is a desire.

In the summer of 2015, I lived in the lush tropics of Costa Rica's Nicoya Peninsula, immersed in a 300-hour vinyasa yoga teacher training. There, I studied anatomy, physiology, spiritual discipline, and the ancient philosophy of yoga—eventually becoming a certified Jivamukti teacher.

The training was transformative. It deepened my understanding of the five tenets of Jivamukti: *shāstra* (scripture), *bhakti*(devotion), *ahimsa* (nonviolence), *nāda* (sound), and *dhyāna* (meditation). But it was the fifth Niyama, *Ishvara-Pranidhana*—surrender to a higher purpose—that stayed with me. To root deeply into the earth while aligning with something vast and unseen. To let go of self-imposed limits and step into the life I was meant to live.

Nosara, one of the world's five Blue Zones, radiated healing. On one side, the Pacific; on the other, wild jungle. I was surrounded by seventy classmates from across the globe, all seeking transformation. And yet—even in paradise—trauma surfaced.

I still felt it in my body: fear of my own power. Fear of leadership. Deep down, I knew I was meant to embody courage, to empower, to heal. But that purpose terrified me. The psychogenic voice disorder, the dyslexia, the hyperactive PTSD—it all collided, forming a silent, immovable barrier inside me.

I struggled with something so simple: speaking. The most basic yoga instructions—Sun Salutation A, Sun Salutation B, the Jivamukti *Spiritual Warrior* sequence—became impossible to articulate. I was standing in the center of a class, thirty people moving in *Downward-Facing Dog*, waiting for me to guide them. My mind went blank. I stumbled over my words, lost in nervousness—not because I lacked the knowledge, but because San Francisco had conditioned me to believe my voice was powerless. That no one would listen. That no one cared. I needed to unlearn the silence I had been forced into. To recognize my own voice as something worthy.

In the *pranamaya kosha*, the energy body, there are 72,000 *nadis*—channels through which prana, or life force, flows. Three are most important: *Ida* (left, lunar, feminine), *Pingala* (right, solar, masculine), and *Sushumna*, the central axis of the body. When prana moves freely through *Sushumna*, the mind stills, and the yogi finds balance. But if energy is blocked in the *nadis*, it cannot rise. There must be a process of unraveling, of releasing, of purging stagnation so that the path becomes clear.

Awareness reveals that energy does not move at random—it follows patterns, pathways, conditioning. *Ida* and *Pingala* embody duality: the interplay of Shiva and Shakti, masculine and feminine, light and dark. *Sushumna* is beyond duality, beyond identity—a space of pure potential. It is the void from which transformation is born. And I was standing on the precipice of that void, ready—or perhaps finally willing—to step through.

HOW CAN THE 8-LIMB PATH BRING HAPPINESS?

This is how we get people to connect with their authentic self. They have to go through all these layers of conditioning. They don't know how to evolve their authentic selves so we start giving them tools and feedback. You have to break out of your box of conditioned response and learn how to do this from your authentic self instead of from your conditioned self. Anna Forrest

In Master Patañjali's first yoga sutra he writes in Sanskrit "Atha yoganushasanam," which means now begins the instruction of yoga. I will explain to you how divine concentration made possible by following the 8-Limb Path can help you rediscover the happiness that intrinsically lives within you. Life is multidimensional and challenging, finding one's true happiness within the chaos is an art. I believe nothing is perfect besides Fibonacci numbers and the golden spiral. And, the real or imaginary terrors of everlasting meaninglessness can seem daunting especially when all we want to do is excel, live powerfully and work to manifest our dreams into reality.

In the *Yoga Sutras of Patañjali,* Master Patañjali divided his philosophical knowledge into four chapters and is the structural framework of yoga. The objective of this ancient text is to assist the practitioner into a more profound and more meaningful awareness of themselves and the connectedness they share with all of existence. Peace, good health, and harmony with the greater whole.

It takes great balance and equanimity to live a mindset of The 8-Limb Path also known as *Ashtanga* is a yogi map, and is a set of powerful rituals to live by which will bring radical change.

The first limb is Yama. It is one's ethical standards and integrities, i.e., the golden rule "do unto others as you would like done to you." There are five of them.

1. Ahimsa — compassion for all beings or non-violence
2. Satya — a commitment to truthfulness
3. Astaya — non-stealing, take nothing that doesn't belong to us
4. Brahmacharya — sense control, preserving prana to enhance a heightened spiritual connection 5. Aparigraha — letting go of our attachment to things, understanding impermanence

The second limb is Niyama. It is self-discipline and spiritual observances. Niyama means "rules" or "laws." These are the rules prescribed for personal observance. Like the yamas, the five niyamas are not exercises or actions to be simply studied and are more than an attitude. Compared with the yamas, the niyamas are more intimate and personal.

1. Saucha — cleanliness and purity
2. Santosa — contentment, modesty and feeling content with what we have
3. Tapas — disciplined use of energy, keeping the body fit with burning desire to learn
4. Svadhyaya — self-study, let go of self-destructive behavior
5. Isvara-Pranidhana — surrender the fruits of your actions to God or a higher power

The third limb is Asana, which translates to "seat." To the ancient Egyptians, the Goddess Isis was the divine quintessence of perfection. The hieroglyph for Isis resembles a chair or seat, and it represents the connectedness to the Earth that enabled Isis to remain whole.

Yoga can restore and ground the practitioner to remember what is important. B.K.S. Iyengar adds, "the needs of the body are the needs of the divine spirit which lives through the body. The yogi does not look heavenward to find God for he knows that He is within." Using asanas to challenge and open the physical body enables us to connect with the unseen elements of our being and ultimately shape and empower our lives through our responses to the outside world.

The fourth limb is Pranayama. It is breath control awareness that is designed to gain mastery of the respiratory process. Pranayama controls the energy (prana) within the organism, in order to restore and maintain health and to promote evolution. Our prana flows up and down the Ida and Pingala, inhaling as it rises in the Ida and exhaling as it descends in Pingala. As the yogi follows the proper rhythmic patterns of slow deep breathing ", the patterns strengthen the respiratory system, soothe the nervous system and reduce craving. As desires and cravings diminish, the mind is set free and becomes a fit vehicle for concentration."

The fifth limb is Pratyahara. The word ahara means "nourishment"; pratyahara translates as "to withdraw oneself from that which nourishes the senses." Pratyahara is the key to the relationship between the outer and inner aspects of yoga; it shows us how to move from one to the other. Swami Sivananda said Pratyahara is the most important limb in yoga sadhana. A sensory withdrawal technique is to focus the mind on inner impressions, thus removing attention from external impressions. We can create our own inner impressions through the imagination.

The sixth limb of Patanjali's Ashtanga Yoga is Dhāraṇā. We develop our powers of concentration in the previous three limbs of posture, pranayama, and withdrawal of senses. When you practice Dharana, sit in a comfortable position, close your eyes and focus on something within you, and your mind becomes peaceful because you are essentially focusing on one thing at a time.

The seventh limb is Dhya‾na, which means meditation. The mind is still, and it is a form of non-sensual happiness. The purpose of practicing meditation is to achieve "oneness" or communion with the universe...where you can pull away from the limitations of the body and mind to connect with infinite potential.

The eighth limb of this practice is Samadhi or the absolute state of ecstasy or pure consciousness. The mind and the intellect have stopped, and there is only the experience of consciousness, truth, and unutterable joy. Samadhi means "to bring together, to merge," where the conscious mind drops back into that unconscious oblivion from which it first came.

CHAPTER 24: SFPD LEGAL DEPARTMENT

San Francisco Police Department
6 January 2021

Rose Visjonær
San Francisco, CA

Reference: #P020041-113020
Re: Public Records Request, dated November 30, 2020

Dear Miss Visjonær:

The San Francisco Police Department (SFPD) received your Public Records Act request, dated November 30, 2020. You requested:

"Dear SFPD Public Records Portal, I would like a copy of my CALEMA 923. Forensic Medical Report Sexual Assault Examination and toxicology report. When I spoke with Sergeant V. at the SVU (March 2019) I found out for the first time it was finally tested in 2016 and a DNA-profile of the assailant was developed from the evidence. She told me to go to the Legal Department to request it and I did and they told me they would not give me a copy of the forensic medical report on a Tox Screen. So I went to the San Francisco General Hospital Medical Records Department ('November 2019) and requested the CALEMA 923. The Office Manager said that ONLY the SFPD have a copy and that she felt concerned that SFGH Medical Records did NOT have a copy. Next I had a meeting at the DA's Office inside the HOJ with Sergeant V., DA O'Conner and the Victim Services Associate (December 2019). The Sergeant told me that she already showed me a copy of the CALEIvIA 923 in our last meeting but she never did.When I asked all three of them if I could have a copy they told me to move on. I prepared folders of medical evidence that I was able to retrieve from the SFGH Medical Records and one of them asked if they could "shred the folders and to not give this anymore thought. "This has been a confusing process; I need a copy of it for my health records. Can you please send me a copy of the CALEMA 923 and the toxicology report from the date of the crime (02-23-2010)? I sought medical care for my injuries immediately at SFGH ER and was therefore the 6hr examination. Sincerely, Rose Visjonær"

Dear Miss Rose Visjonær,

Subject: CALEMA-923 — Forensic Medical Report and Toxicology Results

Please be advised that the forensic medical examination and toxicology report are protected from public disclosure under California Government Code § 6254(f), which exempts information that may compromise an ongoing investigation, related investigation, or law enforcement proceeding.

If you have any questions, please contact Sergeant Sullivan at (415) 837-7898. Thank you for your attention to this matter.

Sincerely,
Lieutenant R. Andrew Smith

DEPUTY DISTRICT ATTORNEY MARSHALL KENT

Do not appeal to people's mercy or gratitude. Appeal to their self-interest instead. — Robert Greene, The 48 Laws of Power

March 2021: During a call with Advocate Ms. Belrose from the Victim Services Division at the DA's Office, she disclosed the name of the Deputy District Attorney who had reviewed the detective's incomplete investigative file. Without hesitation, I looked him up and dialed the office of Assistant District Attorney Marshall Khine.

The phone rang. He answered directly.

"Hi, is Mr. Marshall Kent available?"

"This is he. How can I help you?"

"Hello. I recently learned that you were the Deputy DA who reviewed a drug-facilitated sexual assault case in which I was the victim. Would it be possible to receive a letter from you stating why the case was dismissed, and when?"

"Yah, generally we do not issue letters like that. The SFPD Incident Report is more often than not the information that victims are able to obtain. There was not a formal warrant presented to our office; rather, it was a consultation with the department at the time."

"I have a copy of the Incident Report. You mean a consultation with the Special Victims Unit detective?" I asked.

"I'm not even sure it was called the Special Victims Unit back then," the ADA replied. "The department name has changed over time."

"Is there a form I can fill out—something your office could complete—that states when the case was dismissed and why? It's just that—"

The ADA cut me off. "Sophia Belrose, the Victim Services Advocate, typically handles those kinds of questions. Let me check with her and have her reach out."

It was a familiar move: deflection through bureaucracy. Still, I pressed. "She's actually the advocate I've been working with. But will it be possible to get that letter?"

"No," the Deputy District Attorney said flatly. "I'm not aware of any form or letter our department has ever issued to a survivor indicating what was discussed with the assigned detective."

I paused, then asked carefully, "Mr. Kent—did you base the charging decision on what the SVU Detective presented during that consultation?"

"Correct. Your case did not advance beyond pre-filing. You'll need to speak with the advocate."

Mr. Kent showed little regard for accountability, often circling back to the same logic: *The case didn't proceed because the evidence wasn't sufficient—because the case didn't proceed.* It was circular reasoning, wrapped in legal formality, devoid of transparency.

Contra spoliatorem omnia praesumuntur—disadvantage is presumed against the wrongdoer. This legal maxim underscores a core principle: the duty to preserve evidence, especially when litigation is foreseeable.

But the SFPD failed that duty. Their mishandling of the DFSA-investigation led to the loss—*the spoliation*—of critical toxicology evidence. It was a violation not only of ethical standards, but of California law.

Under Government Code § 6254, investigative records must be preserved. Their failure also contravened the Victims' DNA Bill of Rights, codified in Penal Code § 680. These are not obscure policies—they are mandatory legal obligations. Yet the system treated it as optional. Justice demands evidence—not narrative control or bureaucratic deflection.

Was that delivered here? No.

What emerged was a pattern of evasion, omission, and indifference.

I once believed the system was built to protect us. Instead, survivors are left with fractured lives and missing evidence—while the system looks away. Lady Justice is meant to be blind. Not complicit.

CHAPTER 25: CIVIL RIGHTS ATTORNEY

Injustice anywhere is a threat to justice everywhere. We are caught in an inescapable network of mutuality, tied in a single garment of destiny. Whatever affects one directly, affects all indirectly. — Martin Luther King Jr.

Esq. J.D. M.A. Attorney Atticus adjusted his tie, leaning back in his chair. He was sharp and commanding—a tall, poised African American man with warm, intelligent eyes and an understated confidence that came from years of courtroom experience. He exuded an aura of confidence, honed from his stellar academic career as a top graduate of UC Berkeley, where he had cultivated the effortless poise of one accustomed to being listened to, respected, and sought after.

"Yeah, things are good," he said. "I'm staying safe during the pandemic. It's kinda hot outside today—for the city at least. So, you're meeting with the DA's office tomorrow—what time?"

"Four o'clock. It's a Zoom meeting. I can forward you the link if you'd like."

His office in San Francisco's Dogpatch neighborhood was sharp and minimalist—floor-to-ceiling bookshelves, a sleek walnut desk, and a framed diploma from Berkeley Law mounted on the wall behind him. It caught the light just enough to be noticeable—a quiet reminder of the authority he carried.

"Yeah, send it to me."

"Okay, four o'clock. How long do you think it'll last, Rose?"

"I think around forty minutes."

He drummed his fingers on the desk, thoughtful.

"Forty minutes. Alright. And you want me to observe? See what direction they're taking the case?"

"Yes, that would be incredible. I've spoken to the SVU Sergeant, and I've spoken to Managing District Attorney O'Conner. It would just be really helpful if you were there. I feel like they'd take the situation more seriously if you were present. You have a strong presence." I paused. "And maybe, finally, we can hold them accountable for their misconduct. Maybe they'll actually move forward and press charges against Henry. They always have some excuse. But if they don't, can you?"

Atticus sighed, adjusting his cufflinks.

"I don't have the authority to prosecute, but I can litigate. In recent cases, I've pushed for police accountability for jail inmates and advocated for public policies to address systemic and institutional injustices."

He leaned back, considering.

"Now, the police and the DA? They're the ones who go after him criminally. Put him in jail, prison, whatever. A lawyer like me—we go after him for money. Civil damages. I can't throw him behind bars, but I can get a jury to say he owes you something for what he did."

I nodded. "I have medical records—SFGH, UCSF, the SART Nurse, the OM... but I don't have the actual rape kit. That's something you can subpoena from the police department, right? They'd have to turn it over?"

Atticus tapped a pen against his notepad.

"That's correct. Once a lawsuit is filed, the court has subpoena power. As an officer of the court, I'd be able to request any relevant documents—including the kit. They'd be required to produce it."

Then he paused, leaning back slightly as if choosing his words carefully.

"We know through painful experience that freedom is never voluntarily given by the oppressor; it must be demanded by the oppressed," he said, then glanced at me.

"Martin Luther King, Jr.—*Letter from a Birmingham Jail*, 1963."

For a moment, it was as if the room dissolved and I was staring into a black-and-white broadcast on TV. Dr. King stood at the podium, the edges of the screen trembling with static. His voice rose like a bell, carrying conviction that cut through the grain, each syllable echoing with urgency. The flicker of the image made it feel less like a recording and more like a visitation—history breaking through the static. His eyes, immortal and resolute, cut through the grain of the silver screen—spanning decades, piercing past the crowd and the camera, locking onto me as though time collapsed.

I nodded. "A powerful message. Thank you for joining the Zoom call with the District Attorney on April 29th."

"Right," he said. "I'll check it out, Ms. Rose. That's fine with me." He glanced at his calendar. "Just send me the Zoom link when you get a chance, and I'll be there."

"Yes, I'll email it to you."

Atticus adjusted his watch and leaned back in his chair.

"Alright. I'll be there at four o'clock for the Zoom meeting with District Attorney Boudin. We'll take it from there—see where it's headed. Afterward, you and I can go over everything, figure out the next steps. But for now, I'll observe, listen in, and see what's going on."

I exhaled, a little pressure lifting. "That's good news. Their negligence led to the spoliation of material evidence—which qualifies as willful suppression, right?"

Atticus smiled. "Yeah, that'd be one of the allegations. Sounds about right—seen it before."

He let out a dry chuckle. "This is definitely gonna be interesting. We'll see how they handle it. I'll check it out. Make sure to email me the notes for the meeting with District Attorney Boudin."

Twenty minutes later, I sent him an email.

Subject: *Notes for the Upcoming Zoom Meeting – April 29, 2021*

Hi Mr. Atticus,

As discussed, here are the points I plan to raise during the *ZOOM* videoconference with District Attorney Boudin, Assistant District Attorney Marshall Kent and many others.

Opening Statement: "Hi, I appreciate your time to meet with me today. The purpose of this meeting is to gain clarity on how we can move forward. Mr. Boudin, I'm hoping you will consider filing charges against the perpetrator. The SFPD's investigation was compromised."

Statement of Support: "Mr. Boudin, thank you for your leadership on SB 1220. I support this action to ensure law enforcement reports officer misconduct—prosecutors need that information to meet constitutional duties and restore public trust."

Question: "As a former public defender, you've often stated that prosecutors not knowing about officers' misconduct is unacceptable. Would you be willing to review a case where a Detective—who has a prior history—withheld evidence and interfered with a potential felony prosecution?"

Observation: "The Detective accepted bribes from criminals and was illegally involved in a multi-million dollar sports betting ring. He was placed on a 60-day leave of absence and required to attend an 18-month gambling treatment program. The department considered firing him due to dishonesty. He was also accused and investigated in connection with the murder of another police officer."

Speculation (Contextual Thought): "I've wondered if he took a bribe from the assailant? On March 24, the ADA said: *'There was no formal warrant—just a consultation with the Detective at the time.'* No affidavit. No warrant. This wasn't a clerical error, it felt orchestrated. The silence around it wasn't just negligent. It seemed protected."

Due Process and Civil Rights Violation: "In 2016, California eliminated the statute of limitations for felony sexual assault cases. Yet in 2019, during three meetings at the Hall of Justice, officials, including Deputy District Attorney O'Conner of the Felonies Division, misrepresented that I had gone to a different ER in order to exclude my medical records and avoid opening a criminal case—gaslighting me to shield the assailant from prosecution."

Writing this, and living it, makes me feel sick—because it was not neglect, but a calculated betrayal of duty. Thank you for your support. Having you here means more than I can say.

Sincerely, Rose

Hi Rose,

Thanks for sending this over—I'm reviewing your notes now, and everything looks well thought out and focused. You've done an excellent job outlining the key points and presenting the timeline clearly. I'll be there on the Zoom videoconference as planned, and I'll listen closely to how the District Attorney responds.

Let's see what direction they take. After the meeting, we can regroup and go over the next steps together. I'll follow up with any thoughts or observations that might help strengthen your case from a civil standpoint as well.

Talk soon, Atticus

I closed my laptop, the city's hum buzzing in the background. I took the last sip of my iced coffee, sitting quietly inside Blue Bottle at 1 Ferry Building, San Francisco.

You may not control all the events that happen to you, but you can decide not to be reduced by them. —Maya Angelou's *Letter to My Daughter*

I had found resilience in the face of tyranny and survived the darkness—now, I'm ready for the light and liberty ahead. Seeking justice isn't just about victory. It's about making sure they never get to rewrite the past.

END OF BOOK ONE

www.ingramcontent.com/pod-product-compliance
Lightning Source LLC
Chambersburg PA
CBHW060319310726
48976CB00007B/2386